JUICY

JUICY

NOELLE MACK

APHRODISIA

KENSINGTON PUBLISHING CORP.
http://www.kensingtonbooks.com

For JWR, for fun

1

Bliss Johnson checked her things-to-be happy-about calendar. Today's page listed beach roses and sailboats and velvety black skies filled with stars. Lovely. But not part of summer in New York. Almost everyone found a way to escape the hot sidewalks and gritty air sooner or later and her office building seemed oddly empty. Except for a few newcomers, recent college grads whose evil parents were forcing them to seek gainful employment.

Like her assistant—oh, make that her former assistant. Bliss ripped the page off the pad and crumpled it into a ball, attempting a tough diagonal throw into her wastebasket. She missed.

Okay, she would pick it up later, when her energy returned. When she finished flipping through the calendar to see if it said anywhere that going to Pittsburgh was something to be happy about.

Kayla wouldn't think so. The baby-faced intern, three credits away from a BA in media studies, had been Bliss's assistant at Lentone Fitch & Garibaldi for only a week. Viola Lentone had hired her. Kayla was so enthusiastic at first, eager to learn all there was to know about advertising. She was so young, so fresh, so new . . . and she seemed to think the office was an extension of her dorm. Kayla kept her laptop open on her desk to check her Facebook site, posting despairing messages. *Sav me!! Ths jobb sux!!!*

Unfortunately, Vi'd been looking over Kayla's shoulder when the intern wrote that one. Bliss saw Vi flick the laptop closed with one red-lacquered fingernail and stare at Kayla without speaking.

"Well, the job does suck," the intern said at last.

"And why is that, sweetie?" Vi asked calmly.

"I thought I was going to have more to do."

Fatal words. Kayla, the underachieving daughter of Violet's best friend, was assigned to filing contracts and disappeared into a room filled with high metal cabinets. The occasional sound of clanging drawers was all that was left of her.

Which was why Bliss had to do all her own prep work for the Hot Treats account presentation. She was booked on a flight tomorrow to do a search-and-recon mission on the company, which was smack in the middle of nowhere in Pennsylvania. Bliss reviewed her game plan: Visit the factory. Flatter the execs. Come up with brilliant ideas for selling their new line of fruit pies to skittish, carb-conscious consumers. The flight was short, but she would have to travel in a rattletrap taxi all the way from Pittsburgh to tiny Leonardville, where the factory was. One hour on the plane, another hour in the taxi . . . there was no cure for the summertime blues.

Crowded into a coach seat, Bliss looked through the HT press kit, making notes in the margins and wondering who wrote their copy.

The friendly folks at HT are called food scientists—and millions of busy moms sing their praises for inventing the toaster pastry and other delicious extruded snacks!

She winced and drew a line through the word *extruded*. Bliss wasn't sure what that meant, but it sounded awful.

A photo of a group of nerdy people in white lab coats caught her eye. They were brandishing long wooden spoons and wearing checked chef's hats. Cute. Too cute for words, in fact. The HT marketing campaign was in need of a major overhaul.

She reviewed the photos of the board members and execs, amused by the way their kind smiles didn't match their cold stares. They looked more like hired killers than friendly pie people. They needed Lentone Fitch & Garibaldi, fast, and she needed to land this account even faster. Bliss would have to come up with an innovative concept to do it. Traditional media approaches didn't cut it these days.

Maybe it was time to explore a new career path, she thought glumly, and look for work that was less venal and soul-destroying than advertising. Like designing stuffed animals or something like that. But stuffed-animal designers were probably no less miserable than anyone else. Maybe more so. All those button noses and beady eyes would get her down sooner or later.

Bliss turned to the back of the press kit, reserved for a message from Alf Sargent, the retiring CEO and son of the company's founder. In a few brief paragraphs, Alf shared the highlights of his years at HT and introduced his replacement, Jasper Claybourn, whose photo—a lot smaller—was off to one side, along with a brief bio. *He* didn't look like a corporate stuffed shirt and he didn't look like a killer. He looked hot. Bliss studied the photo and sat up straight. That smile was real.

Easy as pie. In its industrial application, the phrase took on a whole new meaning. Bliss Johnson was on the official tour of the HT factory, observing the process from start to finish. She peered down from a walkway into huge vats that held hot fillings, noting the bubbles rising sluggishly from the depths. Ploop. Plurp. Ploop.

Bliss tried to think of something to say, feeling a little queasy. The fruity smell was overwhelming. But she managed a faint wow. The head pie guy, a giant in white coveralls and an incongruous hairnet, beamed at her. Bliss adjusted her own hairnet, tucking an escaped strand of dark brown hair back under its elastic edge and smiled back, even though she knew she probably looked like a cafeteria server in the damn thing.

Her loaner coveralls were rolled up at the wrists and ankles, and the seat drooped unglamorously. So much for her short skirt and sleeveless red sweater. Bliss looked down at the toes of her high heels and sighed inwardly. Underneath it all, she looked fine. Her body was firm and her breasts were bouncy and her legs were toned and she looked better at thirty than she had at twenty. Underneath it all.

Her escort didn't seem to care what she looked like, because he was too busy talking. He made a joke about genetically modified fruit that could hop from vine to pie, and explained the software code that produced the perfect squiggles on cup-cake icing, and couldn't be stopped on the top-secret subject of Nutty Balls, a product name from hell if anyone was interested in her opinion.

Apparently Alf Sargent was convinced that Nutty Balls were going to be bigger than cupcakes, bigger than pies, bigger than anything in the history of extruded snacks, and no one argued with Alf. The retiring CEO wanted to honor the memory of his recently deceased mother, who'd invented the recipe.

He'd shown Bliss all the framed news clippings about his mom, a legend in her home state of Iowa. Back in the 1950s, Mrs. Sargent, a young widow, won first prize in a nationwide bake-off, her Nutty Balls beating out Miss Mimi Abarbanel's heavily favored Camel Humps and Mrs. Elwood Clip's Secret Spice Snaps in a thrilling upset victory for the rookie from Des Moines. With tears in his eyes, Alf had pointed out the black-and-white photo of his mom in cat-eye glasses and a teeny flowered hat, clutching a check for $25,000 and being hugged around the shoulders by the emcee.

Just looking at the photo inspired him to give Bliss a hug too. Around the shoulders . . . but even so. She eased out of his grip as soon as she could.

The prize money had been the beginning of Hot Treats, which Mrs. Sargent built into a food-industry powerhouse over the next four decades, amassing a multi-million-dollar personal fortune while she was at it. Bliss, who had a weakness for supermarket tabloids, vaguely remembered a few articles about her. Mrs. Sargent had handed the company over to her son and moved to Paris to collect gigolos, which didn't keep Alf from referring to her as "my sainted mother."

But hey, the old lady had worked hard all her life and it had been her money. There was plenty left over to build this gleaming new HT factory, which provided jobs for a whole lot of people. Bliss wasn't going to judge the late Mrs. Sargent, not for one minute.

She took a last look down into the immense vats and stepped gingerly on the walkway to where the giant in coveralls was waiting for her. He waved her through a door that opened into a cavernous hall. The noise was deafening, and the giant offered her a tiny, airline-style package of earplugs from a receptacle mounted on the wall. Following his example, she hastily unwrapped them and stuck them in her ears. They skipped the extrusion unit at her request and came out on a high, grated walkway near the ceiling. She looked down at a wide conveyor belt carrying filled, baked fruit pies that chugged past in endless rows, moving under nozzles spraying a sugar glaze as uniform and thick as car paint.

Bliss could feel her eyelashes sticking together, even though they were thirty feet above the belt. She nodded to the giant and they walked on, coming to another door and entering a corridor that led to the executive office suites.

A man was walking toward them. Make that six-foot-four of gorgeous man, Bliss thought. With a cocky, confident walk. She liked a man who swaggered a little.

Whoever he was, he wasn't going to pay much attention to her, not dressed like this. He was wearing Armani himself, unless she missed her guess. She edged back behind the giant and got the earplugs out, sticking them into a pocket.

The man reached them in a few swift strides, glancing at the giant but making eye contact with Bliss. His voice was deep and warm. "You must be Bliss Johnson. I'm Jaz Claybourn."

She forced her lashes to unstick. No wonder she hadn't recognized this godlike being as the new CEO of Hot Treats right away. Jaz thrust out his hand and she took it, enjoying the feel of his strong fingers clasping hers despite her embarrassment.

What a smile. It was even more effective in person. Bliss squirmed and sweated inside her coveralls, wishing she could rip them open and kick them aside, whipping off her hairnet while she was at it and letting her hair tumble free.

"Aren't you hot?" he asked, looking straight into Bliss's eyes.

"Melting." She met his gaze. His eyes were an intelligent shade of green, and fringed with lashes as black and straight as the hair that fell in a shock across his forehead. His features weren't perfect but they sure as hell were bold and sexy, something she'd noticed in the press kit photo. Bonus points for reality: he was at least a head taller than she was in heels.

"Well, take that thing off and come into my office," he said genially. "I'd like to talk to you about the new campaign."

Bliss got to work on the Velcro tabs immediately. The ripping sound was definitely unsexy, like little-kid sneakers or nursing home restraints. But Jaz wasn't looking her way, so it didn't matter. He clapped the giant on the shoulder. "Thanks for showing her around, Earl."

"No problem, boss," the giant said, too loudly. He still had his earplugs in. Earl nodded to Bliss and ambled away down the corridor. She clutched the bunched-up coveralls around her waist, not sure if she should just let them fall down and step out or what. She would probably trip if she did.

"Need a shoulder to lean on?" Jaz asked in a friendly way.

Of course she did. One to lean on and one to cry on would do it for her. "No, thanks," she said, reaching out a hand and bracing herself against the wall. She let go of the coveralls and they collapsed around her ankles. Bliss struggled to get a foot free, and lost her shoe. She stepped out of the coveralls on that foot and kicked the other foot free, but the folds of fabric swallowed the second shoe too.

Jaz reached down and plucked them out with his left hand as she steadied herself, as if he had a lot of practice returning high heels to women who'd kicked them off.

Bliss gulped. An instant vision of his bedroom came to mind, strewn with satin-doll dresses and fuck-me shoes. Smiling down at her the way he was, it was easy to imagine him—big, built, and buck naked—sprawled out on a king-size bed with his head resting on his crossed arms, a lazy grin on his face as he watched his date get dressed to go home.

Date. Not a girlfriend. Not a wife. *Taken* wasn't the word that popped into her mind when it came to Jaz Claybourn. But maybe that was just wishful thinking. She looked at the hand that still held her high heels—he wasn't wearing a wedding ring, for what that was worth. Bliss blushed and accepted the shoes, still bracing herself against the wall as she slipped them on. She straightened her skirt and pulled down her red sweater.

"Thanks," she said breathlessly.

Jaz nodded again, then reached out one finger and gently pulled off the hairnet she'd forgotten about. "That's much better," he said with a smile. He tucked the net in his jacket pocket.

"Oh, geez. I must be a mess." Bliss quickly finger-combed her thick, tousled hair.

"You look fine. In fact, you look great. Ready for the second part of the tour? My assistant picked up your things from the changing area after you left with Earl. She put them in my office."

"Oh. I don't think I met her but—sure. Lead on."

He turned and headed back down the corridor the way he'd come. "Fair warning. My office is a train wreck." He held the door open for her, and Bliss entered a spacious, mahogany-paneled executive suite with an immense, gleaming desk in its center. A leather chair with studded trim was behind that, and a long sofa in the same studded leather took up the space beneath a billboard-size plate glass window. There wasn't a piece of paper in sight, or a computer, for that matter.

"This isn't where I work," he said. "Right this way." He pushed on a section of panel that swung open into a much smaller space with four flat-screen monitors displaying different things: spreadsheets, commodities trading reports, agricultural weather reports, and international news. The floor-to-ceiling shelves held reams of printed-out reports, organized and labeled by factory department.

Bliss silently noted his framed MBA from Dartmouth. It hung next to a Young Executive of the Year award from some other company, near a shelved tennis trophy topped by a silver guy executing an overhead smash.

There were personal photos, too, placed here and there. Several of Jaz—broad-shouldered and bare-chested and gloriously buff, wearing frayed chino shorts far enough down on his hips to reveal the muscle in his groin—on the beach somewhere with a pack of happy-looking people around his age. Friends? Siblings? Hard to tell from where she was standing. One great big guy did resemble him, but his hair was blond and long.

She noted Jaz and his mom, who looked very much alike, in a formal studio shot that nonetheless glowed with feeling. Bliss looked around discreetly for a matching photo of him with his dad, but didn't see one. Mama's boy? Child of a broken home? Orphan wolf boy raised by random grandma, resemblance coincidental? Could be issues there. She wanted to stop but she couldn't.

Jaz waved at the cluttered room with obvious pride. "This is it. Operation Strawberry Pie. Our latest and greatest hot treat."

Bliss looked around. "Alf seemed to think that, uh, Nutty Balls were going to be your next big thing."

Jaz shook his head and pulled out a small swivel chair for her. "They might catch on in limited distribution. Sometimes you can get away with a product name like that in Southern markets. But not nationwide."

She smiled. "I agree."

"Can't change the name," Jaz said resignedly. "That was his sainted mother's recipe. I guess he showed you the picture. Alf shows everybody that picture."

"He sure did."

He spun the swivel chair around with a laugh. "Sit down. I'll explain the business side and then we can do creative brainstorming on the product launch. Want coffee?"

"Okay."

Jaz sat down right next to her in a much bigger chair, and pressed a button on a small intercom console. "Dora. We need some coffee in here. How do you take yours, Bliss?"

"Black, please."

"You got it. Two black coffees, Dora. Thanks."

For no particular reason, Bliss imagined Dora as a motherly, efficient type in sensible shoes. Two minutes later, she was not thrilled to find out that Jaz's assistant was a leggy blonde with ice-blue eyes. Perfectly poised, Dora brought in an ebony tray that matched her close-fitting suit, and positioned it low enough for Bliss and Jaz to help themselves to the two china cups on it.

"Thanks," Jaz said politely, taking his cup and studying the spreadsheet he'd just pulled up. Bliss murmured her thanks as she took the remaining cup, momentarily unnerved by the look of cool appraisal that Dora gave her.

"You're welcome," Dora said.

"Did you two meet?" Jaz asked absently, glancing from one woman to the other. "Bliss, this is Dora. Dora, this is Bliss."

"I figured that out," Dora said, a faint note of affectionate mockery in her voice. She turned the empty tray sideways against her well-toned thigh and walked out. Bliss didn't quite get the subtext. Jaz's nonchalance could very well mean that he was fooling around with his assistant. Or not.

Bliss sipped her coffee, which was very good and freshly made, and focused on the columns of figures. She tried not to glance down at Jaz's thighs so close to hers, spread wide to accommodate athletic-looking muscle and the intriguing bulge between his legs. He was hung. Totally hung. Not that he had an erection, of course. Yet. All she would have to do was run her hand along one solid quad and touch him there . . . no, no, no, she told herself. This is a client. Hot Treats is a big account. You want to land him, not lay him.

I want both, said a wicked, womanly voice in her head. *He has to be the hottest treat of all.* Her inner she-devil was reacting to Jaz's nearness in a big way. Bliss pressed her knees together, feeling a sensation of pleasure fire up between her legs.

A few hours later—she had no idea how many, the reports piled on his desk covered the time display on his main computer—they had covered a lot of ground without ever leaving his sanctuary. He was fascinated by the viral web-marketing campaign she outlined for him, even if he wasn't sure that YouTube-obsessed teens and blogging moms would send quirky videos about strawberry pies to everyone they knew.

But he did agree that the company needed to develop more flavorful fillings to gain competitive edge and sell a snack-to-the-max experience. They didn't see eye to eye on the packaging: Jaz wanted to update the label but what he had in mind was too subdued for a grab-and-go treat. Warming to her subject, Bliss explained that appealing colors and trendy graphics stimulated impulse buying. He agreed that the gingham wrapper had to go, ditto the chubby cook on the label. Even the Pillsbury Doughboy had lost his gut, Bliss pointed out.

She was feeling a whole lot better. Intense verbal back-and-forth with a very interested and brainy guy did wonders for her ego. The combination of intelligent business discussion, creative concept talk, and, hell yes, hot and heavy flirtation had pretty much dissolved her own brains, though. Just squirming in a swivel chair right next to a powerful, turbocharged male body made for sex was all the foreplay Bliss needed.

But she couldn't act on impulse, couldn't just jump in his lap, despite the fantastic chemistry, despite the fact that she liked Jaz—a lot. Goddamn it.

Dora was a big question mark but since Bliss was resolved to sidestep a potentially problematic affair, whatever was going on between him and his assistant wasn't her problem. Because Bliss and Jaz were going to be friends. Friendly friends. Not *very* friendly friends.

"Whew. That was an amazing session," she finally said. "But I have to go. I'm on the last flight out of Pittsburgh."

He tapped a key and the flight schedule for Allegheny Air appeared on one of the monitors. "It just left. It's later than you think."

"Shit."

"Stay over. We can go out to dinner. I'll ask Dora to book a room for you at a local B&B. Great place. You'll like it. I've stayed there myself."

"Don't you live around here?" Bliss couldn't help asking.

"Nope. I live in Manhattan, same as you. So does Dora. She goes back and forth when I do. But I won't be staying at the B&B tonight."

"Oh." He wasn't forthcoming about where else he stayed in Pennsylvania or who with and she couldn't exactly ask. New York was a safer topic. "So . . . East Side? West Side?"

He named an address at Columbus Circle. Bliss had seen the building. It was new, sheathed in shimmering blue glass, with wraparound views of Central Park and the Hudson River from the upper floors.

Not the same as her Chelsea studio, a sublet. Bliss told herself often enough that she should be able to buy her own place at the age of thirty but she couldn't. New York was just too expensive, that was all there was to it, and you didn't get much for the money. The studio had a microscopic terrace that served as extra storage space. And a stop for pigeons, which promenaded on the terrace rail, cooing madly to each other. So much for the al fresco barbecues she'd imagined having.

But her friend Anna, whose name was on the lease—and who had joined the Peace Corps and was still somewhere south of the equator digging holes for latrines—had pointed out the rusty hibachi behind the bicycle with the flat tire. Just in case Bliss wanted to buy a steak small enough for its tiny grill and four charcoal briquets to cook it with.

"Sit tight. I'll go talk to Dora." Jaz got up and headed out to wherever it was that his cool, ice-eyed assistant sat. Probably on an ice floe, Bliss thought unhappily. Was there any reason he couldn't just talk to Dora on the intercom? Did he have to make excuses for taking Bliss out to dinner?

She reached down into her bag and flipped open her laptop, wondering if wi-fi worked this far from civilization. Wonder of wonders, it did. Fully booted up, she accessed her office e-mail and found a message from Vi.

Did you nail him? I know Jaz Claybourn is a dish.

Bliss frowned and rested her fingers on the edge of the keyboard. How did Vi know that? The answer drifted to the surface of her preoccupied mind. Her boss had probably leafed through the extra copy of the press kit on Bliss's desk. Viola Lentone didn't miss a thing.

I think I got the account, Vi, if that's what you mean.

She could just see her boss's long red fingernails poised to reply. In less than half a minute, Vi did.

Good work, Bliss. Take a day off tomorrow. Enjoy Pennsylvania. I understand that some people do.

Bliss replied with a smiley face and signed off. At least Vi valued her employees. She wasn't easy to work for, but Bliss knew how to get on her good side after seven years at Lentone Fitch & Garibaldi. Bliss had signed on when it was still a boutique firm with a reputation for original work and bare-knuckles aggression.

Bliss didn't know what had happened to Fitch or Garibaldi. Vi had always run the company pretty much by herself. But she was billing millions of dollars a year now and proud of her take-no-prisoners nickname: The Violent One. Of course, a lot of the money went back into the business, especially their office space, which took up an entire floor in a posh building. In advertising, image was all.

She sighed and closed her laptop as Jaz came back through the office door.

"You're all set. Your overnight stay is on HT, by the way. Sorry you didn't make your flight. I should have paid more attention to the time. We can get great burgers or a decent steak at the restaurant in town. What do you say?"

The big, bold, mighty CEO actually looked eager to take her out. Bliss could not think of a single reason to say no. "Okay," she said at last.

She gathered up her things and let Jaz lead her out of the building through a maze of corridors that he seemed to know by heart. The factory never shut down and she could hear the machinery humming in the quiet evening air. They walked past the security guard glued to a small TV, who gave Jaz a wave without looking up from World Wide Wrestling.

"Female division," Jaz whispered to her. "He loves a good cat fight."

"Sweet. So I guess he's not going to tattle about you and me, huh?"

Jaz grinned broadly. "Guess not. We haven't been doing anything to tattle about." He used the key remote to pop the trunk and stow her carry-on bag and laptop before he opened her door for her.

She settled in, providing him with a peek at her upper thighs as she shifted in the seat. Might as well make the most of the magic. It wasn't likely to last. "Thanks. You're a gentleman."

"My mama raised me right."

Even though she was teasing him, she still loved the attention and his old-fashioned courtesy. Bliss had dated one too many loudmouthed rejects from the Planet of the Frat Boys not to appreciate it.

The restaurant in town served exactly what she expected: plain but tasty home cooking. On Jaz's recommendation, she ordered steak, like him, but the side dishes came first. She put a pat of butter at the top of her mashed-potato volcano and watched it melt and trickle down the sides, then ate the whole damn thing in big bites, which made him smile.

"Good, huh?"

"Mashed potatoes are the best."

"How about a bottle of wine?"

"Sure."

He ordered one for them to share and there was a rosy glow on her face by the end of the excellent meal.

"So where are you from?" he asked, not looking at the check the waitress brought. "You never did say."

Evidently he didn't want their time together to end. Bliss was pleased.

"I grew up in a small town in upstate New York. Thurbeck. You probably never heard of it."

"Is it famous for anything?"

She thought for a few seconds. "Strawberry pie, come to think of it. Mary Donovan ran the diner and made them every summer but only when strawberries were in season. Three dollars a slice, which was big money in Thurbeck. But people were happy to pay it. It was amazing pie."

Jaz nodded thoughtfully and folded his arms on the cleared table. "What was the secret?"

"Really good strawberries. She grew her own."

He shrugged. "Lots of people do. She had to have a secret ingredient. Maybe something we could add to HT pies."

Bliss only laughed. "Love. Those strawberries knew they were special."

"I'm not following you."

"Mary's husband fenced in the patch and slept on the porch with a shotgun to keep the raccoons away. He fired it off into the sky a few times a night."

"Hmm. Maybe the strawberries were just afraid. But love is good. And the FDA doesn't make you add it to the nutrition breakdown on the package."

The waitress came over with a coffeepot and two mugs in the other hand, and gave Jaz an inquiring look. He shook his head and pulled out his wallet, leaving two twenties and rising when Bliss did. He gestured for her to go ahead of him. "After you, Miss Bliss."

"Thanks for dinner." She picked up a mint from the bowl by the cash register and tucked it into her cheek. "That was fun."

"I enjoyed myself too. And oh—one more question. How did you get that name, if you don't mind my asking?"

"My real name is Melissa. My baby brother couldn't pronounce it and so after a while everybody called me Bliss, just like he did."

She sauntered ahead, going out the double doors and savoring the last blast of air-conditioning. Rural Pennsylvania was cooler than New York but it was still muggy outside.

Jaz handled everything involved with checking in at the B&B, while Bliss did a little exploring. She would be staying in a tiny cottage apart from the main house but identical to it in every architectural detail. She stepped carefully on the mossy bricks of the path that led to the front door, under an arbor draped in June roses in full bloom, and heard Jaz's quick footsteps behind her.

"Hey, this is great."

"Told you." He handed her the key. Bliss slid it in the lock and swung the door open, instantly charmed by the simplicity of the décor and its airy color scheme.

Jaz set her carry-on bag and laptop on an armchair and put his hands on his hips, looking a little awkward.

Make that big and strong and sexy and a little awkward, she thought happily. He looked like he was waiting for her to make the next move. His gaze was fixed on her as she drifted around the room, making small talk, fiddling with the drapes, knowing that she had changed her mind about fooling around with him. Might be the wine. Maybe it was him. But she could. Just for one night.

Bliss turned and walked boldly up to him and his arms went around her waist in an instant. He opened his mouth in surprise, then leaned down and kissed her eagerly.

"We shouldn't be doing this," she murmured when he stopped.

"Why not?" he asked, and kissed her again.

She broke it off. "What if my boss finds out? There will be consequences." Even though Vi had practically egged her on.

"I won't tell if you won't."

Bliss knew he meant Vi, but she thought again of Dora's appraising look. What did it mean and did she care? Hell no. Not right now. Bliss wriggled against Jaz, and skipped the rest of the question-and-answer for a hot five minutes of luxurious rubbing up against him and being kissed some more. He stroked her back and her hips, pulling her closer until she could feel the awesome erection swelling inside his pants.

Let the rationalizations begin, she thought. "This is just for tonight, Jaz. Only once. Over and out."

"Okay. Whatever you say."

Bliss smiled. As if a man with a huge hard-on and sexually hungry eyes was going to argue with her. She reached for his tie, pushing the expensive silk up through the Windsor knot and working it loose with one finger. He slid the unfastened tie through his collar and flung it aside.

She moved on to the first three buttons of his shirt. Bliss planted a kiss on the bare skin just under his collarbone, inhaling his warmly male scent with a slight but happy sigh.

She undid the remaining buttons one by one, stroking the light fur on his chest and the tapering trail that disappeared beneath his belt buckle.

His belly was tense and flat, as muscular as the rest of him, but she could feel him tremble ever so slightly at her touch. Then Jaz yanked the shirt tails out of his pants with Superman speed and bared his chest to her exploring hands. She traced a finger over one taut nipple and then the other, and he shuddered with pleasure.

He kissed the top of her head, running his hand through her dark brown hair with sensual abandon. "Ready to get messed up, Bliss?"

"I'm ready." But she tipped her face up to his, craving another kiss before they went any further.

He obliged. Then he raised her skirt, put his big hands under her butt cheeks, and lifted her up, holding her with ease. Bliss let out a little yelp and clung to him, clasping him around the waist with her thighs. Her short skirt provided no coverage—and neither did her thong underwear—but there was nothing she could do about it now. Anyway, she didn't want to.

Being shameless felt good. Amazingly good. She wasn't drunk and she wasn't desperate—she just really wanted this man. And he wanted her.

Holding her carefully, he walked her over to the mirror to admire the treasure he had in his hands, even spreading her cheeks apart a little more. Not that easy when she had pantyhose on, but he managed.

Bliss clutched his shoulders and gripped harder with her thighs, arching her lower back to give him a better view of her pussy from the back.

"Uh-huh," he said in a low voice. "Show it off. That thong is already wet. I want to get it even wetter. I want to suck your sweet juice right through it."

He let her slide down and Bliss heard her skirt rip. She didn't care. Her breasts rubbed against his hard, bare chest, the soft knit of her sweater providing sensual stimulation to the aching nipples inside her sheer bra.

She took a step away from him and unfastened the zipper, letting the ripped skirt fall to her ankles and standing in front of him in just her pantyhose, thong, and top. And her high heels.

Jaz didn't wait. He pulled her sweater up over her breasts, taking both her nipples between his fingertips and rolling them tightly, using the sheer material of the bra for extra-sexy friction. But he was strong. The bra was going to suffer the same fate as the skirt if she didn't stop him and take it off.

Bliss reached behind her back for the clasp, a move that thrust her tits into his cupping hands. Jaz groaned and bent his head down to tease one nipple with his tongue. She got the clasp undone and he pushed the bra up and away, suckling hungrily on the nipple, which perked up between his lips. The intense sensation went right to her pussy. Bliss slid a finger down inside her thong. He was right. She was soaking wet.

He must have looked down to see what she was doing to herself, because he let her nipple pop out of his mouth, glossy and red. "Don't stop," she said weakly. He barely nodded, then suckled the other one just as hard, making her sway on her high heels.

"Half dressed and hotter that way," he murmured when he raised his head. "But I am going to get your clothes off. Inch by inch." He patted her on the ass.

"What about your clothes?"

"Oh yeah. Gotta get those off too." He winked at her. "We need a level playing surface. What do you say we move to the bedroom?"

Bliss didn't bother pulling down her sweater, which was all tangled up with her unfastened bra anyway. "Okay with me."

He took her by the shoulders and turned her around. "I want you to walk in front of me. Make your hips sway just like you did when we left the restaurant."

She cast him a look over her shoulder and grinned. "And I thought you were such a gentleman for letting me go ahead."

He grinned back. "Now you know. I'm not. Do you know how good you look from the rear? Not that there's anything wrong with the front view of you either." He patted her ass again. "Walk that way."

Bliss made it last, taking small steps, her hands on her hips. She could almost feel his eyes burn into her flesh and the thought that he was looking, just looking, with such lustful intensity, made her even more aroused.

She paused at the door. Make him wait for it. What the hell. Bliss took a stance with her legs apart and her hands braced on the doorjamb, hoping that he would keep on coming if she stopped—and push the big cock straining inside his pants against her. He didn't disappoint her. In fact, he had unzipped his fly while she walked in front of him and pushed down his briefs, letting his cock out.

She still hadn't seen it or touched it, but she could sure as hell feel it. He was super-long and thick too. Jaz pinned her wrists with his hands. Tall as he was, he had to press his throbbing shaft against the small of her back. She could feel his heavy balls, tight and ready to burst, bouncing between her cheeks.

"I should pull down those pantyhose right now," he growled softly in her ear. "Bare your ass and have you bend over. Or you could get on all fours on the bed."

"You'll have to let me go."

"But I like you like this. All spread open . . . with your back to me. You're not sure what I'm going to do next, are you?"

Bliss gave in to a sensual shudder that went through her entire body. "Make it good," she whispered.

Jaz let go of her wrists and used both his hands to pull down her pantyhose in one swift move. The thong stayed where it was. Startled, Bliss gave a little cry, even though she knew he was playing a game with her. She kept her hands where they were, as if he had tied her in place, letting him caress her bare buttocks with sensual skill.

She tossed her hair, aware that he had kneeled behind her to stroke and kiss her legs, rolling down the pantyhose—inch by inch, as he had promised—and touching the skin he uncovered with tender brushes of his lips and hands.

Bliss stepped her feet apart. The thong still contained the damp ringlets of her pubic hair, but she wanted him to see it all and have the best view possible of her juicy pussy if he was going to take his sweet time.

Again, he didn't disappoint her. Two thick male fingers slid over the cleft, staying on the panty side and barely—just barely—brushing the tip of her clit. The subtle stimulation made her dizzy and Bliss clung to the doorway. He clasped her waist, nuzzling her ass playfully before he crouched down to slip her shoes off and remove the pantyhose completely.

Bliss stood on the carpet, poised to enter the bedroom at last, barefoot. But Jaz stood up and got one big, muscular arm around her waist and the other between her legs, lifting her up and tossing her gently on the bed. Bliss laughed as she landed, and rolled around, removing her bra and sweater while he shucked his pants and briefs.

His crisp shirt was gone, probably lying in the hall. Bliss feasted on the sight of the huge cock jutting almost straight up to his bellybutton.

"Like what you see?" he asked softly. He took his shaft in one hand and began to stroke it slowly from base to the plum-like head, increasing its girth.

Her eyes widened. "Shouldn't I be doing that for you?"

"I like it when women watch. I'm not going to come, don't worry. Just want you to really look at what you're going to get."

The man knew the power of a good visual. And his very male pride in his body was understandable. He was packing something to be proud of. Bliss sat up and scooched to the end of the bed. "Then give me a better view. You're too far away."

He grasped himself firmly right under the head, making it turn a deeper color as more blood rushed into his erection, stiffening the flesh he held so tightly. Then he came closer.

He really did like it when women watched. He kept his eyes on her face, aroused by her focus on his cock. Bliss touched soft fingertips to his balls and Jaz drew in his breath. "Ahh. Go ahead." He changed his stance, keeping his muscular legs well apart so she could treat him to caresses on the sensitive skin between his thighs.

Bliss stroked his balls, which tightened up, as if he were about to shoot his load. A drop of cum pulsed uncontrollably from the hole in his cock head, then another. Jaz let go of himself and pushed her away gently. "Condom time. Unless you want me to eat you all up."

"Please do," she said softly. She grabbed the thin elastic straps of her thong panties and wriggled them partway down her hips before he stopped her.

"Leave those on. I want to suck your clit through that fine material. But go ahead. Play with your panties."

She kneeled in front of him, entwining her fingers in the straps and pulling the wet material between her labia. Bliss pulled slowly, back and forth, up and down enjoying the scorching-hot desire that flamed in his eyes when he watched her masturbate with her delicate panties.

"Go, Bliss. Get good and wet. That little clit of yours is going to get hard. And you're going to come in my mouth."

"I want to," she breathed.

"Then lie back," Jaz said.

She did as she was told, spreading her legs wide open. He reached down to grab her ankles and pulled them together again, dragging her down so that her butt was at the bottom of the bed. He set her feet far apart and kneeled at the end of the bed, as if he were waiting to see what she would do next.

Bliss, more shameless than ever, reached down inside her thong panties and spread her pussy lips wide apart, just as if she was home alone and about to put her favorite big dildo in and give herself a good solo fucking, using her underwear to hold it in while she rode a pillow. Knowing that his cock was even bigger than that cherished sex toy was making her wild for him.

He was smoothing the front part of her thong over her pussy. "There it is," he said, using a fingertip to spank her clit. "Hot and up."

Jaz brought his mouth down on her, swirling his warm tongue around and around very gently. He slid his hands under her buttocks, squeezing and releasing in the same rhythm as his incredibly sensual oral sexing.

Bliss lost all awareness of the room around her, lost in the feeling, knowing only that her one-night-only lover was capable of giving her the ultimate in pleasure in whatever way she chose to be pleasured.

A wave of erotic sensation seized her body, and Bliss writhed.

Jaz slid his hands out from under her ass and reached up to pinch her nipples, bringing her to an intense climax without stopping what he was doing with his mouth.

Uncontrollably, she pushed her hips into his face, coming for him hard, bouncing her ass on the edge of the bed until the waves of pleasure died away. He wiped his wet mouth on the inside of her thigh, leaving her there, panting with satisfaction, her eyes half-closed.

She heard him pick up his pants and get a condom out of his wallet. Bliss couldn't resist watching him roll it on. She heard the foil rip and opened her eyes, watching the thin latex roll down and sheathe his huge penis. True to form, he watched her watching him—and got even bigger.

Bliss got rid of her soaked thong panties and scooted up on the bed not a second before he pounced, on all fours above her, ready to rock. He kissed her neck, her cheeks, her tumbled hair with ardent eagerness, reaching a hand down to position his cock at her still throbbing pussy.

"You're so wet, Bliss. And so swollen. This is going to feel like heaven to me. I almost came when you did, baby."

"No," she whispered. "I want you inside me. I want to come again. Give it to me. All the way."

He did. Inch by inch.

Pinned by his powerful body above her and a shaft that throbbed like a jet engine, Bliss reached her second climax in a minute or two, hanging on to his muscular ass, stroking his back, kissing him like a wild woman. But Jaz's excellent control kept him stiff and sure, pounding and thrusting into her tight, slick flesh for all he was worth . . . and not much later, they hit that high together at last.

2

"I think this is the start of something good."

Bliss lifted her sweaty head from the pillow and shot Jaz a quizzical look. "No, no. You client. Me ad agency slave. This was a fling. Nothing more to it than that."

He laughed and rubbed her belly. She couldn't help arching a little under his caress. "You sure, Bliss?"

He rolled her over, facing him, and took her in his arms. Bliss was eating this up, even though she knew it wasn't going to last. "God, that name fits you," he said. He smoothed her hair back away from her face and blew a cooling breath onto her damp temples. "That's just what sex with you feels like. So when am I going to see you again? I know I agreed to just this once, but I changed my mind. You changed my mind."

She shrugged as best she could that close to his chest. "In New York, I guess. I tend to hole up in the office. The air conditioning in my sublet is geriatric."

He kissed her in the middle of her forehead. "Forget the office. Come out to my beach house. You can catch the train from where you are and have sand between your toes in less than an hour. I have a house on Pine Island, in Breezy Bay. Great place. No cars allowed in the summer months, just bicycles and little red wagons to drag your groceries home."

"Pine Island? My boss has a house there. But I think she said it was near the Summer Club."

Jaz pulled back a little to look down at her. "Small world. That's about half a mile from my house. What's her name again?"

"Viola Lentone."

"Right. Dora told me. I don't think I know her."

"But her married name was different—actually, she's had more than one married name. She's been divorced three or four times. I think she got the beach house from husband number two."

"Describe her."

Bliss's reply was somewhat muffled by his chest, because Jaz was holding her close again. He was a very affectionate guy but sometimes he made it difficult to talk. "Tall. Elegant. Shoulder-length silver hair with dramatic black eyebrows. And she always wears huge silver hoop earrings."

"Hmm. Sounds familiar," Jaz said slowly. "Well, maybe I do know her. I'm pretty sure I ran into someone like that at a couple of deck parties last year. There's only about fifty houses in the Summer Club and Breezy Bay combined. Eventually you meet everybody."

Bliss's heart sank. That was one really good reason to end this fling right now, right here. She wanted to keep her job. Banging a major client wasn't the way to do it, no matter how much fun sex with him was. She wasn't going to take a chance on running into Vi if she took Jaz up on his offer.

"Anyway, you should come out. No law against having fun, is there?"

Bliss struggled out of his arms and sat up, fluffing her hair.

"Maybe." She turned to look at Jaz in all his brawny glory. His green eyes were sleepy-sexy and he reached out a hand to hold hers. "I guess I would if I was sure Vi wasn't going to be there."

She thought again of her cramped sublet and the long summer ahead, and wondered why she didn't just say yes. She wasn't that afraid of Vi's temper.

Okay, she was.

And this guy is too good to be true, she told herself. Once he sees my crummy apartment and how hard I have to scratch just to get by, he'll bow out.

"Bliss, she won't fire you. The HT account is worth millions to your agency."

"That's precisely my point." Bliss rolled away, dragging the tangled top sheet with her, and draping herself in it as she stood up. "Besides, you haven't actually said in so many words that Lentone Fitch & Garibaldi actually has the account."

"You know I want to go with you guys," he said indignantly. "Rolling around in bed with you has nothing to do with my decision. I made up my mind long before I got your clothes off. So did Alf. He buttonholed me while you were taking the factory tour. He likes you a lot."

Bliss nodded, not sure if she should tell him that maybe the outgoing CEO liked her a little too much.

"You picked up the details of our operation in record time and I thought your marketing ideas were amazing—" He broke off and scowled at her. "Goddamn it, do we have to talk shop?"

"Yes." She found two corners of the sheet and tied it in a knot over her breasts.

He braced himself on his elbows and stayed on the bed, looking at her longingly. "Do you seriously think we're going to be satisfied with having sex just once?"

"I didn't say that."

"Good. Now we're getting somewhere. Because that was probably the best sex I ever had."

Bliss held up a hand. "This is not a negotiation. We will now resume our normal business relationship."

He stared at her doubtfully. "You have got to be kidding."

"I'm not."

Jaz swung his legs over the side of the bed and got up, walking over to her. "Don't make me spout a lot of bad dialogue, Bliss. I don't want this to end. I really like you. Come out to my beach house and play. I really, really like you. I could even fall in—"

"Don't go there." Her steely look stopped him in his tracks.

"Okay, okay. I give up."

She watched him warily, hanging on to her security sheet. No way would a man like Jaz Claybourn, hard-driving CEO and bedroom bounty hunter, give up that easily. Bliss took a deep breath, waiting to hear what he would say next. He didn't say anything. In fact, he looked as confused as she felt.

He went into the bathroom, washed up, and came out with a low-slung towel tied around his hips. "Seen my pants? I gotta get going."

She wasn't going to ask where.

Bliss pointed to where he had dropped them on the floor and swept past him into the bathroom, slamming the door on the trailing sheet. She swore and undid the knot, letting the sheet fall off and standing on it. She pulled out the water knob and adjusted the temperature, then yanked up on the knob that switched the flow to the showerhead. She stepped under the pounding spray, but not before she heard him check in with Dora on his cell phone and laugh in an intimate way.

Mm-hm. Suspicions confirmed. Dora saw him nearly every day and there had to be something going on. But Bliss couldn't shake the feeling that he wasn't totally, officially taken.

She soaped up, rinsed off, and got out, wrapping herself in a big towel. Jaz opened the door without knocking and stuck his head in, grinning like a wolf. "Okay. Dora's going to chuck Alf under the chin tomorrow morning and make excuses for me. He worships her, says a blonde gives the place class."

She waited for him to contradict that. Say something post-coital and flattering. *Brunettes are much sexier.* He didn't.

"He'll believe whatever she tells him," Jaz went on, oblivious to Bliss's irritation. "I'm taking a four-day weekend starting tomorrow, which is Thursday, and you're coming out to Pine Island as soon as you can."

"No."

He didn't even pretend to hear her. "You get to fly back to New York first, of course. Tell Vi you nailed me to the wall."

"I would phrase it differently, but go on."

"You have the account. She's sure to give you Friday off. The ferry runs every hour from Havertown on Fridays. Very convenient. Like I said, you can take the train from Manhattan. Transfer at Glenwick for the Havertown train, and take a taxi to the ferry dock. Easy as pie."

"I hate you."

He rested his head on his muscular arm and looked down at her. "I don't think so. You're just nervous."

"You make me nervous." Looking at him naked from the waist up was dissolving her brains again. And her resolve. He seemed to be on the verge of a smile. A very contagious smile. Bliss felt the corner of her mouth twitch.

"We're going to have a great time, Bliss." He put a finger under her chin and tipped her face to his for a long, lovely kiss.

On the general principle of making him wait for it some more, two weeks went by before Bliss headed out to Pine Island. Two weeks of tossing and turning in an empty bed. Two weeks of fantasizing about Jaz. Two weeks of not caring if she did lose her job—because she could get unemployment and another job, but that wasn't going to happen because Vi was jubilant about getting the HT account. She bought a half page in *AdWeek* to gloat publicly and promoted Bliss on the spot, even throwing in a tiny raise.

But Bliss still hadn't found the courage to tell Vi that she was seeing the CEO of Hot Treats. She'd worn sunglasses and a big scarf on the ferry out, just in case. Halfway across the immense bay, Pine Island came into view, stretching east and west for more than forty miles. Bliss had realized how big the island was and relaxed a little.

Jaz had arrived on the island only a couple of hours before, she found out when she called him from the ferry on her cell. He met her at the dock, looking built in ragged shorts and a faded T-shirt.

His house was nestled among low, wind-sculpted pines and she felt safe enough from discovery there. She'd mostly forgotten about Vi when he'd suggested going to the beach, taking what seemed to be a roundabout way to get there.

"Want to see where your boss lives?" Jaz pointed to the house.

"No fair. You didn't tell me it was on this path."

Jaz shrugged. "It's the shortest way to the beach."

Bliss almost expected to see flashes of lightning around stone battlements and flocks of malevolent bats hovering above the Beach House of Doom. But the structure was plain enough: gray-sided trapezoids thrusting skyward, pierced by angular windows, one of which displayed, in an ironic way, a faded prom dress in aqua chiffon with a matching satin sash.

Maybe the dress had once belonged to Violet, who now hung it in her beach house window as a warning to former classmates who had failed to recognize her genius. Maybe there was a bucket of blood suspended above it for those who failed to recognize Violet's genius now. Bliss walked a little faster, dragging Jaz by the hand.

"What's the hurry?" He stopped to get a better grip on their beach chairs and leaned them against Violet's split-rail fence. "Don't you want to stop in and say hello?"

"No."

"Why not?"" Jaz looked up at the house and listened. "Someone's there. Hey, Vi!"

Bliss just gaped at the sight of her boss sliding open a glass door and stepping outside. There was a tall, cool drink in her hand. Bliss prayed that it contained gin. A lot of gin.

"Bliss! What are you doing here?" Vi poked a finger into her glass and retrieved a maraschino cherry by the stem, popping it between her lips and munching it thoughtfully. "Care for a Shirley Temple?"

"Uh—no thanks." Bliss very much doubted that her boss was drinking a non-alcoholic beverage. "I came out with Jaz."

"Hello, Jaz!" Vi said, a little too brightly. She squinted at him. "You look familiar." She turned her head in Bliss's direction. "Enlighten me."

"I'm Jaz Claybourn," he answered before Bliss could reply. "I'm your new client—the CEO of Hot Treats. Pleasure to meet you. But I think we've met before, at the Buchanans' deck party last summer."

"Of course. Now I remember. You were thinking of taking the helm of the company back then. And I saw your picture in the HT press kit. Bliss, you naughty girl, I believe that's a conflict of interest." She downed her drink and licked her lips. "Gin and cherries. Disgusting but tasty. Want one?"

"We're good, Vi. Thanks. We were just heading home." Bliss patted the beach towel slung over her arm, trying to send a telepathic message that home was where the towel racks were. She didn't think her boss would notice that they had been heading in the opposite direction, to the beach. She really didn't want Vi to join them.

Her boss was well past decoding messages, however. Vi

emitted a ladylike burp. "Jaz, didn't your father build a lot of the Summer Club houses back in the day? And didn't you help him?"

"Yes, I did," Jaz said, with a low laugh.

Bliss looked at him with astonishment. He looked as strong as a house carpenter with those broad shoulders and mighty arms, but it had never occurred to her that he could actually accomplish something as down-to-earth and practical as building a house. She tended to think of white-collar executive types as having been born that way: able to decipher complex spreadsheets and forecast the vagaries of the stock market, but not actually able to *do* anything.

Hmm. She was impressed.

"Rocco knew your father," Vi mused. "Your late father, I mean."

"I sure did," a deep voice intoned. "Will Claybourn was my best buddy." A very tall man who had to be well over sixty stepped through the open glass door to stand next to Vi. He had a lion's mane of silver hair streaked with black and soulful dark eyes. Bliss noticed the splotches of paint on his faded denim shirt and jeans, and took him for a house painter. "Hello, Jaz."

Vi set down her drink and took him by the arm. "Bliss, I don't think you've ever met Rocco Camp. My soul mate."

The older man picked up Vi's hand and kissed her fingertips one by one. "*Cara mia.*"

Bliss's eyes widened and her toes curled in her flip-flops. In her seven years at Lentone Fitch & Garibaldi, she had never heard Viola mention having a lover, let alone a lover who was a house painter. Vi had said only that she would never marry again, and Bliss assumed that it was a sensitive subject. But Rocco Camp was a stud for his age, a towering, well-built guy with a devil-may-care smile.

The older couple moved to the impromptu bar set up on the

deck, and Rocco replenished Vi's drink, adding six maraschino cherries and feeding her the seventh. Vi giggled. They whispered sweet nothings to each other, evidently forgetting that Jaz and Bliss were still there.

"He's an artist," Jaz whispered out of the side of his mouth. "His paintings sell for hundreds of thousands of dollars. But he's as eccentric as hell and it's only getting worse. He and my dad used to ride around Pine Island on bicycles, serenading women at night and raising hell, before my dad met my mom."

"Oh." Bliss watched Rocco kiss the fingertips of Vi's other hand.

"Rocco never married. But I think he slept with every woman on Pine Island once upon a time. I didn't know he hooked up with Vi. She was flying solo last year."

Bliss heard her boss sigh with pleasure and decided to get going. She called out a good-bye and caught Jaz by the hand, giving him a second or two to pick up their beach chairs.

Vi hadn't seemed surprised or angry at all to see the two of them. Of course, the older woman prided herself on working long hours, so Vi might be feeling a tad guilty herself about being out here. But Bliss kept her voice low even when they were well out of earshot. "I hope we didn't come out on the same ferry. That's why I had on my disguise."

Jaz chuckled. "I almost didn't recognize you at first."

"Jaz, I looked but I didn't see her. There were a lot of people, though."

Jaz shook his head. "Rocco has his own boat. He probably picked her up at the Havertown dock. Can't miss it that tub—it's painted purple."

"Oh. I guess that's it. But I would have noticed a purple boat."

"People do. I told you, he's eccentric. It's just a big old motorboat, but he'd hire bare-breasted galley slaves to row it if he could."

Bliss nodded, bemused to find out that her boss considered someone like that her soul mate. Maybe Vi wouldn't disapprove of Bliss seeing Jaz once they were all back in the city. But maybe she would. There might be hell to pay on Monday morning. Vi was not exactly predictable.

Bliss walked hand in hand with Jaz, her nervousness eased by the warm pressure of his hand. She was still eager to get to the beach, and not just to avoid Vi. She had gotten only a glimpse of it from his deck after he'd given her a fast tour of his house. It was built in a clean-lined open plan with distinctive woodwork—she realized now that he must have directed the custom-building process. Then she'd changed into her bikini and he'd changed into his trunks, and off they went.

She could hear the waves crashing softly as they came to the high stairs built over the top of the first dunes, well back from the water. The dunes were topped with spiky beach grass that waved in the shore breeze and pink-flowered vines that twined through it.

Bliss took the stairs two at a time. The ocean stretched to an infinite horizon, shimmering in the pale aqua light of early evening. The crests of the waves were bright white, curling neatly under as each rolled in, collapsed upon itself, and spread outward into ankle-deep foam.

She ran down the steps on the other side, heedless with joy, straight to the water. She kicked up the foam as she galloped into it, chasing its receding edge and jumping in again, getting wet all over.

Jaz laughed and she turned to see him drop the folded chairs and run too.

"No lifeguard! Is it okay to go in?" she called.

"I'll save you!" he called back. He bounded through the wet sand and into the water, scooping her up in his arms. He licked the salt water off her neck. "So how do you like Pine Island?"

"So far, so good," she murmured. Bliss twined her arms

around his neck and gave him a kiss that kept on going, even when he had to let her down, sliding her over the front of his body until her feet sank in the compressed sand and swirling water.

Her bikini bottom caught on the stainless steel button on his baggy trunks. "Hang on. We're hooked." Jaz looked around to make sure no kids were watching, or adults, for that matter. Then he pulled on her bikini bottom and cast a lascivious glance into it, admiring the dripping curls. "Can't wait to taste you again, Miss Bliss. Want to go back to the house and fool around?"

"Sex fiend."

"Damn right." But he unhooked her.

"Later, okay? We have all night."

He nodded and slapped her wet ass, giving her a big grin. "I like the way you think. Want to swim out?"

"You go first."

That was all it took to persuade him. He waded out to deeper water and waited for the right wave. With a powerful spring, he dived into the curl just before the wave broke over his head and came up on the other side, laughing and spitting out water. He rode the wave in, sleek and strong as a seal, and paddled over to her. "Want to try it?"

"I'm not that confident in the ocean," she confessed.

"The water's pretty calm. I'll teach you."

Bliss shook her head. "Not ready. Besides, I like watching you."

Jaz rolled on his back and floated. "I try to put on a good show." The water, changing color with the setting sun, gilded his skin and tightened his nipples. Bliss didn't think she'd ever seen a man look so happy or so much in his element.

A small wave moved diagonally across the current and broke, sluicing foam across his body and face. Jaz spouted water through pursed lips, then rolled over and dived again, disappearing under the surf.

Bliss didn't see him come up but she wasn't worried. He was obviously an expert swimmer. But she shrieked when he got her by the knees and toppled her in, laughing and spluttering. Then he rose to his full height, dripping and magnificent, his soaked trunks clinging to his cock and balls, which were hanging in there despite the cold water. He squeezed the water out of his hair with both big hands before he reached down again and hauled her up.

"Told you I'd save you." Step by step, he waded with her in his arms back to shore, scattering the sandpipers at the water's edge.

"Yeah, from yourself." Bliss kissed his gritty cheek—he must have been swimming along the bottom—and let him carry her to the dry sand. He bundled her in the huge, brightly patterned towel, and wrapped a corner of it around her hair, mopping up the rivulets that flowed down her back. He took another corner and cleaned her ears.

"I'm not six years old, you know. I can clean my own ears."

Jaz dropped the corner of the towel and tweaked her nose. "Glad to hear it, princess." A shiver ran over his skin and he brushed away the water and sand on his chest.

"What about you?" she asked. "There's only one towel."

Jaz shrugged. "I'll live."

Bliss rolled her eyes. "Tough guy." She unwrapped the towel and dried him off with vigorous strokes.

"Woo hoo! Feels good. Thanks, Bliss."

"You're welcome." She wrapped the towel around herself again, catching a smile from a couple about their age walking by.

Holy freaking cow, she thought. *We're a couple too.* How and when that had happened, she wasn't sure.

"Uh, what's next?" she said.

Jaz grabbed the folded beach chairs. "Wind's coming off the ocean. Too cold to sit out here. Let's go back to the house and shower. I could use a nap, how about you?"

"I didn't know you ever napped."

"What's that supposed to mean?"

"Um, you're so on top of everything. So hard-driving."

He guffawed. "Don't feed me lines like that, please. How corporate do you think I am, Bliss?"

She didn't know how to answer that question, so she didn't.

He nodded toward the ocean. "Napping is one of the great Pine Island pastimes. It's the sound of the waves—everyone sleeps better out here. Plus you don't have to be anywhere or do anything, you can just kick back and chill however you want to."

"I could use a little of that," Bliss admitted.

"So let's get started. I just want to curl around your clean, smooth body in my big bed and whisper everything I want to do to you in your ear while you fall asleep. You'll be all hot and bothered when we both wake up."

Did that ever sound like a plan. "Okay," she said, impressed by his self-control.

"Then, after a breathtaking interlude of wild, crazy sex, we could check out a few parties, fill up on the cheese and crackers. I told a few friends they could use the house this week, but they didn't replace what they ate. The larder is bare, babe."

"And I thought you were rich," she teased.

He thought that over while he got a better grip on the beach chairs. "Okay, if you add up my salary, stock options, and some interesting perks, I am. But I don't have the clout to get the store by the ferry dock to change their hours and I forgot to stop in on my way to get you."

"I get you that excited, huh?"

"As a matter of fact, yeah." He gave her a hungry look.

"Yum. They're closed for the night and they don't open again until early morning. Mooch we must."

"Got it," she laughed. She heard a rumble from his stomach and patted him there. "But we might have to move a few things in that schedule. When do the parties begin?"

"There's one in progress at the Ark. That's the big group house near mine. A rental. Kind of a zoo, but a lot of nice people. Great food and lots of liquor. We can hose off and chow down right now."

The decks on the Ark were crowded with guests attired in beach black tie, which basically meant whatever was dry, Bliss figured. Tattered shorts for both sexes, skimpy tees or bikini tops for the women, and loose tanks on the men that showed off great biceps and a lot of chest. Jaz had changed into one that made her want to run her hands over his delectable muscles and get started on the wild, crazy sex.

He introduced her to a few people but the music was too loud to really get the names and no one seemed to care. A long wooden table was laden with an array of takeout from Zabar's, a selection of jug wines, and chilled vodka, which a guy in hospital scrubs was funneling into an enormous watermelon.

"That's Stan. He's a heart surgeon. We're in good hands."

"Good to know."

Stan finished his task and patted the watermelon's striped side. "Let that sit for about twenty minutes, people."

A young woman brought out a tray of Jell-O shots, to applause. "These are good to go." Hands reached out and the shots disappeared. She went back inside for more as Stan came over to Jaz, insisting on being introduced to Bliss. "Can I get you guys drinks? Your choice of cheap wine or discount vodka."

"Class act," Jaz said dryly.

"Hey, throw a party on Pine Island and the whole world

shows up. Not like anyone can tell Grey Goose from Schmuckov's after the first drink. So what'll you have?"

Jaz eyed the table. "Vodka. Throw in some fruit juice to make it a little healthier."

Stan nodded. "Coming up. Same for you, Bliss?"

"Sure. Thanks."

He took only a minute to mix two tall ones, and handed them over. "Fair warning. These are mostly alcohol."

"Isn't that the idea?" Jaz said, laughing.

"Yup. Not like anybody has to drive home." He slapped Jaz on the back. "Vodka does the trick. Gotta hand it to the Russians for figuring out a way to get high using fermented potato peels."

Jaz and Bliss circulated for a while, and he pointed out some people he knew. "She's in advertising. He works for NBC. You could network."

Bliss leaned against him happily. "I'm not here to network. I'm here to have fun."

"You came to the right place."

She caught a whiff of pungent pot smoke in the air, but she couldn't see who was smoking and she didn't care. A club mix throbbed through the loudspeakers, and they danced to the sensual beat, drinks in hand, cheered on by guests who quickly joined them. Pressed together and swaying in each other's arms, Jaz and Bliss made their way to the deck staircase, letting the crowd close ranks behind them.

"Ready to go?" he whispered, his arm slung around her shoulder. A little drunk, he reached down and touched one of her nipples with his fingertips.

The sensation shot right through her. "Ready," she whispered back.

Stan came running over with a bulging plastic bag leaking red juice. "Wait! Take food home! I bought a crate of strawberries at the greenmarket and you gotta take some. Careful.

They're on the bottom and they're dripping." He thrust the bag at Jaz. "There's salami and cheese and foccacia in the Tupperware container too."

"Thanks, Mommy," Jaz said.

"I want the container back, dude."

"Sure thing." Jaz unwound his arm from her shoulders and took the bag from Stan. "See you on the beach, pal."

They were no longer starving by the time they finished the food in the container. Bliss found a colander and rinsed the ripe strawberries, tumbling them into a glass bowl she filled with ice.

Sitting outside on his deck, they were waiting for the moon to come up and making do with a citronella candle that smelled nice. Bliss put a huge strawberry between her lips and bit into it.

"Mm," Jaz said. "That looks juicy. You look juicy."

"These are really good," she said innocently, sucking it. "And they're huge."

"Have another one. But just hold it in your mouth for a second."

She did . . . then took it out. "Why did you want me to hold it like that?"

"Because," he said softly, his face shadowed, "that's what you're going to look like with my cock in your mouth."

That was a cue to segue to the bedroom if she ever heard one. After two shots apiece of the very good vodka he kept stashed in the freezer part of his fridge, they shared a fiery kiss . . . and then they went to the bedroom and got naked fast. Kneeling on the bed, Bliss got a grip on his thick shaft and pulled Jaz toward her. She parted her lips to take the throbbing head, licking it with dainty touches of her tongue.

He moaned. The tensing of his belly muscles told her that he wanted to shove his aching cock in her mouth and make her suck hard, pushing her head against his groin . . . but he held back.

Bliss rolled her tongue lasciviously around the head of his cock and just below it in front, lapping tenderly. She wasn't quite naked, but her white cotton panties didn't cover a whole lot of her either. The thong she'd been wearing the first time really turned him on and she wanted that to happen again.

She touched his taut sack with her fingertips, stroking him and squeezing very lightly. One nut up and one nut down. He was close to coming. Bliss gave his cum hole one last lick and sat back on her haunches, holding him just above his waist and looking up at him.

Aroused and massively stiff, Jaz swayed a little. His eyes glowed darkly, on fire with lust. "I can't decide how I want you," he said.

"On all fours," she replied.

"You read my mind. Guess you know I want to pull those panties down for you too. But don't take them off. Tease me."

She moved backward on the bed, spreading her legs open. "These are the cheerleader kind. Snow white and soft."

"Rah rah."

Bliss tucked a fold of the white cotton into her labia, rubbing one finger over the clit he couldn't see. He got down on the bed and got to work on her nipples, sucking them with tender skill in turn, then taking a break to watch her stimulate herself with her panties on.

"Is that what you do when you're by yourself?"

"Uh-huh," she said. "I like to fantasize . . . and I like to masturbate."

He growled and bit her neck. "What women do when men aren't around totally turns me on."

"You'd be amazed," she said wryly. She reached down and clasped his cock. "But the real thing is best."

Jaz pushed her down and got over her on all fours, spreading her legs apart and kissing her roughly, his tongue deep in her mouth while he bumped the head of his cock against the front of her white panties.

"I can feel how wet you are," he whispered. "I think it's time to get those panties down. Turn over."

He scrambled up and let her get on her hands and knees, staying in back of her, breathing hard.

Bliss tossed her hair over her shoulder and looked back at him. "Want me to pull them down?"

"Yeah. Little by little. Like you're all alone in your apartment, thinking about your boyfriend and putting on a show for him when he isn't even there. Getting yourself hot."

"I'm thinking about you. I know how much you like this, Jaz." Bliss rested her blushing face on the cool sheets and reached behind her, hands on her ass cheeks. She touched the panty elastic and rolled 'em down, revealing herself halfway.

"Perfect," he breathed. "Your ass is so round and sexy. C'mon. Show it off."

She used her thumbs to position the rolled panties at the crease below her buttocks, knowing that he was drinking in the sight of her bare behind. Submissively, she clasped her hand over the back of her neck.

"I don't want to touch myself," she murmured. "Not yet."

Jaz came closer and rested a big, warm hand on each cheek. "You into spanking?" he asked.

Bliss smiled into her tumbled hair. "Sure," she said. "A sexy one. Sometimes I really need it."

"Need one now?" He stroked her butt, moving his hands in big circles over her smooth flesh. She could feel a well of moisture rising from deep inside her pussy, soaking the rolled-up panties that held her thighs together.

"Yes," she whispered.

Jaz sucked in a breath and smacked her behind several times, making her cry out with pleasure. He was just forceful enough, hard enough to give her intense stimulation but not hard enough to leave a mark.

"Want more?" he asked. His voice was low and ragged. His cock was swinging and it bumped against her thigh, leaving an exciting hot streak of pre-cum.

"Yes. Yes, please." He gave her what she asked for: bare-bottom discipline that brought her very close to release. A sensual spanking did it for her every time.

He soothed and stroked her ass, parting her cheeks to look at her anus, she knew. Bliss heard him open a bed table drawer, looking for the lube. She raised her hips higher, giving him a do-it wiggle, and burrowed into a pillow.

With one fingertip, he smeared cool lube around the hot hole, pressing it and sensing her readiness, and stroking her back and hips with the other hand.

"Guess you like to get finger-fucked in the ass too."

She nodded into the pillow, pushing back against his probing finger. Thick as it was, it slipped in easily, thoroughly lubed, and Bliss moaned. He began to thrust it in and out of her asshole very gently, but going deep, making sure she knew who was boss this time around.

The anal sensation made her hungry for pussy penetration, but she didn't want to rush it. Ass play done right was delicious, and Jaz did it better than any man she'd ever been with.

He didn't seem to want to talk, just kept doing it. He folded back the rest of his fingers into a big fist that bumped her ass and made the thrusts slower, almost forcing her to push back and get her ass well fucked.

"Good girl," he said. "You like to take it in the ass . . . I like to give it." But Jaz pulled his finger out. "Stay there."

Bliss obeyed. He left and she heard running water; then he came back with a washcloth, scrubbing gently between her cheeks, and wrapping the wet cloth around his fingertip for a little bonus stimulation, laughing when she wriggled. "C'mon. On all fours. I want to see what your face looks like after that."

She rose and twisted around to look at him, her hair hopelessly tousled and her mouth a little swollen from being pressed into the pillow. She stuck out her tongue at him and he grabbed her hair, lightning fast, but it didn't hurt. "You're a brat. But you're a beautiful brat."

He let her go. Bliss arched her back and stretched like a cat. She was ready to get her pussy pounded and threw him a hopeful look. Jaz shook his head. "Not yet. Stand up."

He sat on the edge of the bed, his legs far apart. The size of his erection and the muscularity of his thighs made it impossible to close them and his balls were too big for that. He grabbed Bliss by the hips and positioned her in front of him.

The white panties were bunched below her pussy, wet and succulent. He put two fingers between her labia and brought a taste of her juice to his mouth, then bent his head to lick her clit as lightly as she'd licked the head of his cock.

Bliss closed her eyes and tipped her hips forward, letting her hair swing over her back, enjoying the silky feel of it and the even silkier feel of his long tongue.

She wanted to get her panties lower and stand so he could really eat her out, and she slipped her hands under the elastic, hesitating for only a second.

"Get 'em down to your knees," he ordered. "And get your legs wide apart. Keep those panties stretched, like they're about to rip."

He could read her mind, Bliss thought with satisfaction. She edged the panties down, stepping to keep them taut between her legs. He grabbed her ass with both hands and buried his face in her pussy, going for maximum oral action with upward thrusts of his amazing tongue.

Bliss got her hands into his black hair, holding on tight and crying out. The deep tonguing and wanton licking were putting her over the moon.

And speaking of that, the moon had risen, and the bedroom was bathed in its blue light. Jaz pulled back and looked at her, standing in front of him while he sat, running his hands all over her body and resting his head worshipfully against the crescent of her lower belly, smelling the fragrance of her skin and her sex. He got the panties the rest of the way off.

"Lie down, Bliss," he murmured. "Right in the middle of my big bed. I never wanted a woman the way I want you. Never."

He slid on the condom he had at the ready and they tumbled back into the sheets, rolling around wantonly. "Didn't you want me on all fours?" she asked.

"Yeah," he gasped. "Oh, yeah. I did. You make me lose my mind."

She rolled off him and let him go, getting on her hands and knees, then resting her head on the sheets so she could use her hands to spread for him. He made a sound that was half growl and half groan, and she felt the sheathed tip of his cock pop between her swollen pussy lips.

Jaz grabbed her hips and pulled her back, making her use her hands to balance. His cock filled her to the max, pumping into her snug, juicy pussy. His heavy balls swung free in this position and touched her clit with every powerful stroke. Unh. Unh. Unh. He slammed into her, and she loved it, craved it, screamed his name . . .

The ultimate pleasure was not far away, and both of them felt it at the same time, crying out with animal joy.

3

A few hours later, Bliss woke up, noticing that the room was still bathed in faint moonlight. Jaz's big body was next to hers, his chest against her back and his powerful thighs cupping hers. His arm encircled her waist and held her tight. The safe feeling of his embrace was heaven. She couldn't think of a single reason not to stay exactly where she was until the sun came up . . .

They hadn't closed the curtains and she squinted her eyes against the pink glow that came through the window.

"Here comes the rosy-fingered dawn," she murmured.

"Fuck it," Jaz said sleepily.

"Are you saying you're not a morning person?" She waited for at least thirty seconds but the only answer she got was a soft snore.

Bliss eased out from under his arm, and went into the bathroom. She closed the door and started the shower, holding her hand underneath the spray to check the temperature. The water was freezing. Well, she would just let it run . . . and look around for shampoo, because there wasn't any in the shower stall.

She opened a cabinet crammed with guy hygiene items, and paper goods bought in bulk. There was a whole shelf just for toilet paper.

A smile crossed her face when she saw the brand of razors he preferred: Mach Daddy. Oh, please. The package was unopened, propped against a bold black-and-red can of shaving cream that was probably pretty effective for waxing a car. Men would buy anything that promised a turbocharged thrill. She moved a few things and found an ancient plastic bottle with daisies on it. Bliss scratched the dripped crud off the label with a fingernail.

Shampoo with conditioner. Good. There was about an inch of thick liquid at the bottom. Bliss felt a sneaky thrill that the bottle was so old. Finding a cache of deluxe girl stuff would have triggered jealous feelings she didn't want to have.

It wasn't her business—not yet, anyway—if he was seeing someone else. She mentally amended that statement: it was her business if he was seeing someone right now, but not if he had recently been seeing someone, but wasn't seeing her anymore.

Screwing off the cap on the bottle wasn't easy, but she managed and took it into the shower with her, indulging herself in a long one and undoubtedly using up all the hot water.

Not a problem. Jaz was out cold and she doubted he would wake up before ten.

She toweled off briskly, rubbing the water from her hair and not even bothering to look for a blowdryer. Might as well get into town right when the store by the ferry dock opened and get something to fix for breakfast.

Bliss padded quietly back to the bedroom and stopped to take in the wonderful sight of her big sleepy guy. Jaz had rolled onto his back, his legs open and his arms stretched sensually over his head in a way that defined the muscles. His soft cock was flipped up onto his lower belly and his balls were beautifully relaxed. He shivered ever so slightly in the cool breeze coming through the window, and the light of early morning cast his body in radiance that made him look like a god.

The god was still snoring blissfully, of course, reminding her that he was very human. And all male.

Bliss found her shorts but not the white cotton panties. Then she spotted them . . . under his butt. No biggie. She had several pairs in her weekend bag but just the shorts would be fine for a fast walk to town and back. She looked around for her top, couldn't find it, and swiped his T-shirt instead.

She put the T-shirt up to her nose, enjoying the way it smelled . . . like him. Bliss slipped it over her head—but not her shoulders. She had only one bra and where the hell was it?

Over the back of the chair. She put it on and pulled the T-shirt down. It almost covered her shorts. Bliss took one last, long look at Jaz, and blew him a kiss.

She went down a few dead ends before she remembered the way back to town. Pine Island was flat and the narrow streets led every which way, especially in Breezy Bay.

A five-foot trellis of beach roses blocked one path and someone had left a small sailboat in the middle of another. But Bliss didn't mind the detours. The morning air was fresh and clean, with a sharp tang of the sea.

There were a few other early risers out, some on bicycles. Bliss realized that she was passing through the Summer Club, where Vi's house was, and walked a little faster. Then she slowed down, remembering the gin-and-cherries concoction her boss had been enjoying. Not a chance Vi would be up this early.

A vague memory told her to turn left and she soon found herself on the main street of town. The owner of the small market was just opening the doors, and the irresistible smell of fresh coffee wafted out. And something was baking.

"You're my first customer," the woman said. "You're new, aren't you? My name's Bunny."

"I'm Bliss."

The store owner laughed in a friendly way. "Then we both have funny names. But at least people don't forget them. Come on in."

Bliss stepped up onto the smooth wood floor, took a shopping cart so small it seemed like a toy, and found bacon and eggs and orange juice. She lingered over the neatly stacked heaps of fruit, choosing nectarines and plums, and then went to the back counter, where Bunny was setting up a takeout coffee service.

Bliss inhaled the fragrance of some very small, very plump pies resting on a platter. They had obviously come out of an oven less than an hour ago.

"I do the baking before it gets hot," Bunny said. "Try one. They're cool enough to eat. And they go quickly."

Bliss got a paper picker-upper from a slotted box and helped herself, nibbling the flaky crust and licking the apple filling that began to ooze out. "Mmm. These are fabulous. And so small you don't feel guilty about eating them."

The older woman grinned. "That's the idea. People buy them by the dozen. I usually sell out by nine-thirty."

"I'll take four," Bliss said. "Plus this one."

Bunny bagged them and moved to the cash register to ring up her groceries. "Want to start a charge account, hon?"

"Uh, no. I'll pay cash." Jaz probably had a charge account, but breakfast was on her after a night like that. He would probably protest, but that was tough. She wanted to treat him.

She picked up the bags, and thanked Bunny, only glancing at the lean young guys in running shorts and sneakers who stopped at the front door of the store.

"Gotta hydrate," one said, wiping his red face with the back of his hand.

"You can come in," Bunny said amiably. "But don't sweat on my peaches."

"We won't," the other runner gasped. "Got any of those little pies? I need the carbs."

"Sure. Berry or apple?"

They all seemed to know each other. Pine Island was a very friendly place. She paused to look at the headlines on the newspapers racked outside, and glanced at the weather summary on the upper right corner of a front page: *90 degrees and humid. Air quality alert.*

Not here. The real world seemed delightfully far away.

Jaz was walking around out on the deck when she got back, sipping coffee. He put the cup down when he saw her and ran down the deck stairs to help with the bags.

"They're not heavy. But thanks." She gave him one.

"You should have left me a note. I didn't know where you were. Is that my T-shirt you're wearing?"

"Yeah."

"Looks good on you."

"Looks better on you." She patted his butt. "I thought I'd be back in time to surprise you with breakfast in bed. You were snoring like a bear."

"I snore?"

"Like you don't know that?"

"Okay, I confess. Thanks for the goodies. I hope you charged them to my account."

"Nope."

"You should have, Bliss."

"I wanted to treat you." They walked into the kitchen together, and Bliss swung the bag she was carrying up onto the counter.

"Did you meet Bunny? She usually opens up, Fred likes to sleep late."

"Who's Fred?"

"Husband of Bunny. He's a lucky man. She makes the world's best teeny-weeny pies."

"I know. There are four in the bag. Actually, I got five, but I ate one."

"Then there's two for you and two for me," he said nobly. "You walked into town. So you get the extra pie."

"Thanks very much," she said, laughing. "But I don't need the calories. So it's three for you and one more for me."

Jaz found the bag of warm pies and ate his first. "Mmm," he said through filling and crumbs. He devoured another.

Bliss left the other things in the bags, not quite ready to cook breakfast. "You know, those pies gave me an idea. Why not do the same thing at Hot Treats? Sometimes people are willing to pay more for what they aren't getting."

"Huh?" He washed down the pies with a swig of coffee and looked at her over the rim of the mug.

"Less calories." She picked up a plump little pie and examined it.

"That's because there's less pie."

"Duh. That's what makes them cute. Cute sells. Taste keeps people coming back for more. Can I have some coffee?"

He finished his and set down the mug. "Of course. Please forgive me for being a rude, greedy, selfish beast. Just thought I'd say that before you did."

"Thanks." She nibbled thoughtfully on her second mini-pie of the morning. "It's a really good concept, Jaz. Think we could test-market it?"

He filled a cup for her. "Black, right?"

"You remembered. Aww."

"Anyway, back to what you were saying, we could, sure. We have a separate baking unit set up for limited production runs and test batches. Gotta run a cost analysis by the bean counters, though. They'll say nothing doing but they always say that. Innovation is a very, very scary thing to bean counters."

Bliss ate her pie in two bites, and picked up her mug. "Going small could be big."

"I like the way you think, Bliss." He put his arms around her, coffee and all, and hugged her. "Oughta let you run the company."

"I wouldn't want to."

They brainstormed some more over breakfast, which he insisted on making, shooing her out of the kitchen to get some sun before the day got too hot. Jaz brought their plates out to the deck. Swallowed by an Adirondack chair, Bliss couldn't get up too easily and stayed where she was, balancing her plate on her lap to devour the bacon and eggs. She craved protein, especially after the morning after sex like that. "Mm—I saw a couple of runners at the store." She took one more bite of eggs. "They were practically begging Bunny for pie."

He gave her a sideways look. "Yeah, so?"

"You could be missing an important market. Does Hot Treats have an energy bar in the works? Jocks are obsessed with health. And they love carbs. "

"Hey, just between you and me, our products are junk food."

"But do they have to be?" she reasoned. "You wouldn't have to change the basic recipe that much to make an energy bar. Throw in vitamins and yummy hydrolyzed soy protein."

Jaz made a gagging sound.

"Cut the portion size and you cut calories. Hype the fruity goodness. Health-conscious types are suckers for fruity goodness."

"Gee, that sounds cynical."

"Could be good for the bottom line, Jaz. And you really have to go after the moms, too. They want their kids to eat better."

"Hmm," he said thoughtfully. "Gotta digest." He stretched out on a wooden lounge chair and patted his belly. "That was good."

"Do you think those are viable ideas?"

Jaz put his arms behind his head and stared up at the clouds in the sky. "Sure. Worth a try. I'll call Dora, ask her if she'll talk to the plant manager Monday, get things started—what's the matter?"

Nettled by the mention of Dora's name, Bliss didn't answer right away. She slid down a little further in the Adirondack chair so he couldn't see her expression. "Oh, right. Your ace assistant."

"Well, yeah," he said mildly. "Who else would I ask?"

"So is she in charge of the entire freaking factory while you're gone or what?"

"No." He got up quickly and came over to her, resting his hands on the wide, flat armrests and looking down at her with a smile on his face. "I do believe you're jealous."

"Not in the slightest," she said huffily. But she was. Sex with Jaz got her more emotionally opened up than she wanted to admit to him or herself. She just about couldn't stand the thought of sharing him with anyone else, not even this early in the game.

"Don't be. There's no reason for it. I'm into you."

The bland statement wasn't as reassuring as she would have liked, but her pride kept her from asking for more. Jaz reached down to take her by the hand. Bliss wasn't going to sit and sulk, so she let him pull her to her feet.

"Come on. We don't have to talk business. Time to play." He led her down the deck stairs past the brightly colored beach towels fluttering on the line. She followed him to a ramp that curved around under the house, and into a basement that wasn't really a basement. The house rested on pilings that had been driven into the sand and enclosed.

Bliss looked around. She was in handyman heaven. Every

tool she'd ever seen or heard of was hanging on the walls or stowed in plastic bags. Lumber was stacked up high in long rows overhead, and there were milk crates filled with wood scraps in all shapes and sizes. "Your workshop?"

"Yup. Wanna build a birdhouse?"

"You have to be kidding." She thought of the grubby pigeons on her New York terrace for a moment and how unimpressed they would be by a friendly little birdhouse.

"Yeah, I am." Jaz went over to a huge, sagging heap of blue and yellow plastic and shook it out. "You're gonna love this."

"I am?" She didn't see anything to love about it. "What is it?"

"A raft."

"It doesn't look like a raft."

Jaz sighed. "Believe me, it's a big, round, rubber raft. We gotta get Rocco to blow it up. He has an air compressor, uses it for airbrush work."

"Ah—no. I really don't want to go over to Vi's house."

"Why not?"

"I just don't." Bliss didn't want to be the one who woke Vi up after she'd been drinking gin. And eating way too many maraschino cherries. Those things killed.

Jaz only shrugged. "Just asking. Anyway, Rocco doesn't live at her house. I'll take this over. Be right back." Clutching the deflated raft, he kissed her on the nose, and headed out the way they'd come in.

Left to her own devices, Bliss poked around the cellar, impressed all over again. He undoubtedly knew how to use all these tools, and many looked like they'd been handed down. Someone had driven nails into the cellar walls to hold them, and outlined their shapes with black indelible marker.

She touched a carpenter's plane, the paint on its handle nearly worn off. Like most of the tools, it was heavy and solid. It was easy to imagine Jaz's dad teaching him how to use it—

but she didn't have to. A faded snapshot pinned to the wall over the workbench caught her eye, of a guy putting the finishing touches on a model boat with two sturdy little boys. They had to be the Claybourn men—the family resemblance was unmistakable. His father had the same broad shoulders and pleasantly wicked grin.

The photo had been pinned up a long time ago. She looked more closely at it and saw this same sandy basement in the background. If she had to guess, Jaz's house was built atop the foundation for an older one, the one where he'd spent his summers growing up. Maybe he'd lived here year-round, if his father built so many houses out here.

She remembered the photo of him with his mother in his office. But he resembled his dad, too, and so did his brother. Or maybe the family features just blended nicely. The younger boy was blond. She read the neat feminine handwriting at the bottom of the photo: *Jaz and Joey with Dad. 1976.*

So he was a big brother. That fit. His take-charge, capable air had probably been handed down from his father, just like the tools. She wondered where his mother lived and if she owned a place out here, or just visited sometimes. Uh-oh, she told herself. You're not at the meet-the-mom stage yet. It's going to be a while before he meets your parents and vice versa.

Bliss ran a hand over the workbench, scratched and scarred by countless projects, and the massive old vise clamped onto its edge. Absently, she spun the little metal rod that opened and closed the vise, and smiled at the carefully labeled drawers of saved screws and nails that weren't new.

He had hung onto all his father's stuff, and it said a lot about him. He was good with his hands, he was thrifty, and he could be sentimental about a drawer full of old nails. She looked again at the photo, smiled, and went to the doorway to go back up the ramp and wait for Jaz.

He was just coming from the main walk, the fully inflated raft slung over his head like a gigantic halo. He held the ropes on each side to keep it from swinging and grinned at her like a kid. "Ready to ride?"

She looked down at her shorts and T-shirt. "Should I change?"

"Doesn't matter. You're going to get wet no matter what you have on."

"Then I won't change."

"Good. I like you the way you are." He winked at her and padded down the walk to the beach, his bare feet all that was visible under the raft from the back. A passing dog looked at him and barked wildly.

"Take it easy, pooch," she said and ran with light steps to catch up with Jaz. He turned the raft sideways to get up and over the wooden stairs over the dunes, and went down the stairs on the other side in the same way, struggling to hang on to the ropes in the brisk breeze.

Once at the water's edge, he lifted it off his head with a little help from Bliss, and set it down in the foam, keeping a fist curled around the rope. The undertow of the retreating wave made the raft bounce in the water. "Hop in," he said with a grin.

"Are you going to dunk me?"

"I promise I won't." He bent down to hold it steady for her, and Bliss climbed in on her hands and knees, getting as comfortable as she could with her back leaning against one rounded wall and her feet braced against another. She heard a wave crash, and the surge of foam that spread out from it lifted the boat and made it spin a little.

Jaz let out some of the rope and it spun a lot more. Bliss only laughed. He dragged the raft with her in it out a little farther, waiting for the next wave and positioning the raft for maximum effect. The wave hit much closer than the last, and the raft swung around crazily, half-filling with icy, refreshing foam that swirled between her legs and splashed her clothes. She was drenched and loving it.

He spun her several more times, laughing as much as she did, then dragged her back to shore, scraping the raft bottom along the sand. "So how was that?"

"Fun. Big fun. I want more."

He tightened his grip on the rope and pulled her back toward the wave. "I have a feeling you're insatiable when it comes to pleasure."

"You're right."

The breeze picked up suddenly and the waves got bigger. Jaz spun her over and over, giddy with delight, until a wave he'd misjudged crashed over the raft and capsized it. Bliss came up spitting sand and seawater.

"You okay?" He looked at her anxiously, holding on to the raft and reaching out a hand to her.

"Yeah." She brushed the gritty mix out of her eyes. "That was great—oh!" Another wave knocked her in the back of the knees and Bliss went down a second time.

Jaz let go of the rope and hauled her up. "I think you've had enough—"

She flung herself into the raft. "No! Spin me again!"

He obliged. Breathless and laughing, Bliss caught a glimpse of a group of little kids, waiting at the very edge of the water, waving and calling to Jaz.

"You started something," he said. "They want to ride."

The children's parents were setting up umbrellas and beach towels, staying near the community lifeguard, who climbed into a tall, slatted wooden chair and began his shift on watch.

"Okay. Bring 'er in." She slapped the sides of the raft and sent drops of seawater into the air in a glittering spray.

"Aye, aye, Cap'n Bliss."

"Oo, I like the sound of that."

For the next hour, she sat on the beach, watching Jaz give the kids rides. He made them ask their parents first, and he didn't take them out to where the waves were breaking. But he spun them in the shallow water fast enough to make them scream with delight and beg for more too.

Good with kids. Good in bed. Good-looking. Good at what he did and successful on his own terms. Bliss tucked her arms under her folded legs and rested her head on her knees. She had to squint into the sun to watch him, but she didn't want to take her eyes off him for a second.

Boxes of food had arrived while they were down at the beach, left on the deck in a row of five.

Bliss took a sun-warmed towel from the line and wrapped it loosely around her hips. She shucked her wet, sandy shorts underneath it and pulled off his T-shirt. "Okay if I walk around in a bra?"

He let go of the raft and kissed each of her taut nipples. "Hell, yes. Be my guest."

She gestured at the boxes. "How'd the food get here?"

Jaz leaned the raft against the deck railing. "Standing order. The delivery boy brings it over in a Boston whaler."

"Oh, is that one of those little flat-bottomed boats?" Her nautical knowledge wasn't extensive but she did know that much—and she had seen several tied up at the small marina near the ferry dock.

"Yup. He pulls it up at the end of the walkway on the bay side and brings the boxes down in a Pine Island Cadillac."

Bliss smiled. "You mean a little red wagon." She was getting used to seeing them everywhere, tied up to the front fences of houses. Some were rust buckets painted in motley leftover colors, and some were brand-new and as shiny as nail polish.

"I do indeed."

"Where's yours?"

"Down in the basement. I didn't get around to taking it out."

Bliss went to the sliding glass door and opened it, then stopped, not wanting to go inside with sandy feet.

"Rinse-off station is over here." Jaz went to a low outdoor faucet fitted with a showerhead on a flexible nozzle and she padded after him. She lifted up her towel to bare her legs, and he rinsed her off first, sluicing sand and dried seawater off with the cool spray.

She took the nozzle from him to do her face, then bent over to rinse her breasts right through the bra. When she straightened, her nipples were erect and clearly visible. Jaz's green eyes widened with male appreciation.

"Good enough to eat." He didn't waste time with his own ablutions, doing his big feet quickly, wiggling his toes and getting in between. He hit her toes with the spray again, just for the hell of it.

Bliss lifted her towel higher. And then higher, revealing her pussy. Where they were and the way she was standing, no one could see them.

"Uh-oh. Sandy crotch. Can't have that," he said. Jaz sprayed her there, carefully, so as not to soak the part of the towel that covered her butt. Bliss shivered. The water was cool but the gentle spray was soothing. And stimulating.

"Stand with your legs apart. And spread your pussy lips with your fingers," he whispered. "Let me really get in there."

She did what he said, and Jaz came closer, looking intently between her legs and fixing the showerhead ring on pulse. He positioned the spray so it would get her clit, then looked up.

Bliss put her hand over his to keep the spray where it would feel best, and tipped up her face to his for a kiss. Jaz hadn't shaved and his face showed sexy stubble that she stroked with her other hand. His tongue felt warm, deep in her mouth, a sensual contrast to the spray pulsing on the tender flesh of her clit.

Jaz reached up to squeeze and caress one breast, kissing her harder. "Can you come like this?" he murmured against her lips. "Do you masturbate in the shower?"

"Sure," she whispered. "That's what these things are for, right?"

He rubbed his stubbly cheek against hers and she could feel him grin. "Right."

"Let's go inside," she said, laughing. "What if someone comes by and catches us like this?"

Jaz nodded. He let her go and turned off the water, hanging up the showerhead carelessly and not picking it up when it fell off the hook with a thunk. "After you." He slapped her towel-wrapped ass, not all that gently.

Bliss went inside and led the way to the bedroom, somewhat hampered by Jaz unhooking her bra on the way. She jumped on the bed when she got there, on all fours. The towel fell to one side, leaving her ass and thighs bare.

"Stay like that," he said.

She arched her back, presenting herself to him like a cat in heat. He kneeled in back of her and rammed his tongue into her waiting pussy in one thrust. Thick and strong, slick and soft, his tongue got busy cleaning her more deeply, from the inside out.

Bliss moaned, pushing back into his face to take every inch of his delicious tongue. Her skin felt damp and cool, but her pussy was throbbing with hot desire that made her long for what he had given her last night: a super-stiff cock inside her as far as it could go, thrusting at maximum male speed.

He paused and pulled back, spreading her labia far apart gently with both hands. He looked at her there—she could feel his warm breath like a loving little breeze. Then he licked a few grains of sand from her inner labia with just the tip of his tongue. She heard him spit into his hand or something, then he resumed the royal treatment, orally pleasuring her until she wanted to scream with excitement.

"Lie down, Bliss." She turned around and rolled over onto her back, looking at the huge hard-on that popped out when he unzipped his shorts. He wasn't wearing underwear either, something she'd noticed while he was spinning her in the raft. If there hadn't been people on the beach, she would've reached right up his shorts and played with his cock while they were fooling around in the breakers.

She didn't doubt he was going to let her play with it now. The thick shaft bobbed a little when he took it in his hand, masturbating while she watched, for a change.

"Let me suck you," she said softly. "Get over me the opposite way and hang that big cock in my face. So I can't move. I want to open wide and swallow you. You can lick and finger-fuck my pussy while I blow you and lick your balls."

"Oh, baby. Oh yeah. Here I come."

He was over her in a flash, his strong thighs on either side of her face. All she could see was his cock and balls, and his muscular ass spread open so she could see his tight anus too. Bliss reached for a pillow to hold her head higher and got in position. She wiggled her hands up through his legs and stroked his buttocks while she applied her tongue to his nuts first, licking lasciviously and thoroughly.

Jaz moaned with pleasure, not paying quite as much attention to her pussy as he had done. But she didn't want him to, didn't want to come too fast.

"Move back a little," she told him. "Cock next."

Staying on all fours above her, he scooted back so she could get his shaft into her mouth. But he was so stiff it wasn't easy. Bliss wrapped her fingers around the veined, throbbing flesh and guided his rod between her lips, sucking eagerly and hard.

The inside of his thighs trembled and she tasted pre-cum, salty-sweet. She used her free hand to stroke his tightening balls, pinching the sac gently in her fingertips and drawing his balls tighter against the base of his cock.

Swelling more and more, the flesh in back of his balls looked like an even longer extension of his shaft. She ran her fingertips over it, stroking from just below the sensitive puckers of his anus to the base of his cock and squeezing that when she came to it.

Jaz had forgotten all about her pussy, surrendering totally to what she was doing to him. But he kept some measure of self-control, not thrusting so hard that he made her gag but staying with the rhythm of her cocksucking. Bliss worked her tongue and lips so that his shaft was tightly wrapped in the slick flesh of her mouth.

She felt his cock twitch and pulse slightly. Jaz gasped and his belly hollowed out. His powerful groin muscles tightened, preparing to shoot out the cum he was trying to hold back.

Bliss was thrilled. He was on the verge of a strong orgasm and she wasn't so lost in her own pleasure that she would be deprived of the experience of seeing it in every detail.

She sucked harder, looking up. Jaz began to moan uncontrollably, bucking above her like a stallion. Even that far gone, he was still careful not to gag her, still kept his cock from touching the back of her mouth, just enjoying the fantastic blow job he was getting.

Bliss let go of his cock and got both hands on his buttocks, squeezing muscle that was almost too hard to squeeze. She used her fingernails, clawing his ass wantonly, and that did it. Jaz shot his load right into her mouth, crying out with frantic pleasure, calling her name.

She hung on, sucked and swallowed, relishing the hot semen, pouring from deep within his body into her waiting mouth. He shuddered and pulled out, letting her touch her tongue tip to the hole in the head of his cock and squeeze out just a little more.

Then she let him collapse beside her and nestled her head on his shaking thigh. They were crosswise on the bed, lying in tangled sheets. Jaz was breathing hard, his chest rising and falling with the force of it.

"You didn't let me do you, Bliss," he said at last, opening his eyes and looking down at her. His head was pillowed on her thigh.

"Whenever," she said lightly.

He stretched away the ebbing sexual tension in his body, then buried his face in her pussy while she luxuriated in the touch of his tongue. She was so aroused by seeing him come that hard, so ready to come herself. Bliss pinched her nipples when he got to her clit, pulling on them hard, enjoying a little punishment in contrast to the soft sensations happening between her legs.

Jaz lifted his head to look, wiping off his wet mouth. "You have a thousand ways to do yourself, don't you? Mind if I watch? Gets me hot."

"No," she whispered, pinching her nipples harder. She pulled on them even more, loving the electric thrill that made her pussy clench when she did it.

Jaz thrust two big fingers into her to feel it too. "Do your tits," he growled. "Make yourself hot. Your pussy is all filled up and you're spread open like you just don't care. Anyone could walk in here and look at you, and you wouldn't care."

She fantasized another man, a friend of Jaz's she didn't even know, entering the room, and watching her get fingerfucked. The stranger would be naked too, as strongly built and as hung as Jaz, sliding his hand tightly over his cock while he watched Jaz make her come, helpless from the pleasure she was getting—and even more stimulated because another man was looking on.

"You're getting hot," Jaz said softly. "Your pussy is big and swollen. Feels like it's pulling my fingers up inside. You like deep fucking, don't you? Here it comes. Nice and deep and slow." He pressed his fingers in harder, making her moan. She moaned louder when he touched his thumb to her clit.

Bliss let go of her nipples and clutched the sheets, writhing. Jaz kept his fingers inside her and moved his thumb, softly sucking her extremely sensitive clit while his tongue flicked over it inside his mouth. She screamed when her orgasm happened, shimmering through her, shaking her body from head to toe.

Bliss floated away, seized by an intensely erotic wave of feeling. In another minute, she opened her eyes, looking at Jaz, who slid his fingers out of her pussy and wiped them on the sheets.

"Beautiful," was all he said.

4

On the ferry back to Havertown Sunday night, Bliss nestled into Jaz's encircling arm, swoony with happy tiredness. They had an upstairs bench in the back to themselves. No one else wanted to sit where the prevailing wind occasionally sent up a blast of spray from the boat's wake, but they didn't mind. He'd pushed her bag under the seat in front where it wouldn't get wet, and lined his bags up next to it, including a bombproof laptop case made of brushed aluminum.

Jaz had apologized when he'd booted up the laptop late Saturday night instead of taking her to a party but Bliss hadn't minded. She was curled up with a book on the built-in sofa he'd designed, looking at him every now and then while he took care of business whatevers, studying the screen in front of him.

With black-rimmed glasses on and an air of ferocious concentration, he looked every inch a Young Executive of the Year. Except for the bare feet and baggy cargo pants, of course. And the black T-shirt sporting a pirate skull-and-bones and a funny motto: *The Beatings Will Stop When Morale Improves.*

Bliss was quite content to be alone with him; he had no reason to apologize. As far as she could tell, Pine Island was a nonstop party for those who were into it, but once a week was enough for her.

They'd stayed up until well after midnight, no great feat considering they'd slept the afternoon away. A few of his friends, male and female, had stopped by while they were sleeping and left notes in the door that fluttered in when he opened it.

Hey, dude. Since when do you lock your doors? Can I borrow your electric drill? I couldn't find it. See ya on the beach. Dave.

"That's because I hide it, Dave," Jaz said, ripping up the note. "Not like you ever return the tools you borrow."

Jaz, this is your engraved invitation to a potluck brunch next Sunday at the Webbers. Bring orange juice, OK? You can't cook worth shit. Ginny W.

"I like that," he said. "You thought my bacon and eggs were okay, right?"

"They were fabulous," she assured him.

"Then I'll bring bacon and eggs. That'll shock the vegans."

"Who's Ginny?" Bliss asked and wished she hadn't the second the question was out of her mouth.

"If that's code for 'is Ginny married,' the answer is yes. Happily."

"Busted."

He gave her a reassuring squeeze and unfolded the next note.

Took fifteen nails from your basement. Will replace. Did you know that labeling everything is a sign of an obsessive-compulsive disorder? You might want to talk to someone about that.

"That's Bernie, our resident shrink," he said. " I get a free diagnosis every time he swipes my stuff. Geez, I hope he didn't hear us going at it."

Bliss nodded. "How come everybody leaves notes? Don't you people have phones?"

"Of course we have phones. But it's so easy to just drop by

everyone's house and keeping a cell phone in a beach bag is a good way to get sand in it. Locking the doors in Breezy Bay basically means don't knock. Everybody got that message."

He grinned and enveloped Bliss in a head to toe hug, crushing her against his chest. She was very happy to be there, smushing her nose into his clean T-shirt and smelling him.

You're all I ever wanted, she thought. *Hope this lasts for at least a summer* . . .

The memory of that moment came back to her as she rested on his chest again, one hand over his heart to feel the beat. The thrum of the ferry's engines made conversation hard and she didn't feel like yelling "What?" back and forth. She tipped her face up to look at the stars lighting up the black velvet sky instead . . . until he looked down and kissed her.

Monday morning at Lentone Fitch & Garibaldi went as slowly as it usually did. Bliss got in early, and set a tall cup of takeout coffee on her desk, popping off the complicated plastic lid with more sipping options than her brain could handle. Half flip and a tuck, full flip and a rip. There was such a thing as too much product engineering.

She turned on her computer and opened the file for Hot Treats, adding the ideas she and Jaz had brainstormed, then closing it and looking through her cut-and-pastes from food Web sites.

The industry was huge, and the market research was conflicting. When it came to what they ate and drank, people were often irrational. One thing stood out: they were willing to pay premium prices for healthy food, or at least food they thought was healthy.

Bunny's tiny pies, with real fruit fillings, were a great idea— if recipes like that could be re-created for industrial baking. That part of the process would be up to the white-coated nerds in the Hot Treat labs and test kitchens.

Bliss opened up an illustrating program and fooled around with design elements, tweaking the Hot Treats gingham into larger and smaller patterns, and jazzing up the logo in different ways.

More than anything, she wanted to wow Jaz with great ideas that his company could use. And Vi too, of course. She fired off an e-mail to her boss, wondering if Vi was even in the office yet. A two-word reply came back with breathtaking speed.

Stop by.

Bliss studied it while she sipped her coffee. Those two little words could mean a lot of things.

I am absolutely furious with you for fooling around with the most important client in the history of LFG. Stop by so I can hand you a pink slip in person.

Or:

What's Jaz Claybourn like in bed? Good going, Bliss. Your commitment to LFG is admirable. How about another raise? Stop by for your monogrammed bag of gold.

Bliss finished her coffee and decided that Vi's message meant exactly what it said.

Stop by.

She walked down the hall to Vi's office, stopping to chat with a few colleagues on the way. Lentone Fitch & Garibaldi had a lot of different clients, and a lot of account executives at every level to take care of them all.

"I heard the Violent One wants to see you in person," Alexandra Kassanian said. The associate copywriter was chewing on a pencil, paging through a paperback thesaurus and using a highlighting marker to underline possible synonyms for *fresh*. Next to *new*, it was the most overused word in advertising. "Whadja do, Bliss?"

"Nothing, as far as I know."

"You must have done something. She gets on my case for chewing pencils." Alexandra put down the pencil hastily when

Vi poked her head out of her office two doors down and waved Bliss on. "Good luck."

"Hello, Vi. What's up?" Bliss kept her tone nonchalant, especially since Kayla was standing in the office.

Vi resettled herself in her Aeron chair, swiveling to face the intern. "Be with you in a sec. Kayla, you can file those." Vi pointed to a two-foot-high stack of papers that Bliss knew had been on her windowsill, undisturbed, for the last two years.

"Okay." Kayla picked them up, cradling the stack in one arm and looking through the topmost pages. "But these aren't contracts. Where do you want me to file them?"

"There are empty drawers in the contracts room," Vi said. "In the back, at the bottom."

Where it was dark and dusty, if Bliss remembered right. Where that big waterbug used to live.

"Are there file folders in the drawers or should I get some from the supply guy?" Kayla asked.

The intern was stalling for time, Bliss realized. And trying to drive Vi crazy for sticking her with meaningless work.

"Just combine some of the folders that are least at five years old and recycle the empty ones."

Points to Vi. Bliss looked at Kayla.

"How would you like me to label the folders?" the intern asked politely.

A truly irritating question. Bliss couldn't have done better at Kayla's age. Bonus points and a free throw to Kayla.

"However you like," Vi said. "Feel free to create new categories. Use colored markers. Alexandra has some." Her smile was big and bright, followed by a dismissive wave.

Game, set, match to Vi, for implying that filing was creative work that an upwardly mobile intern would want to do.

Kayla sighed and left the office, not bothering to say anything to Bliss.

Vi spun around in her swivel chair. "What else can I do with her, Bliss?" she asked. "Sorry, rhetorical question. You know she's my best friend's daughter. Full of excuses and complaints. I have to keep her out of my hair."

"I guess so." She was secretly glad that Vi had something else to worry about besides the fact that Bliss was seeing Jaz. But her boss was bound to bring it up sooner or later.

"So how did you like Pine Island?" Vi asked, trying to doodle on a memo pad with a dried-out pen from her desk set. The original set was enshrined in the Museum of Modern Art, or so Bliss had been told. "This damn thing is out of ink. But God, is it perfect." She replaced the useless pen with reverent care and folded her hands.

"Oh—it was great. Very nice."

"And did you stay with Jaz?" Vi asked blandly.

"Um, yes. I did."

"How sweet."

"What exactly do you mean by sweet?" Bliss asked cautiously.

"Considering that a romantic relationship with him might jeopardize a multimillion dollar account, do you think it's wise to enter into it?"

Bliss could sense the steel behind the words. She took a deep breath before answering. No gin-swilling, cherry-munching, artist-fucking . . . she still couldn't believe the totally together Vi was dating a crazy artist and she paused to let the breath out. Anyway, no one was going to make her give up Jaz.

Other than that, she really didn't know how to answer Vi's perfectly reasonable question.

"Oh, it's all right, I suppose," Vi said suddenly. "Happens all the time. Good Lord, if I had a nickel for every sexy exec I went to bed with back in the day—" She broke off when she noticed Bliss's fascinated look. "I won't go into the details."

"Okay then." Bliss hated the nervous chill that crept up her spine. She felt exactly the way she used to feel when she was standing on the carpet in her high school principal's dismal office, being chided for the umpteenth time for dressing like a rock star or kissing a cute senior in back of the bleachers.

When, exactly, did human females get to have fun without someone disapproving of said fun? She reminded herself that Vi had not disapproved. Bliss had received only a tactful reminder and her boss had let it go at that.

She edged toward the door.

"So what do you think of Rocco?"

Bliss glanced at her boss, whose voice had switched from steely to soft in an instant.

"Am I crazy, Bliss?" The older woman looked up wistfully at her.

"N-no, not at all," Bliss stammered. "He seems like a lot of fun. He kissed your fingertips. I thought that was kind of cool. Go for it, Vi."

Her boss sighed and rested her chin dreamily in the palm of her perfectly manicured hand. Only then did Bliss notice the stars and flowers that adorned her nails, painted with a miniaturist's skill.

"Nice manicure," she said.

Vi extended both her hands across the desk. "Do you like it? Rocco did the painting. He had to use a magnifying lamp, but I thought it turned out very well. He says that women need stars and flowers."

The silver-haired artist might not be so crazy, Bliss decided. She smiled quite sincerely at Vi. "Can't argue with that."

Back in her office, she scrolled through about twenty new e-mails, deleting most but keeping the one from Jaz.

Good morning, Blissful. Flying out to Chicago to meet with money people. Back Thursday. Hope to see you in the city. Your place or mine? Love from your Jazcat.

Love, huh?

Her fingers hovered over the keyboard as she thought about her answer. *My place.* The signoff took her a lot longer. *Love, Bliss,* she typed at last. Then she clicked Send.

Just why she had decided to meet him at her studio sublet escaped her at the moment. Something to do with her pride. But her memory was melting in the 90-degree heat and the grocery bags she had to carry up ten flights of stairs weren't helping.

The elevator was on the fritz and the elevator repair guys were on strike. The building's manager, a young guy, had decamped to Montauk, about as far as you could go on Long Island without actually ending up in the Atlantic, and he wasn't answering calls to his cell phone.

Bliss stopped on the third floor. She made her way down the hall to Maisie Frankel's apartment, 3-B, and knocked on the door, listening for the sound of shuffling slippers.

"Who is it?" a quavering voice asked. Bliss could just see Maisie's blinking eye through the peephole.

"Bliss Johnson," she answered. "Here's your stuff from Gristede's." She handed over two bags of groceries to the ancient woman who opened it.

"Thanks so much, *bubbeleh.* Sorry to make you wait. Would you like a glass of pink lemonade?"

"No, that's all right. I have company coming over."

"Oh," Maisie trilled. "A young man?"

Bliss smiled sheepishly.

"How nice. Oh, I remember the days—but never mind. It's very kind of you to bring up my groceries. Thank you again, Bliss."

"No problem." Bliss hoisted the three remaining bags and went back to the stairwell, clumping up seven more flights, wishing she had decided on a nice, light supper of plain rice cakes and tap water, instead of the hefty sirloin and baking potatoes and two bottles of burgundy that were weighing her down.

It was too hot to drink burgundy. It was just about too hot to breathe. She staggered up the last flight, hoping her geriatric air conditioner would last through the sweltering night.

Bliss unlocked her door and dropped the grocery bags on the tiny kitchen table. Thank God the apartment was marginally cool—she walked over to the air conditioner and patted it.

With a mechanical sigh, it breathed its last. Bliss heard the fan whirr, then slowly come to a thumping stop. Shit oh shit oh shit. She prayed the heat outside would not creep through the walls until after Jaz had gone.

She couldn't possibly invite him to sleep over. If they had sex, he would slide off her faster than a downhill ski racer going off an ice overhang.

Ice. That was the only thing that sounded sexy right now. Bliss went back to the fridge, opened it and stuck her face inside for a few minutes, savoring the supercooled, faintly stale air that blew over her skin. Then she put the steak in, still in its plastic bag, and closed the door.

She took the potatoes out, scrubbing them thoroughly in the mini-sink and piercing them with a fork. Bliss hoped Jaz didn't mind nuked potatoes. No way in hell was she turning on the oven.

Then how are you going to cook the steak? her inner Martha Stewart asked.

She wasn't going back down those stairs and up again. Ann had left the phone number of the upstairs neighbor, a burly outdoorsman who did a lot of illegal barbecuing on his terrace when he wasn't dressing up in women's clothes. Ann had declined to say how she knew this.

Bliss went to the phone and drew out the phone list under it, dialing Rodney's number. She was prepared to loan him any item in her closet or chest of drawers, just so long as he didn't stretch out the back of her bras.

A ruggedly male voice answered by the fifth ring. "Hullo."

"Rodney?"

"Yup."

"Hi, this is Bliss. From downstairs. You wouldn't happen to have any extra charcoal briquets, would you?"

"Sure thing. Will half a bag do? Gawd, do I sound like a drug dealer or what?" Rodney chuckled long and loud. "Be right down."

A few minutes later, Bliss heard a knock on her door and prayed Rodney wasn't going to treat her to a look at him in frilly underwear or start a discussion about where to buy size 14 high heels.

To her relief, he was dressed in jeans and a tank top. A Hello Kitty tank top. She took the bag of charcoal he held out and mumbled something about being right in the middle of, you know how it goes, thanks so much.

Rodney saluted her and ambled back down the hall. Bliss went to the terrace door, opening and closing it quickly to keep the precious cooled air inside the apartment. She kneeled, set down the bag, and, watched by a few lethargic pigeons, dragged the hibachi from behind the bicycle with the broken tire.

The hibachi wasn't too rusty. She could scrub it with steel wool, fire up those briquets with a little lighter fluid—she shook the can that was next to the hibachi, there was some left—and grill that sirloin like a pro.

That she had never barbecued or grilled anything in her life didn't faze her. Just because her dad never let anyone touch his $700 gas-powered, professional-grade Roaster Boaster machine or the long, gleaming weapons that dangled from the rack on its side didn't mean she couldn't do it.

She lined up the briquets like little black pillows on a

deathbed and shook the last of the lighter fluid over them, forgetting that she was going to scrub the grill part.

Up here on the unshaded tenth floor the heat was intense. *Match make spark*, she told herself, feeling somewhat addled. *Spark make fire*. Bliss looked around for a box of matches or a firestarter, spotting a red-handled wand in an empty flowerpot. She took it out and clicked it a few times, quickly putting it next to the briquets when it emitted a shaky blue flame. It only lasted a few seconds, but the lighter fluid caught and blazed up.

Bliss leaned back. *Woman make fire*, she told herself proudly. So far she wasn't doing too badly. But she was too nervous about leaving the fire unattended to shower.

Jaz would just have to accept her as she was, melted eye makeup, sweaty skin, frizzy hair and all. She got up and pushed away the objects near the hibachi, just in case.

The briquets seemed to be doing their thing. She peeked through the humidity-streaked glass of the door for a time check. Jaz would arrive in twenty minutes, so she could put the steak on the hibachi in about fifteen, and check the thing from the cool side of the door.

She opened it just wide enough to squeeze through it and shut it. Bliss went to the kitchen to open the microwave, tossed the potatoes in, and set the timer. Then she tidied up the place, tossing old magazines into a paper bag and putting it under the foldout couch, and punching the pillows for that freshly punched look that was all the rage in interior decorating.

Attacking the bathroom surfaces with a blitz of spray-cleaning products was next. When she was done, she took a look at herself in the mirror and gasped. Her face was beet red and those wisps of hair floating around her face were anything but sexy.

She ran to the glass door to check the hibachi. It didn't seem like it was about to explode, but she couldn't tell. No shower, she told herself sternly, setting out a stack of small folded towels on the rim of the bathroom sink.

Bliss turned around and surveyed the place. It looked okay. The downstairs intercom rang. The place looked terrible all of a sudden, but it was too late. She went to the intercom and buzzed Jaz in when she heard his cheerful hello, explaining about the elevator situation.

Ten flights. He wouldn't take long but she figured she just had time to freshen up without messing up the bathroom. Once it was clean for company, you couldn't use it. Her mother had taught her that. Bliss put the stopper in the kitchen sink and dumped a tray of ice into it, filling it with water and tossing in a clean dishtowel. She splashed the wonderfully cool water over her face and neck, and swiped at her torso under her top with the wrung-out dishcloth, using it to dampen her hair, which she pulled up and fastened into a neck-baring twist.

Earrings, she thought. Wear big jangly earrings. He won't notice what the place looks like if all he can see is your earrings.

She looked in her purse, found a two-dollar pair with about a million moving parts and got the wires through the holes in her ears just as Jaz knocked on the door. Bliss pulled her top down and put a smile on her face.

"Hi!" she said, flinging open the door. Jaz was leaning on his arm, sweating hard but looking happy to see her. He handed her a bunch of gorgeous summer flowers: purple-blue hydrangeas and small sunflowers and pink lilies and white snapdragons all mixed together.

"Hi yourself. You look great. Love the earrings." He looked around, taking it all in. "So this is where you live. Nice place."

"No it isn't. But thanks for the flowers. I hope I have a vase that's big enough." She didn't. "You don't mind if I put them in a bucket, do you?" She squatted by the sink and pulled out a shiny galvanized bucket. It didn't look like anyone had been using it to wash floors.

"Of course not."

She used a pitcher to fill it up, then plunked the glorious bouquet into it, letting the flower stems spread out by themselves and putting to one side of the couch. Then she went back to the kitchen, wrung out the dishcloth that she'd tossed back into the ice water and patted the sweat from his handsome face.

"Ahh. The geisha treatment. Thank you, Blissiko. I feel cooler already. So what's for dinner?"

"Oh, a really good steak and baked potatoes, and burgundy."

"All right. Sounds great."

So far, so good, Bliss thought. Was it really this easy? Her last dates, with a forgettable guy, had been spent in buffet-style restaurants mostly listening to him talk. She hadn't ever cooked a meal for him or anyone else.

She looked over Jaz's shoulder at the glass door. No billowing clouds of smoke. The bicycle with the flat tire was where she had left it. "Guess I better get the meat on the grill," she said.

"Want help?"

"No, no. You sit down. How about a glass of wine?"

He held up the bag in his other hand, which she hadn't seen. "I brought a six-pack of Coronas. Cold. I'll start with one of those."

"Sure. Need a bottle opener?"

"Nah."

He got settled on the couch and twisted off the cap on one of the Coronas, letting her put the rest into the fridge. Bliss took out the steak, hauling the heavy package of meat from the plastic bag with one hand and grabbing a serving fork with another. Jaz watched her walk by the couch, a gleam in his eye as he swigged his cold beer.

Bliss eased open the glass door to the terrace and Jaz grimaced at the gritty breeze that blew in. "Ugh. Hot out there."

"This won't take long." She closed it behind her after she stepped through and looked at the briquets on the hibachi.

They were light gray with glowing red edges. Bless their ashy little hearts.

She used one tine of the fork to split the plastic wrap on the package of steak and peel it back carefully. Then she jabbed it, hoping to lift it and place it on the grill in one go, realizing that she hadn't brought a platter or seasonings.

Bliss looked up to see Jaz, who had gotten up to watch her. She didn't see the steak unfold as she lifted it but she felt it begin to drop off the big fork and hastily tossed it in the general direction of the hibachi.

It was bigger than the package it had been in, and covered the grill completely. In fact, it hung over the sides. The hibachi looked like a miniature bed with a meat quilt on it.

Bliss swore under her breath. Jaz laughed on the other side of the glass door and pressed a hand against it to slide it open. He came out, holding his bottle of beer, looking a lot more amused than she was.

"Think you should cut that in half? We can cook it in pieces."

"I guess so." She jabbed the fork into it again but it didn't budge.

"Hold on. Let me get a plate. You can't just wave a raw steak around. You might drop it."

She tried to lift it, just to see if she could. "I'm not even sure it's going to come off."

"Honey, there's a reason that this is man's work. Women are too smart to do something as stupid and boring as barbecuing. Mind if I take over?" He kneeled beside her and gave her a kiss on her flushed cheek, pushing a wisp of hair behind her ear with one finger.

His smile was so beguiling that all she could say was yes.

"Go get me a plate. And get yourself a beer."

By the time she came back, he had pried the meat off the grill and was studying its stripes with a curious look. "Hm. Did you clean this grill before you lit the fire?"

"I meant to. Why? Doesn't the fire burn all the crud off?"

He cast a glance at the last pigeon strutting on the terrace feeling. "I have a feeling that the pigeons have been using it for a roost."

"Oh no. That is totally disgusting. I am so sorry, Jaz. I didn't even think of that. Shoo!" she shrieked at the startled bird. "Shoo!"

The pigeon flew away and Jaz let the steak droop over the grill again. "Well, so much for that. Not a problem. I'll take you out. Or we can go over to my place, pick up takeout at Whole Foods, or order in from Shun Lee, and start over."

Bliss felt tears well up. She could blame them on the smoky little grill, her own disappointment, him being so nice she couldn't stand it, but she couldn't blink them back.

A big, juicy teardrop rolled down each cheek.

"Are you crying?" he asked with astonishment. "What in hell for?"

"Several reasons. I'm hot. I spent forty dollars on food and ruined it. I live in a crummy little apartment with pigeon crap on the terrace."

Jaz took a swig of beer and looked at her thoughtfully. "Got it. Well, I can't change the weather and you wouldn't believe me if I asked you to marry me so you could live happily ever after. But we could go out. Or move this party to my place."

She hardly heard what he said. "What do I do with the hibachi? Put it in the bathtub? The whole building could catch on fire if I leave it alone."

He patted her on the back. "Let's get back inside. I want you to drink that beer. We can eat the potatoes mashed up with butter. That'll do."

"I forgot to get butter." She sniffled up snot.

"Then we'll eat them plain." His voice was soothing. "C'mon, in you go." The touch of his hand on the small of her back was even more soothing as he guided her through the doorway. He paused to fork the slab of raw meat onto the plate, and took it to the kitchen where he pressed the foot pedal of the garbage can and dropped it in. "Sayonara, steakysan."

Bliss sat on the sofa, twirling the cold beer bottle in her hands. "I blew it. And you're being too goddamn nice."

"No one has ever accused me of being too goddamn nice. Not even Dora."

Aha, said a voice in her miserable mind. He just had to mention your archrival with the ice-blue eyes and unfrizzable blond hair. Bet Dora cooks steak perfectly. Bet she cooks for Jaz all the time.

He sat down next to her and pressed his thigh against hers. The warm contact and the sensual feel of the powerful muscle under his lightly furred skin broke through her unhappy obsessing. Bliss patted his big, bony knee.

He clinked his beer bottle to hers. "Drink up. And stop worrying about Dora. Every time I mention her name, your eyes start going in concentric circles, did you know that?"

Bliss frowned and tipped up the bottle against her lips, drinking as fast as she could, even though she knew the bubbles would make her hiccup if she did.

She finished it off and managed a silent but unpleasantly beery burp behind her hand. "Now w-what?"

"Pour some water on the hibachi and leave it to the pigeons. We're going to my place. You need to get loved up."

"Could work."

Later, much later, they lay naked in the moonlight streaming through windows shut tight and climate-controlled. The noise of the streets was barely audible. Though he lived in one of the most expensive buildings in New York, his place wasn't all that big. But it was bigger than hers. He did mention that HT kept a suite of offices in the same building and she figured they underwrote the cost of his apartment as a corporate perk for him.

The décor was just as masculine as his Pine Island house. Of course, he'd designed most of the furniture and had it built to spec. HT hadn't paid for that. The New York pieces were upholstered in textured black wool, handwoven by Scottish cottagers, from sheep with ancient pedigrees. The look was sophisticated but not as nice, somehow, as his Pine Island house. Indulging in a *Trading Spaces* moment, he'd shown her pictures of the sheep, which had imperturbable stares to go with their ancient pedigrees.

No floral prints anywhere. No needlepointed mottos on pillows. No shopping magazines. Nary a trinket in sight and no cute photos of pug dogs in sunglasses on the fridge. No makeup in the bathroom, no conditioner or shampoo meant for blondes only.

Giving in to her lamentable curiosity, she'd done a little fast snooping while he'd ordered dinner in from Shun Lee. There was no trace of female habitation at either place, but that didn't fully reassure her.

Jaz was just too great a guy not to have women chasing him night and day. But their affair was too new for her to be asking bitchy questions about where he went and who he saw, and it wasn't like he was asking her things like that.

Lying in his arms, looking up at his strong, sweet face as he dozed, she counted up the few dates they'd had, factored in the incredible sex, remembered the exhilaration of fooling around like a couple of high school kids on the beach, recollected how peaceful she felt around him when they weren't doing anything at all, not even talking . . . and wondered if she could do without him.

Oh, shut up and just let him hold you, she told herself. And hold him back. For all you're worth.

She slid her arm around his middle and fell asleep against his chest.

* * *

Since the Fourth of July fell on a Friday, Vi let everyone at LFG leave early on Wednesday afternoon to get a head start on a four-day weekend. Except for Bliss, who earned a big hug and overtime pay in advance from Vi for volunteering to work through the holiday.

At the beach. With Jaz. Hot Treats was the main sponsor of the Pine Island Fourth of July children's parade. Some of the New York staff came out to help distribute hundreds of free samples of the new mini-pies to all the mini-marchers, and their moms and dads and relatives and friends.

But not Dora. Even though Jaz told Bliss his assistant sometimes visited friends on the island, she was somewhere on Cape Cod for the big holiday weekend, much to Bliss's relief.

The promotion got results. By Saturday, the Pine Island paper ran a color photo with a caption that made Bliss very, very happy.

Jaz Claybourn, a lifelong Pine Islander from Breezy Bay, treats youngsters to free mini-pies at the annual Independence Day parade. The photo showed Jaz with two cute kids munching away, with an adorable dab or two of filling on their cheeks and behind them, the company banner displaying the product name: MyPies.

Yes, the photo was next to an in-depth article on the mating behavior of horseshoe crabs, and no, the Pine Island paper wasn't exactly the big time, but it was still good publicity.

Bliss had worked late hours with the Lentone Fitch & Garibaldi art director to design a new wrapper for the MyPie launch. And geez, was the packaging ever cute and happy. Jaz thought it was too cute and happy, but the art director pointed out that a black wrapper wouldn't sell a whole lot of pies.

All in all, they gave away about one thousand MyPies, baked, packaged, and shipped direct from the Leonardville factory to the Havertown dock without a hitch. Jaz and Bliss spent the next day sacked out on the beach when they weren't throwing themselves into the waves. Sun, surf, sex—the combination cured a lot of things.

That's what she told her mother, when she checked in with her parents via phone, leaving out the sex. Edie and Bill Johnson had celebrated the Fourth the way they always did, watching the traditional parade down the main street of Thurbeck, and eating barbecue at several different parties.

Jaz spent at least an hour on the phone with his mom, who was in Vermont at a rented place on the lake with her college friends, reading the Bill of Rights and the Constitution aloud to each other. She treated her son to a snippet of the Gettysburg Address, since he was nice enough to listen, then went back to mixing margaritas for her politically conscious pals.

But by Sunday, the breeze in Breezy Bay and points east and west ceased to blow. The mosquitoes and biting flies made it impossible to sit outside or on the beach. The line at the ferry dock was doubling back on itself by noon, and Jaz and Bliss waited to leave along with everyone else.

She reached down to pick up her bags when the line began to move forward, and gave Jaz a big smile. He did the same. "Ready to go home?"

She nodded.

"I'll take you out to dinner tonight someplace swanky. You can get dressed up and show off your golden tan."

She stuck a finger under her waistband and scratched. "And my bug bites."

"On you, bug bites are beautiful."

"Not exactly," she laughed. "But sure, let's go out to eat."

Jaz had the town car driver drop her off in Chelsea after he got out uptown, promising to pick her up at eight. Fine with her. She walked over to the big housewares store on Ninth

Avenue and bought the last air conditioner in stock, paying $50 extra to have it delivered and installed in an hour.

The delivery guy was waiting at the door of her building with a huge box strapped to a hand truck by the time she got back. Bliss had shopped at the produce markets along the way, enjoying the colorful explosion of flowers for sale along with fruits and vegetables stacked in neat pyramids.

She let him in, glad that the elevators were finally fixed. The delivery guy bumped the big box through her door and got to work, taking out the dead one and installing the new one. He turned it on full blast and showed her how to work the vents.

She could have figured that out herself, but she gave him an extra $20 anyway. He flashed a gold-toothed smile at her and departed. Bliss brought a folding chair from the kitchen and set up a footbath in front of the air conditioner, getting ready for a poor girl's pedicure. The new air conditioner pretty much ate her overtime check but it was well worth it.

She sat down in the chair and slipped her feet into the sudsy water, flipping through a magazine devoted exclusively to the pleasures of shopping that was under a pile of paperback romances. Models decked out in inexpensive versions of runway couture were her inspiration. She had some things in her closet that could be loosely defined as swanky.

Bliss wiggled her toes in the water, then set aside the magazine and got busy with the pumice scrubber. Keeping her feet pretty during the summer was work, but it felt awfully good.

She stepped out onto the thick folded towel by the chair and used another to dry her feet. Then she went to the closet and pushed the hangers to one side until the dress she had in mind was visible.

It had a mostly mesh bodice, with light, flexible boning that allowed her to breathe, and a detachable, swishy skirt. That dress lifted her boobs like nothing else. She wanted to turn Jaz on with it, make him stare at her cleavage while she sat across a table in a posh restaurant and flirted like crazy with a cute waiter, if the place had one. In New York, that was usually a given.

She hummed as she rifled through her dresser drawers next, deciding against pantyhose as she lifted out a garter belt, moving it to and fro and making the delicate garters sway in mid-air. It was perfect for a night of seduction and sex.

The stockings that went with it were sheer, with lace tops that actually did stay up by themselves. But the garter belt was too sexy to do without. Bliss also decided against wearing panties. No, she was going commando tonight.

Jaz called her from the car and jumped out to open her door when she came down to the street, not letting the driver do it. His eyes widened when he saw the dress and he put both hands around her waist to give her a sensual kiss right there on the sidewalk. Two gay guys walking by hand in hand applauded, but Bliss noticed they weren't admiring *her* butt.

"You look amazing, babe. Let's go." He handed her into the back seat and got in around the other side, ignoring the blaring horn of a homicidal taxi driver swerving around the double-parked town car. Jaz gave him the finger and gave his driver the restaurant's name and address, then closed the clear partition between the front and back seats.

Bliss had never been there but she'd heard of it. "Posh place."

"The poshest of the posh. And we'll have it pretty much to ourselves. I know the owner. Gustave only stays open in summer so he doesn't have to lay off the help, but most of his regulars are out of town living it up in the Hamptons."

Bliss nodded and smoothed her dress over her knees. Jaz rested a hand in her lap and pulled the material back so that her thighs were bared. "Don't worry, the driver can't see." His hand moved appreciatively over the lace tops of her stockings and the garters. He smiled wickedly. "No underwear, huh?"

"No," Bliss said. They indulged in discreet sex play as the blocks rolled by outside the tinted windows. Jaz's cock rose to the occasion and his pants were tenting. She put her hand over the bulge and squeezed lightly.

Jaz drew in his breath. "Better not. We're almost there."

Geographically, that was true, but they hit a traffic jam on Madison Avenue that kept them in the town car for another fifteen minutes. The driver let them out and drove off to wait nearby until it was time to take them home.

Bliss stood on the sidewalk, her light dress blowing around her legs, stirred by a breeze that did nothing to cool the air. She kept her hands by her sides and controlled the swishiness, not wanting to flash the maitre d' when they went inside.

Jaz opened the door for her and followed her in, nodding to members of the wait staff, who all seemed to know him. As he'd said, the place was nearly empty.

But it was gorgeous, and the walls seemed to breathe money. Fin-de-siècle French mirrors adorned elegant wood paneling and gave the room some sparkle, but the lighting was low and rosy. The white damask tablecloths seemed whiter because of it.

The maitre d' led them to a table, chatting unobtrusively with Jaz, and bowing to her as he pulled out a rococo chair upholstered in pale silk brocade at the table Jaz chose. Bliss felt positively royal as she sat. It was good to be the queen.

Jaz sat across from her, accepting a leather-bound wine list adorned with an extravagant tassel, which the sommelier brought over and handed to him with a bow.

"Quite a lot of bowing in this place," she whispered when the sommelier withdrew.

He shrugged and studied the wine list. "They're looking

down your dress. Can't blame them." He read off the names of a few wines. "Any preference?"

"You pick. I wouldn't know one from another."

Jaz took another minute to decide and the sommelier materialized at his side. He ordered a vintage burgundy and the sommelier nodded, taking back the list with yet another discreet bow and walking away without making a sound on the thick carpet underfoot. Bliss had never been in a restaurant like this, but that was because she didn't have an expense account. She secretly liked the way everyone did their bidding, as if nothing pleased them more.

Jaz clasped his hands on the table, studying Bliss with undisguised lust. "So. What fantasy would you like with your *amuse-bouche*?"

"My what?"

"That's fancy French for appetizer. Literally, a mouth tickler."

"Um." Bliss wriggled in her seat. "I don't know. You can pick that too."

He cast a glance at a young waiter standing near the wall, menus in his hand, waiting for the moment to present them to Bliss and Jaz. "How about him?"

"Huh? I'm confused. Aren't we talking about food?"

"We don't have menus yet."

Bliss looked in the direction he had. The waiter was about twenty, with dark hair and soulful eyes, and an innocent but very sensual face with full, soft lips. Tall but not as tall as Jaz. Slim. Oh geez, she thought, he is pretty.

"Will he do?" Jaz inquired.

"What do you mean?"

"Fantasy time. Play along. Don't worry, nothing's going to actually happen. But your eyes lit up when you looked at him."

Bliss blushed.

"I don't mind. You get respectful attention from a handsome

young guy, I get to tell you what he wants to do to a beautiful woman he can't touch, and we both get to eat."

Bliss was nonplussed. Like every other female on the planet, she'd had her share of fantasies about young guys who lusted after more experienced women, but she'd never done any cradle robbing and she didn't intend to.

Still, what Jaz had in mind sounded like fun.

"And then I get to take you home when you're hot and juicy, and make you come two or three times." He broke off when the sommelier came with the wine, and quickly got through the business with the cork and the first taste. He nodded and the wine was poured. They were alone again.

Bliss sipped hers, feeling a buzz almost immediately. Unless that was the atmosphere of the place. The low lighting put her in a languorous mood. The mirrors reflected into each other and she saw the profile of the handsome young waiter in several, from different angles, as if he were a character in a dream. One of her wilder dreams.

Jaz let her finish her first glass of wine without saying anything more. His proposal for a shared fantasy appealed to her. The young waiter didn't have to know.

He came over with the menus and gave Bliss a shy smile, but only nodded to Jaz. When he went away, Jaz winked at her. "Told you. He's been standing over there looking at you. I had a feeling the feeling was mutual."

Bliss only smiled and looked over the menu. She picked something easy to eat, since Jaz planned to get her involved in a fantasy that had yet to unfold. He chose the same, and the young waiter came back to take their orders. "M'sieu, madame, my name is Jacques," he said with a slight but charming accent. "Please call on me if there is anything else you require."

"Thank you. We will," Jaz said with a grin. He turned his attention back to Bliss when Jacques walked quietly away. "They cook everything to order and it's going to take a while. Shall I start?"

Bliss was rosy-faced from the wine and feeling just a touch of embarrassment. A fantasy involving a real person who might overhear at some point was not something she'd ever thought of doing. "Go right ahead. But keep your voice down. Way down."

"All right." He moved his chair closer to hers and spoke softly, heightening the sense of intimacy. "You and Jacques are in a chateau, but you're the mistress."

"Then who is he?"

"Ah—a new house servant who considers himself privileged to wait on you. And he saw you nearly naked once, but you didn't know it."

"Where was I?"

"In your bedroom. With your maid. Who was, um, helping you get dressed and lacing your corset."

"Where was Jacques? Can I have more wine?" She twirled her glass by the slender stem.

"Sure. He was someplace where he could see you without you seeing him." Jaz thought it over. "In the closet. He came in before you were finished with your bath in the adjoining room. He was told to bring you something and he didn't want to get caught looking at all the beautiful things on your dressing table." He poured the deep red wine into her glass, nearly filling it.

"So he's watching. Now what?" Bliss was amused despite her initial reluctance. This *was* fun.

"You tell me. This is an improvisation. Jump in anytime."

She sipped her wine, aware of how close he was without actually touching her. Just his nearness was erotic. She opened her legs under the tablecloth where no one could see, and pressed her thigh against his.

"I instruct my maid to pull the laces tight," she said at last.

"She braces her foot against the bed and winds them around her hands, giving me a smaller waist. My bare breasts pop over the top of the corset, and I laugh, trying to push them back down."

"Yes."

"What I don't know is that she's looking at my behind."

"Naked or not?"

"Naked, of course. I haven't put on my drawers yet." Bliss patted his cheek. He placed her palm against his lips and pressed a kiss into it. The few members of the restaurant staff in the room pretended not to see and drifted away, leaving them to their tête-à-tête.

"The maid is a virgin when it comes to men, but not women. She has always desired me, her voluptuous mistress, as much as Jacques does. But Nanette has served me longer, although I knew nothing of the kind of service she wants to provide."

"Mmm. You're good at this."

"You got me started," Bliss laughed.

"Go on."

"Nanette clasps her hands to keep from touching me between my legs. I'm flushed from the effort of breathing in the corset, but the tightness is exciting too. I turn to her and ask her to push my breasts down so the nipples at least will be covered. She handles me with feminine gentleness, tucking the nipples into the lace."

"And Jacques sees it all," Jaz picked up the thread of the story he had started. "He slides his hand into his breeches. His cock is unbearably stiff and hot. He squeezes it roughly, hurting himself so as not to ejaculate in his new doeskin breeches. The head manservant would take them down and give him a whipping if he ruined them."

Bliss looked at him with surprise. "What the hell have you been reading?"

"Former girlfriend of mine was a romance addict. I read a few."

Bliss nodded. "Okay. Well, I would never let anything bad happen to Jacques. If I saw him handle his cock like that, I would stop him at once."

Jaz poured himself some more wine. "And you would have to take him into your private chamber to take care of him, and talk to him kindly. Just the sound of your voice would be enough to make him get an uncontrollable erection again. Right in front of you."

"This is getting me hot."

"Good. It's supposed to."

Bliss looked around for the real Jacques. He had disappeared, fortunately. She wasn't sure she could look him in the eye when he brought their entrées.

"Okay. Back to me and the maid. Nanette drops to her knees in front of me to help me put on my drawers. It's beginning to dawn on me that she is sexually excited and scarcely able to conceal it. She clasps my ankle and lifts my foot into one leg of the drawers and then the other, pulling them up over my thighs and bare behind as she rises, facing me.

"I try to look into her eyes as she pulls the drawstring and ties it in a bow at the waist. But she won't meet my gaze. Dropping a curtsy, she asks my permission to go."

"Are you sure you want her to go?" Jaz asked, looking a little disappointed.

"Yes. Because I just spied Jacques in the closet and I don't want her to see him. She would see to it that he was punished properly. Perhaps even sent away. And I don't want that. Because at that moment, I realize how lovely he is."

"And here he comes now," Jaz whispered, moving fractionally away from her.

Bliss turned scarlet when the young waiter set down the plates with European deftness, not making a sound, like everyone else in the elegant restaurant. She looked at the flowers on the table, and at Jaz, but not at him.

"Excusez-moi. Fresh pepper?" he asked, picking up a long mill he picked up from a nearby wait stand.

She had to look at him. She prayed he would think that drinking wine on a summer night had crimsoned her cheeks. She met his eyes. Soft, brown, and questioning. "No, thank you."

"That will be all for now," Jaz added. Jacques gave a little nod and set the pepper mill on the stand, leaving them alone. Bliss didn't even know what was on her plate. Something in sauce.

"Close call," Jaz murmured. "This looks good. But finish up the story. We can have the maid for dessert."

She smothered a laugh that broke the tension. "You're really bad, you know that?"

"Guilty as charged. I love the way you fantasize."

"Takes practice," was all she said. No need to tell him that she hadn't gone totally without sex for nearly a year before they met. Not with her burgeoning collection of erotic romance, historical and contemporary, which she had kicked under the foldout couch the night he came to visit. She put the tines of her fork into the sauce and tasted it. "This is good. But anyway, back to Jacques."

Looking at her with amusement, Jaz drank his wine while she considered the possibilities of her imaginary servant. "I close the door behind Nanette and go to the closet. But Jacques has stepped out. He knows that I saw him and that by dismissing her, I saved him from a whipping. He begs my pardon, hanging his head in shame.

"I lift his chin. My fingers brushing his face undo the reserve he has been trained to show and he parts his soft lips, startled by my touch. He kisses me, shyly and tenderly, like the inexperienced boy he is. Nonetheless, he is almost a man—and the kisses grow bolder.

"His hands come up and he touches my nipples. He is curious but not sure of himself. Sighing in his arms, I see that my breasts have overflowed the tight corset again. I lie upon the divan and open my arms to him. He lies beside me, burying his face in my breasts and suckling like a child. I have never experienced the pleasure of physical love with so young a man and my body aches for him. Wanton thoughts race through my mind of just how I ought to pleasure him and what a thrill it will be to see him climax for the first time. I want to witness every second of it. I want him to ejaculate into my cupped hands, like a gift to me, so I can rub his hot essence over my bare breasts. I know that he will not come so quickly the second time, and I want to make sure that he gives me a hard, long ride."

"You are very, *very* good at this." Jaz's voice was charged with sexual heat.

"I'm channeling Virginia Hammermill."

"Who's she?"

"A romance novelist with a very dirty mind. Who were you channeling?"

"Ah, I was just making it up as I went along. I only read a couple of those books. Go on."

"I wonder whether I should confess my secret desire—I wish to serve him as humbly as he has served me. Without my husband knowing, of course."

"Where'd he come from?"

She looked at him, puzzled. "My imagination, like all the rest of this. He thinks women should obey men without question and he ties me up and takes a paddle to my behind if I don't. His dominating sport arouses me unbearably and I am never satisfied. So . . . that's why I want Jacques. For a little while, behind closed doors, he may be the master if he wishes. I will do anything he asks.

"But Jacques doesn't give me a chance to confess. He lifts his head from my breasts and kneels beside me on the divan, taking his cock out of his breeches. He begs me to initiate him sexually—"

Jaz clinked his fork against his plate. "And here he comes again."

"M'sieu, madame, is everything to your satisfaction?" the real Jacques asked. He cast a polite glance at their untouched entrees.

This time Bliss looked right at him. "Oh, yes. We were just talking."

Jaz cut and ate a bite of whatever was swimming in the sauce. "Delicious. Thank you, Jacques." He waved his fork at Bliss when the waiter moved across the room to see to another couple who were ready to order. "Better eat some of that. Gustave will be over next, and the chef will get yelled at if you don't."

She picked up her knife and fork. "Not a problem. I'm starving. But we can skip dessert and coffee."

"My thoughts exactly. I want to get you naked and I can't do it here."

Finishing a bottle of champagne on top of the wine they'd had at the French restaurant left them both feeling restlessly sexual. Once they moved from the living room to Jaz's bedroom, he wasted no time. His voice was rough and he seemed different somehow, on edge. But his touch was still gentle.

"Tie me up," she said softly. She had taken off the detachable skirt to the dress and the boned bodice made a perfect fantasy corset. "Let's finish the story. Master and mistress." Bliss pulled her breasts out and let them overflow the top. She handed him the stockings she had peeled off and unfastened the garter belt.

"Whatever you want."

He went out of the room and came back with a chair. The curved back was made of a single piece of narrow wood, with an open space below that. "Sit down," was all he said.

She sat on the smooth surface of the seat, hands on her thighs, looking up at him. He was dressed but his shirt was open and his solid chest invited her touch. She reached up but he pushed her hand away. "You're not in charge. Scoot back on the seat. I want to see your ass."

Bliss obeyed, into this game too, and trusting him implicitly. He knew how to be just rough enough when she wanted that and he had proved it several times over. She rose halfway and sat firmly in the chair, thrusting her bare buttocks back as she sat down again, opening her legs wide.

"Good girl. That's the idea. You can't hide what I want from you. If you're wondering if I designed the chair for this, I didn't." Jaz used the stretchy stockings to tie her ankles near the bottom of the chair legs. "But it does the trick."

Bliss arched back, letting her hair brush the back of her neck. The champagne was making her feel dizzy and decadent. The position tipped her breasts up and out. Jaz stopped what he was doing to suckle and nip at them. Wild with desire, she dug her nails into his shoulders until faint lines of blood appeared. He pushed her hands away again, pulling hard on the stocking and tying her hands to her thighs.

He shucked the rest of his clothes and turned the dimmers down low, coming to stand before her. In the half light, his muscular body looked massive and dangerously sensual. His huge cock was smack up against his taut belly. She longed to touch it but she couldn't.

She opened her mouth, hoping he would let her suck his shaft and calm him down, but he didn't seem to want that. He reached down and took her nipples between the finger and thumb of either hand, rolling and tugging them. "Feels hotter when you can't move, doesn't it?"

"Yes," she whispered.

"You don't have a lot of inhibitions."

"That storytelling session was your idea."

He shook his head. "I have to admit the way Jacques looked at you made me a little jealous."

"He was only looking."

"I know. He had no idea of what we were doing. I left him a good tip. I have him to thank for getting you this hot, I guess."

"Jaz, you make me hot."

His body tensed visibly. "And you're going to do the same for me. Open your mouth."

She did. He slid his cock between her welcoming lips, letting out the breath he was holding when her tongue fluttered around his shaft and her mouth tightened around it. He shuddered with pleasure and the tension in his body eased a little. Stroking her hair almost tenderly, he thrust his cock into her mouth with the care for her that he always had.

The he sighed and stopped. He walked over to the long dresser and took something out of the top drawer. A smooth piece of thin wood about six inches wide. A paddle. Somehow she'd known that he would have one.

He came back with it in his hand and stood to one side of her. "Master and mistress, huh? How far do you want to go, Bliss?"

"All the way. Use that on my bare ass. I want you to." Bliss closed her eyes. They hadn't ever gone this far, but she still trusted him.

"You sure?"

"Yes." She felt the rush of air on her skin first, before the first crack of the thin wood paddle landed on her exposed ass. Bliss braced herself against the back of the chair. Pleasure and pain mingled into one intense sensation that rocketed through her.

"Can you take it?" he said softly.

"Yes," she whispered.

"Four more. Five in all."

Two. Three. Four. Five. She counted mentally, straining against her bonds. But each smack heightened the sensation of the one before it. She came almost without knowing it, feeling the seat wet and slick beneath her open pussy.

"That's enough." Jaz dropped the paddle on the floor and knelt to untie her. He rubbed her wrists and hands, kissed her palms, and released her ankles. Then he picked her up as if she weighed nothing at all and carried her to his bed. He laid her down on her back on the cool sheets. She was still wearing the mesh bodice. Her bare breasts bounced free.

"Open your legs. Spread your pussy lips with both hands and stay that way."

Her hot buttocks tingled, and the sheets beneath her felt wonderful. Without saying a word, she watched him sheathe his huge cock with a condom, struggling to roll it on. Paddling her had aroused him deeply.

He got on all fours over her, kissing her soft mouth, kissing away the teardrops at the corners of her eyes as she reached up to him. Then he rammed himself into her, twisting his hips with each thrust, gasping with pleasure, going full tilt to make her come again.

Bliss scratched at his back, on fire with the same crazy need that had engulfed him, wanting to take and be taken. He cried out when his orgasm hit him hard, only seconds before hers. She clutched his iron butt and drove him into her, raising her legs to take him all the way, screaming his name.

He collapsed in her arms, pumped muscles slick with sweat. Slowly, slowly, the wildness ebbed away from both of them. "Goddamn it," he said, gasping. "You are my weakness, do you know that?"

"No," she whispered.

He kissed her forehead when he got his breath. "Bliss, Bliss," he murmured. "What the hell am I going to do with you?"

* * *

She woke with him curled around her as he had been on the first night they'd shared a bed at Pine Island. Like then, she felt completely safe in his embrace. His thighs cupped hers and his soft cock and balls rested against her warm, still tingling behind. One big arm clasped her waist and he was breathing into her hair. He felt her stir and he came awake at once, still filled with the nervous energy of their rough love play.

"Hey, angel," he murmured into her hair. He moved his hand down to feel her ass. "How's that beautiful behind? Did I paddle you too hard?"

She smiled into her pillow but didn't turn around. "I'm going to remember it for a few days when I sit down, put it that way. And when I think about you. Anyway, to answer your second question, no, you didn't."

"Good." He caressed her whole body with long strokes, pausing to savor the curves and squeeze her where she was softest. "You got me a little crazy. Tell me to stop next time."

"I didn't want you to stop," she answered truthfully. "I think we're just going to be into doing that sometimes. I don't want to analyze it."

He was silent for a minute or two. He nuzzled her hair when he spoke again. "Just so you know, I wouldn't ever do anything you didn't want me to do."

Bliss wanted to tell him again how much she liked him to be that aroused. But not now and not here. "Go to sleep," she whispered. "Everybody needs to get wild once in a while."

He was quiet again and she thought that he had fallen asleep. But he said one more thing, in a growl so soft it was hard to hear. "I think I really do love you."

"Same here," she whispered. She pulled his arm around her and luxuriated in his warmth.

5

"I suppose we'd better get some work done this summer," Vi grumbled. "I say we. I mean myself. You've been plugging away at that HT campaign, Bliss. Any new developments?"

Bliss looked up from the file on her lap. "No. Not really." *Just that Jaz and I are crazy in love, and playing sex games that get a little out of control sometimes.*

"You mustn't mix business with pleasure," Vi said idly, fixing the back of one of her huge silver hoop earrings. She pulled the mirror on her desk closer to her face and frowned. Then she smiled. Both expressions looked artificial.

"What do you mean?"

"We want to retain that HT account. By we I mean we."

"Got it. Hey, did you see that the *New York Times* picked up the parade photo from the Pine Island paper? They cropped Jaz out, but you could still see the kids eating pies and the MyPie logo on the banner."

"How fabulous," Vi said. Her eyes glowed with fervor. "How are sales?"

"Too early to tell anything definite, but Jaz said the distributors are ordering MyPies for convenience market accounts."

"Brilliant."

Bliss closed the file on her lap. "I've been working on new ways to get media attention for the pies."

Vi pondered that for a few moments. "We could hire desperate, out-of-work actors to dress up like Wizard of Oz characters and drop them from a hot-air balloon."

"The actors? I don't know any that desperate." Bliss tapped her pencil on the closed file. "I take it back. I could get you a few."

"I meant the pies. But I don't suppose potential customers would enjoy being pelted with them."

Bliss had to agree. "Well, no. But the balloon concept is interesting."

"No, no. Forget I said that. Printing a logo on a hot-air balloon is too expensive."

"We could use a big vinyl banner. Wouldn't cost that much."

"Bliss, dear, please don't take me up on terrible ideas. Yes, Kayla, what is it?"

The intern came into the office with her arms full of bulging files. "You said you wanted me to move these from the bottom drawers to the top drawers. But the top drawers are full."

"Then empty them and stack those folders on the floor," Vi said patiently.

Kayla made a face and turned around, heading back to the contracts dungeon.

"We're never going to be able to find anything in there again," Bliss pointed out. She felt sorry for Kayla and gave her boss a look of reproach.

"I have to keep her busy," Vi insisted. "There are less than seven weeks of summer left. By the way, are you and Jaz going out to Pine Island this weekend?"

Bliss nodded. "Yup."

"Me too," Vi sighed. "Rocco is about to test his latest theory. He thinks that Pine Island might have been settled by Vikings."

"Did he—find runes on a clam or something?" Bliss wasn't quite sure whether to laugh out loud, or act like there was something to it. Vi was obviously crazy in love herself.

"Nothing like that. But he found an old map in a book about Vikings, and he wants to see if they could have sailed this far south from Newfoundland and back again. I have to keep my eye on him. He's building a longship on my front deck."

"Really?" Bliss had seen Vi's deck only once but it was as uncluttered and tasteful as the rest of her beach house. It was hard to imagine Rocco in paint-splotched jeans being allowed to mess it up. What women did for love . . .

Jaz and Bliss sat on opposite sides of the town car's back seat. He was absorbed in the files open on his laptop when they came to a jolting stop, stuck in sluggish traffic on the eastbound Long Island Expressway. They were still in Queens, en route to the Havertown ferry dock. His hand came down in the wrong place on the keyboard and the display disappeared. "Goddamn it."

Bliss tried to capture the papers that slithered out of the file on her lap. Most of them ended up at her feet.

"Sorry, Mr. Claybourn," the driver called back. "The moron ahead of me slammed on his brakes so he wouldn't hit the moron ahead of him. Want me to try the service road?"

"No," Jaz said. "This will clear out after we get past this merge. I hope."

The driver nodded and the town car inched forward.

"How are you making out?"

"Trying not to get footprints on the presentation for the HT board."

He reached down to collect whatever papers he could reach and handed them to her. "At least you didn't lose your work. I think the MyPie file I was working on is gone."

"Give me the laptop," Bliss said. He handed it over and she pulled up a few menus, did a little jiggery-pokery on the keyboard and retrieved it. "There you go."

"Wow. I'm still tempted to let you run the company."

"And I still don't want to."

"Why not?"

"I find that underpaid, soul-destroying work suits me best."

Jaz snorted. "You could go back to college and get an MBA or something. Then you could find overpaid, soul-destroying work." He closed the programs he was using and shut down the computer, stashing it safely in the pocket behind the driver's seat. "That's enough of that."

Bliss finished gathering up her papers and stashed them in a zippered tote bag. "Why do I have the sudden feeling that you're not the happiest CEO in the world?"

"Aw, you noticed."

"Is there anything I can do?"

He closed the clear partition between them and the driver. "I think that getting a blow job is illegal on the expressway, so the answer is no." He blew out a weary sigh. "Sorry. That was kinda crude."

Bliss slid over as far as her seat belt would allow and patted his hand. "I'm listening, Jaz."

"It's like this," he said after a while. "The closer I get to Pine Island, the better I feel. But I can't run the business from there. It wouldn't be fair to the HT board or the company employees."

"Are you experiencing—"

"Drum roll," he interrupted her. "A midlife crisis. Yes."

"You're still in your thirties."

"I'm thirty-nine. And I like to get a head start." He smiled at her. "I'll be okay, Bliss. I've got you. And I could always go work for my brother."

"Oh." Bliss thought back on the blond boy she'd seen in the old snapshot next to Jaz. "What does he do? You never really said."

"He started out as a house carpenter, took over my dad's business. But he's a major contractor now. He and his crew just finished a big job on the east end of Pine Island, a twenty-room house for a movie mogul. That's why you haven't met him yet."

She looked at Jaz curiously. "I know you're not serious about working for him. But—you sound serious."

"I'm not. I can swing a hammer with the best of them, but I don't want to do it for a living. I can't complain, though. HT's done right by me. If I put in fifteen more years, I can retire early."

"Why would you want to retire?"

Jaz's face grew thoughtful and sad. "My dad died too soon. Cancer. There were a million things he wanted to do with the rest of his life, but he didn't get a chance. Maybe you noticed that photo of me and my brother and my dad down in the cellar at Pine Island—"

"I saw it," Bliss said quietly.

"I've been meaning to take it down, have a copy made for my office. Just to keep my mind on what's important."

She remembered wondering about why there was only a photo of him and his mom in Leonardville, but she didn't mention it.

"Anyway," Jaz said, "I haven't. That photo's been there for years. My mom framed it and hung it by his workbench so he could remember what was important." He gazed out the window of the town car. "She doesn't ever come out to Pine Island. Too many memories."

Neither of them noticed that the traffic had lessened. They

weren't whizzing along, but they were getting where they were going.

"You miss him, don't you?" Bliss said at last.

"Yeah, I do," Jaz said. "But he's gone and that can't be changed. One thing about him, he didn't allow any whining. One whiny word and he'd have us scraping old paint off the siding or something like that."

Bliss nodded. "My dad was the same way."

"What did he do?"

"Sold insurance in a small town. He still does."

"How about your mom?"

"She was a schoolteacher."

"My mom too," Jaz said with surprise. "She taught high school history. "

"Bet they were both proud of you," she said softly.

"Well, yeah. I put myself through school working weird shifts as a stockbroker trainee, handling trades in foreign markets that opened hours before the NYSE did. Got my MBA, got tapped to head up smaller companies, and then I got the HT job."

"You're a rising star." Her tone was light and teasing but she meant it.

He shrugged off the compliment. "Hot Treats snacks would keep on chugging right out the factory door whether I was running the company or not. I'm a cog in a machine. I don't have any illusions about that."

Bliss decided to try a different tack. "What would you do if you had all the money you needed?"

"OK, some people think I can't cook but I'd like to open a restaurant at the end of nowhere on Pine Island. Fill it with my friends every night of the summer. Volunteer for something really worthwhile the rest of the year."

"A restaurant, huh? Interesting."

"You think so? I'll show you where it is."

Bliss was intrigued. "You mean this restaurant exists?"

"It's been closed for years, but yeah, it exists. I wasn't kidding when I said it's at the end of nowhere."

They ran up the deck stairs to the Breezy Bay house, feeling liberated from work and traffic and everything that made life in the real world dreary. A cool wind blew mist in from the ocean, shrouding the walks in soft gray light. Jaz hoisted the box and the disposable cooler for perishables that the delivery kid had left in front of his house and brought them in.

"Bunny is a mind reader," he said to Bliss, checking the contents of the box and the disposable cooler for perishable. "Everything I wanted is here. We're set for the next three days."

"Good thing. I'm hungry," said a deep, unfamiliar voice. Bliss turned around in surprise and found herself blocked by a wall of man.

"Hey, bro," Jaz said, not looking up. "I think she put in your favorite cookies. Bunny thinks you're still four years old. Wait till I tell her you can blow your own nose."

The wall of man grinned down at Bliss. Holy cow. Joe Claybourn was taller than Jaz, and even more muscular.

"Don't tell her that. I can't. But I'm working on it."

"Right, right," Jaz said absently. He pulled out a package of cookies and threw them at his brother. "Knock yourself out. Not a Hot Treats brand, but I know you like them."

Joe caught them in one big hand and ripped open the package with his teeth. Big, white teeth. "So are you going to introduce me to the lady?"

"Bliss Johnson, this is my baby brother, Joe Claybourn."

He held out the opened package to her. "Want a cookie?"

"No, thanks." She smiled back. Joe's grin was contagious. And the rest of him was spectacular. His T-shirt hugged the contours of shoulders that seemed genetically designed for hauling lumber and throwing pretty women over them.

His jeans were faded just right from working in the sun, with white streaks where his thigh muscles pressed against the fabric and some interesting holes and tears.

Workboots, half opened and carelessly tied, that held mighty man feet. Tool belt, slung over hips that . . . this is Jaz's brother, she reminded herself. Do not look any lower than his neck.

"So what's for dinner, Jaz?" He took the cookies over to the long, custom-made table and sprawled in a big chair. Bliss had noticed that most of Jaz's furniture was on the big side. Now she knew why. Every male in his family was big.

"You cooking?"

"No, you are. But don't drag in members of the vegetable family. I don't eat members of the vegetable family. Except French fries and corn on the cob."

Jaz pulled out a bulging bag of fresh, unhusked ears of corn. "That Bunny. She just knows." He held one next to his brother's ear and tickled it with the tassel.

"Quit it," Joe growled.

"Guys, please," Bliss laughed. "Tell you what. I'll cook. I can manage meatloaf. Both of you okay with that?" They looked at each other and nodded. "Grab a couple of cold beers and go sit out on the deck."

"Beer and cookies," Joe said. "Good appetizer."

The brothers slid open the glass door and went to sit outside. Bliss got busy, more at home in Jaz's beach house kitchen than she'd ever been in her own.

She peeled back the clear wrap from the hamburger, got it in a bowl and opened up a package of onion soup mix, dumping that in with a chopped onion and a beaten egg. Five slugs of ketchup, a shake-shake-shake and a whack on the bottom of the breadcrumbs cylinder, a shot each of salt and pepper, and she was done. Bliss steeled herself to squeeze the cold, raw mess together with her hands, and then patted it into a loaf pan.

She went to the sink to scrub up, not realizing Jaz had come into the kitchen behind her until he got her around the waist. "Hey, Joe has to go. But he's coming back. When will the meatloaf be done?"

"In about an hour, hour and a half."

He nodded. "Thanks for making it. You didn't have to do that."

She got her hands clean and dried them with a dishtowel, turning around in the circle of his arms to face him. "Why not? You said you hadn't seen your brother for a while. You guys needed time to talk and I felt like making meatloaf."

"Bet it's going to be tasty."

"Could be the signature dish for the restaurant at the end of nowhere someday." She looked into his eyes as the meaning of her remark registered with him. Then Jaz pulled her close for a long, sensual kiss that didn't stop until Joe clomped into the kitchen.

"Cough, cough. Break it up, you two." Joe set the empty bottle of beer on the kitchen counter.

Secure in Jaz's arms, Bliss looked up at the blond version of the man who was holding her. "Fuck off," Jaz said cheerfully. He rocked Bliss a little and kissed her on the nose.

"Glad to see you so happy, you piece of shit." Joe's tone was just as cheerful. "Later. Thanks for the beer, Bliss. I'm coming back for the meatloaf."

"Bring a fork," Jaz said. "I'm not washing one for you."

Manspeak. Bliss remembered her younger brother talking to his pals the same way. She nestled against Jaz's chest, and waved good-bye to Joe from there.

She saw a different facet of Jaz the next day when the brothers pored over sketches for a shade arbor he wanted to build over the deck.

He really wasn't a cog in a corporate machine, and the rising young executive persona was what he did for money. At heart, Jaz was a man who liked hands-on work and knew how to do it.

Joe set down his flat carpenter's pencil. "Let's get started. We can frame this out today. Just you and me. Like old times."

"I'm getting all choked up," Jaz said, wiping away an imaginary tear.

"If you've got the wood. . . ."

They exchanged a meaningful smile. "To the basement!" they said simultaneously.

Bliss looked up from her laptop and watched them go down the deck stairs. She could hear their laughter and the thunking sounds of lumber being taken down from the racks under the basement ceiling. The quiet moments were easy to figure out. Jaz would insist on checking every piece for warping, and the occasional curse meant a splinter had met flesh.

They tromped back up, tossing four-by-fours into a pile on the front deck. Then they hauled up milk crates of shorter pieces, followed by tools: a portable circular saw, a monster drill, and assorted hardware.

A couple of friends stopped on their way to the beach and shouted encouragement to the Claybourn brothers. "Build, baby, build!"

Joe whipped out a bandanna and waved to them. Then he tied it pirate style around his blond hair, and put on sunglasses. What a big, bad dude he looked like. And how nice he actually was.

From where she was watching inside, she got a look of him peeling off his baggy tank top and a view of the tattoo that spread across his mighty shoulders. The design was Celtic and resembled intricate wings. It made his shoulders look even wider than they were, tapering down into a back ridged with muscle.

Bliss felt a little guilty for looking, but since no one knew she was, it didn't really matter. Joe Claybourn was impossible not to look at.

He walked around on the deck, organizing the elements that would go into the airy structure Jaz had in mind. Turned toward Bliss, he put the wood into order by length, and winked at her.

"Size matters," he called through the glass door.

Jaz came up the stairs with a couple of sawhorses folded and slung over his shoulder. "Are you flirting with my girlfriend?"

"Yup."

Jaz set down the sawhorses and threw a mock punch at Joe, who ignored it. Bliss thought she had never seen any men finer than these two, loose jeans slung low, toolbelts slung lower, bare chests and all.

Joe was much more tanned than Jaz, but then he worked outdoors. But their bodies were so similar—tall and powerful, with an animal grace that came naturally to them—the sight just about melted her.

She went into the kitchen to get something cold to drink and distract herself. The layouts on her computer required her full attention, because the Lentone Fitch & Garibaldi art director wanted to get a go-ahead from her as soon as possible.

The hours slipped by. The brothers went to and fro outside, raising and bracing the supporting beams first and then starting to build the arbor that would create a mix of sun and shade over part of the deck.

They climbed ladders and crawled out on improvised scaffolding, measuring and positioning lumber, hammering and screwing, with practiced speed. She enjoyed watching them, but it wasn't always easy to tell who was who when they were only visible from the waist down, considering they were wearing identical faded jeans and filthy workboots.

Jaz would win the Best Butt contest, she decided. His was fractionally tighter and harder than his brother's.

A falling tape measure hit the deck with a skittering, clanking sound, its long metal ribbon twisting wildly as it went down.

"Could you get that?" Jaz hollered.

Bliss poked her head out the glass door, looking up cautiously. Oh, geez. Both brothers were above her, facing each other, their knees far apart as they balanced on the arbor's main beams. The position strained the seams of their jeans to the max.

Nice view of the classic Claybourn package, she thought. Times two. She picked up the tape and pressed the button that sucked up the tape.

She handed the measuring tape up to Jaz, reveling in how gorgeous the men looked in the sun, their brawny bodies shining with sweat. Jaz's dark but delicate chest hair was wet, and Joe's golden fleece almost sparkled.

"Wanna come up?" Joe asked.

"I'd probably fall off."

"Nah. You could sit on the roof," Jaz said. "Safe enough."

"Well, then—yeah." She'd okayed the layouts and didn't feel like slaving another minute on such a nice day. Bliss put one bare foot on the first rung of one of the ladders.

"Uh-uh," Jaz said. "Put sneakers on."

She ran back in to put on the pair she'd stuffed into her weekend bag. He was right. Even thinking about going up on a roof barefoot was another sign of temporary insanity. But with him, temporary insanity felt great.

Bliss went back out and started up the ladder again. Jaz reached down a hand to pull her up to their level and she popped her head through the beams they were kneeling on.

"Careful now. Get on the last rung and I'll grab you by the back of your shorts. Then swing a leg over the beam when you come up."

She did as he said, feeling his hand slide in to give her ass a quick squeeze before he got a grip on her shorts. One, two, three, and she was up where they were, straddling a beam and feeling very pleased with herself.

"I can see the whole beach!" Bliss craned her neck, keeping her hands on the rough wood of the beam to balance. The endless ocean stretched east and west, dotted with people soaking up the late afternoon sun. There were more people bobbing in the water on the other side of the breakers, but all she could see was their heads.

"Want to sit on the roof?" Jaz asked. Bliss nodded but she didn't let go of the beam.

"I'm going to stand up first. Then you take my hand and stand up, and I'll hand you off to Joe. From him it's two steps to the roof."

"I changed my mind," she said suddenly.

"The trick is not to look down. Just look into my eyes. It's easy. Like ballroom dancing."

Ballroom dancing was about the hardest damn thing she'd ever done and she'd only done it once. "Oh. Okay."

The three of them rose at the same time, and she followed his instructions. For the few seconds it took to get her close to the roof, it did feel like dancing. She wished there was some way to get a picture of herself, one hand in Jaz's and the other in Joe's. Bliss set a foot on the beam to take the last step and someone yelled "Hold it!"

She teetered, righted herself, and looked around to see ... someone taking her picture. Dora. *Dora?* The blonde with the icy eyes was down on the walk, tucking her digital camera back in her beach bag.

"Couldn't resist that shot, Jaz," Dora called. "I'll e it to you."

"When'd you get to Pine Island? Come on up."

"Can't. We have to make an evening ferry. But thanks."

"Where are you staying?"

"With friends."

Bliss noticed the other woman standing in back of Jaz's assistant, with dark hair worn loose like Dora's and a gorgeous body. Not as slender as Dora's but beautiful and strong. Both women wore barely there string bikinis, and a couple of male passers-by did doubletakes, which they ignored.

Hello, competition, Bliss thought. Times two.

The women waved good-bye and kept walking. They didn't seem to have made much of an impression on the Claybourn brothers, though. Of course, Joe and Jaz had to keep their eyes on her or she might fall.

Bliss resented the intimacy implied in Dora's remark. *I'll e it to you.* Obviously his assistant had to e him all kinds of things, but what if her picture made her look goofy? She didn't want Dora snickering over it.

She looked down and wobbled a little. Jaz and Joe held her hands tighter. The brothers handed her off to a flat spot on the edge of the roof, where she sat down. They resumed their work, moving to a mutual rhythm that made them seem almost like an interconnected machine. A muscle machine.

Bliss was closest to Jaz, who was on all fours and hammering at the moment. A tiny drop of sweat hung suspended from one of his nipples and his bare back shone with sweat under the sun. She imagined licking the wet saltiness from his skin, imagined twining her legs around his back while he hammered into her—

The noise of Jaz's hammer stopped. "What are you smiling about?" he asked.

"Oh, nothing," Bliss said.

Joe, taking a break, let his legs dangle from the beam he was sitting on and swigged water from a bottle he'd brought up. "Bleagghh. This is warm. I'm going down for something cold." He scooted over to a ladder and climbed down. Jaz made his way to where Bliss was sitting, a vertical projection that held the skylight, providing just enough shade for the two of them, if they sat very close together.

He patted her bare thigh. "So how do you like your perch?"

"I like it just fine." She smiled.

"Don't fly away." He used a bandanna from his pocket to mop the sweat from his face and leaned back against the vertical. "Whew. Hot work. Bet we'll be done before sundown. Joe and I make a great team."

"You sure do." Bliss leaned out a little. Something over by the Summer Club caught her eye—something long and curved waving above the wind-twisted pine and thick stands of bayberry. If she had to guess, the something was near Vi's house—she recognized its thrusting angles. "Hey, what's that?"

Jaz opened his eyes and sat up a little, looking where she was pointing. Then he squinted. "Dunno. But it's moving."

"It sure is."

They both watched the progress of the long, curved thing through the bayberry bushes.

"Wait a minute," Bliss said suddenly. She stood up for a better look and Jaz put a protective hand around her ankle. "Whoever that is, is going to the back of Vi's house. Could be part of Rocco's longship. Must be the prow—didn't they have dragon prows?"

"Huh?" Jaz had leaned his head back again and closed his eyes.

"Vi said Rocco was going to build a Norse longship. He has a theory that the Vikings settled on Pine Island."

"You're kidding." Jaz opened his eyes, still holding on to her ankle.

"Let go, please. I want to get a better look."

"I don't want you climbing all over the roof." He stroked her calf in an absent-minded way.

"You should look at this thing," Bliss said. "I could be wrong."

"Norsemen. Dragons. Are you sure you're not hallucinating?"

"Hey, strange things happen in your kingdom. Get up and see for yourself."

"That's no way to talk to a king." But he got up, brushing bits of roof asphalt off his butt. He scanned the view toward the Summer Club houses.

A scroll-shaped something popped up in the general vicinity of Vi's house. "Hmm. Maybe you're right. That could be a dragon head. Want to walk over to the Summer Club and see what's going on?"

"Sure."

"Careful." He walked onto a beam and reached out a hand to guide her to one of the ladders. Jaz went down first, and stopped before he reached the bottom, until her sneakered feet were securely on the top rung.

Bliss moved down until her butt was level with his face. He brushed bits of asphalt off her shorts and seized the opportunity to plant affectionate kisses all over the back of her. Bliss giggled. The man just didn't quit.

She heard Joe come out of the house and Jaz stopped kissing her. He got off the ladder and steadied it for her until she was standing on the deck again between the Claybourn brothers.

"Coming down for a cool one?" Joe asked.

"Yeah. And we thought we might walk over to the Summer Club real quick. Bliss thinks Rocco's up to something."

Joe nodded. "He's building a longship on Violet Lentone's deck. I swung by there yesterday to drop off an estimate for an addition."

Jaz and Bliss exchanged a look. "You were right, Bliss. Okay, I have to see this. Can you spare me for one hour, bro?"

"Sure." Joe walked over to the toolbox and rummaged in it for something he needed. "You know, Rocco hired a couple of my guys. They helped him drag the hull of an old clamboat out of the reeds back of Vi's house and they banged together scrap lumber for a half-assed cabin and decking."

Bliss could see that his carpenter's pride kept him from taking a project like that seriously. "I don't think longships had decks or cabins," she said.

Joe chuckled. "This is a clamship. It'll sink ten minutes after he puts it in the water. But he's having fun."

"Rocco always does," Jaz said.

The silver-haired artist was fitting the scrolled thing they had seen into a slot on the clamboat's deck. Rocco gave it a whack with a hammer to get it to go just as Bliss and Jaz came up the ramp. The thing wobbled and tilted to one side.

Bliss got a good look at it for the first time. The dragon head was new, attached to a long piece of curved driftwood.

"Hey, man," Jaz said. "This is amazing." He was a lot more tactful than his brother. "Where'd you get the boat?"

Rocco banged on the dragon-head prow again and set the hammer aside. "I found a wreck back in the bushes. Completely overgrown. Probably tossed there by a hurricane back in the day."

"How about the wood for the deck?" Jaz asked, cautiously running a hand along one side. Bliss noticed that those boards were not scrap but regularly sized and neatly fitted.

"That's from Vi's attic out here," Rocco said nonchalantly. "Don't think she noticed they were gone."

"Oh, yes, I did," Vi said. "But just help yourself to whatever you want, my love." She stepped through the open glass door and acknowledged the presence of Bliss and Jaz with a nod. "Hello, you two."

"Hi, Vi. How are you?"

Her boss only rolled her eyes. She gave the slightest inclination of her head to indicate that Bliss should follow her inside, and she quickly closed the glass door behind them. "How am I? Losing my mind, that's all. Rocco's obsessed. Viking this,

Viking that. He won't shut up about his damned theory. I'm thinking of naming this house Valhalla."

Bliss chuckled. "Good one."

"Rocco is in his sixties, for God's sake. But that doesn't stop him. Do young guys do things like this?"

Bliss wasn't sure quite how to answer that. Jaz Claybourn was hardly an average young guy and she couldn't use him for an example. "Maybe. Jaz and his brother are building a shade arbor over the deck right now."

"But that's useful," Vi pointed out.

"A longship could be useful out here," Bliss said. "You could . . . float groceries in it."

"Sure I could," Vi snapped. "While I howl for blood and bang on a shield. I don't *think* so, Bliss." She heard Rocco calling to her and went back outside. Bliss followed, trying not to laugh.

"Well, this is coming along nicely," Jaz said, winking at Bliss.

"Might be finished by dinner," Rocco said absently. "*Cara mia*, what are we having for dinner?"

"I don't know," Vi said with a tight smile. "How about braised maidens in plunder sauce? Didn't the Vikings eat things like that?"

"I could look it up." Rocco wasn't really listening to her. He set a raised deckboard back into place.

Vi crossed her arms and tapped her foot angrily. "This has gone too far."

Jaz and Bliss exchanged a look. "Don't worry," Jaz said. "You can always use it for a planter." His laugh fell flat when Rocco gave him a stern look.

"Absolutely not. This ship will sail. There is no other way to prove or disprove my theory about Vikings on Pine Island."

"I no longer care," Vi said suddenly. "I want it off my deck. How fortunate that you two happened to stop by."

"Ohhh," Jaz said slowly. "You want us to haul this thing to the water."

"It's not like we can just pick it up," Bliss said. "Be reasonable."

Vi gave Bliss an if-you-want-to-keep-your-job stare and she remembered a little too late that being reasonable was not one of Violet Lentone's strong points. Her boss's stare turned into a glare.

"Right," Bliss said. "We need to get this thing off your deck. Any ideas, Jaz?"

The problem didn't seem to faze him. "We'll have to borrow boat rollers."

"We can ask the gay guys in the dune house," Rocco said. "And they can help with the heavy lifting."

"Doug and Ted," Vi said brightly. "Why didn't I think of them? Let's call." She went back inside while Jaz walked around Rocco's bizarre boat. Jaz still seemed interested in the problem of moving it, Bliss thought, forgetting that it was (a) probably impossible and (b) not his problem. She reminded herself that the eccentric artist had been his father's best friend.

In a little while, two men with close-cropped gray hair came down the walk. Both were wearing tiny shorts with carefully shredded hems and heavy workboots. They were preceded by a female whippet on a thin leash that barked when Vi waved enthusiastically to them. "Doug! Ted! Come up and have some coffee. And then give us your advice on this thing."

The whippet skittered up the ramp, squatting to leave a puddle of pee on the deck when it got that far. Vi pretended not to notice.

"This is a fabulous, fabulous thing," said Ted reverently. He looked more closely at the clamship's garish paint job and ramshackle construction. "Truly, truly fabulous."

"I—" Vi broke off and looked at Rocco—"we want to get it in the water. Today."

"Are you sure?" Doug asked. "I have to say, Vi, as garden ornaments go, it beats a plastic swan all to hell."

Vi sighed. "Jaz already suggested using it for a planter. Rocco won't let him."

"Of course, I can't test my theory if it stays on the deck," Rocco said in a placating tone. He seemed to have finally grasped that his oddball creation was annoying his lady love. "The Vikings didn't colonize people's decks."

Ted laughed. "Come meet our Swedish houseguests. They haven't left ours yet! All they want to do is drink aquavit and fry in the sun."

Doug leaned down to look inside the boat's small cabin. "They can't help it if they're blond. Plus they brought out five jars of that yummy pickled herring. It's addictive."

"Speak for yourself." Ted came to where Doug was standing. "Rocco, is this cabin section connected?"

"Not yet. Although everything in the universe is connected, which is why I can't throw anything out."

"I'm waiting." Vi rolled her eyes. "I know there's more."

"Anything I throw out would eventually find its way back to my studio again," Rocco said patiently.

"He has two houses," Jaz said to Bliss under his breath. "One to keep his junk collection in, one to live in." She nodded.

Ted ended his examination of the clamship's cabin, giving it a slap on the side that made it rock a little. "Okay. This part can be lifted off. That makes things a lot easier."

The whippet looked at the boat with large, startled eyes and barked again.

"Hello, doggie," Bliss said, holding out a palm for the whippet to sniff. "What's her name?"

"Rexi, short for Anorexia. I mean, she eats but not much," Doug said. "She has kibble issues."

"But we love her just the way she is," Ted said. He picked

the dog up and held her in one brawny arm. Rexi tucked her narrow nose in the crook of his elbow and settled down.

"Let's go get the rollers like the good neighbors we are," Doug replied. They strolled down the walk, singing a happy song about helping others, and Vi and Rocco went back inside to get more coffee.

Jaz looked at the mast and the furled sail that was tied to a crossbraced piece of wood. "Interesting. That is definitely a flagpole, but I'm not so sure about the other part." He looked more closely. "Oh. That's the bottom support from a really big easel. Rocco used to do giant canvases. I wonder if he used one for the sail."

"I thought you said his paintings sold for hundreds of thousands of dollars."

"They do. Maybe he used a dropcloth."

"How long do you figure before the whole thing sinks like a stone?" Bliss asked.

Jaz shrugged. "You know, it might not. Rocco and my dad used to do a lot of sailing. He does know a fair amount about boats."

It wasn't long before Doug and Ted returned, without the whippet but with the boat rollers and four very blond, very strong men.

"*Hej hej*," said one, waving a hand. The others echoed him.

"That means hello in Swedish," Doug said. "Everybody, this is Rolf, Haakon, Bjorn, and Ulf. They will be your lifters today and please ask them about our specials."

He explained what he wanted done, and the Swedes removed the cabin and set it on Vi's deck, along with the dragon-headed prow, which Rocco moved out of the slot with a few hard bangs of his hammer. Then the group hoisted the boat by the rope cleats on the sides and carried it down the deck ramp together.

"God, they're magnificent," Doug murmured. "And they're not even gay. Not even bi. Not even curious. Such a shame."

"How do you know them?" Bliss asked.

"Friends of friends. I was an exchange student in Uppsala when I was young. Perhaps you are surprised that I speak their language."

Bliss had wondered about that, but she didn't have time to chat. Jaz grabbed her and they scurried down a different ramp to the path, to hold the rollers steady so the Swedes could set down the clamship. The four blond men went back for the cabin and the prow, laying both down on the boat's deckboards when they returned and clapping each other on the back. The biggest one said something in Swedish and the others all laughed.

Doug translated. "Now we drink."

Ted and Jaz checked out the boat's placement on the rollers. "That should hold," Ted said. "Think you can manage from here?"

"Sure," Jaz said. "It's on wheels. It'll float when we slide it into the water."

Doug and Ted looked a little dubious about that. "If you say so," Doug said. "Call or come by if you need help again." They followed their houseguests down the walk.

Bliss picked up the thick rope at the front of the contraption. "Yo heave ho."

"Give it here," Jaz sighed. "I can't let my dad's old friend give himself a heart attack dragging a boat around."

"You're a good guy, Jaz."

"Stop me next time I volunteer for anything, okay?" He leaned against the rope and the wheels rolled an inch or two forward. Bliss loved the way things just happened on Pine Island. One minute you could be dancing on a roof without a care in the world, and the next, dragging a ten-ton clamship.

"Want me to go back to Vi's house and call Joe?"

Jaz shook his head. "He probably made a meatloaf sandwich, had a couple of beers, and fell asleep on a deck chair."

"Okay. But at least let me help you pull."

He shook his head. "I want you to walk to one side and make sure the boat stays in place."

Bliss rested a hand on a cleat and they waited until Rocco appeared on the path. Then she heard Vi clattering down the ramp in wooden-soled sandals. Her boss held a bottle of champagne in one hand and four plastic glasses in the other. "Wait! You can't launch a ship without champagne!"

"You can't smash a heavy bottle like that on this boat," Jaz said. "You'll stove it in for sure."

"You're right. Well, we can just pop the cork and pour a little over the prow," Vi said. "Is that what you call the front part? The prow? The bow? The wow?"

"In this case, all three are correct," Rocco said.

"I thought so," Vi replied. She seemed a little giddy about getting the boat off her deck. "Then we can drink the rest."

With some help from Rocco, Jaz dragged the boat to where the walk ended at the bay, taking it right off the end of the sloping walk into the shallow water. A small crowd gathered to watch, cheering when the ungainly craft floated free. Jaz got on board and tipped the cabin more or less into place. "You're going to have to bolt this down," he called to Rocco.

"My tool kit's on board," the older man called back. Jaz jumped off into the shallow water and hung onto a rope tied to its bow to step clear of the rollers.

Vi kicked off her wooden sandals and left them at the end of the dock, rolling up her pants and wading out with Rocco. She stopped to pour the champagne into the four glasses as they all stood in knee-deep water. They toasted the successful launch and Vi dribbled the last of the champagne on the dragon-head prow and stacked their empty glasses. She tossed the bottle on board, along with the glasses.

"Useful if I have to bail," she said cheerfully. Jaz and Bliss dragged the rollers out of the water and back onto the walk as Rocco and Vi clambered aboard. The silver-haired artist fitted the prow into the slot he'd made to hold it, and then started the motor. It sputtered, let out an acrid puff of smoke, and roared to life. As an afterthought, Rocco raised the sail, which caught a light breeze and fluttered in the evening air.

The watching crowd cheered once more, and drifted away.

As the artist turned the boat around, Bliss saw the emblem at the sail's center, done in metallic paint: a gold lion rampant with a silver mane and a goofy grin. It looked a lot like Rocco.

A question came to her mind. "How are they going to get back?"

"We're not going to wait here and let the mosquitoes eat us alive. Anyway, there's lots of places they can dock, and he and Vi can always walk back to the Summer Club on the beach. People are going to be curious about that boat and Rocco's going to have a grand old time explaining his crazy theory."

Bliss shaded her eyes and looked at the evening sky, a deepening blue shading to a pale pink, reflected by the calm waters of the bay.

"There they go, sailing into the sunset. They sure look happy."

"Yeah, they do," Jaz said. He put an arm around her shoulders and gave her a warm hug. "That could be us in thirty years."

Buried in his embrace, she wasn't quite sure she'd heard him right. "Huh? What did you just say?"

"Nothing."

"Don't backpedal."

He bent down to give her a champagne-flavored kiss. "Just be my girl. That's enough for now."

They dropped off the rollers at Doug and Ted's house, and waved to the Swedes, whose hosts were nowhere in sight.

A feeling of utter contentment filled her heart as they walked back to the path that led to Breezy Bay. Jaz was mostly right. Spending long summer days with him and being his girl wasn't just enough for now. It was more than enough—more like all she ever wanted.

Two days later, they were back in New York and back at work. Jaz was absorbed in the spreadsheet on the screen in front of him, looking at the monitors to the left and right of it and adding in figures from those displays.

"What fun," he grumbled. "I'm going cross-eyed doing this. But you gotta make bean counters happy."

Bliss could barely see him from where she sat. She was in a paneled conference room that looked just like the one in Leonardville. Sample ad layouts and stapled research reports were spread from one end to the other of a very long table.

Clicking away on a laptop keyboard wasn't her idea of a fabulous way to spend an evening either. But they had to get the big presentation, set for two days from now, finished tonight. She wished she felt a little excitement but she didn't. Not the faintest flicker.

Bliss booted up a clip of a test video for a MyPie commercial and studied the child actor. Freckle-faced. Gap in his grin. Striped T-shirt and a baseball cap. Cute kid. Too bad he was looking at the MyPie in his hand with disgust.

"No, no, no," she murmured to herself. "You're supposed to look like you love it. Like you would sell your skateboard to buy more."

Jaz came up in back of her. "Who is that brat?"

"Not sure. Our art director shot this. We have a set-up in one of the back offices, so that's why the lighting looks kinda screwy."

"I wouldn't know."

"Well, the lighting doesn't matter all that much in a test shoot. But you want the actor's personality to come through."

"It's coming through, all right. Meaning he's all wrong. Which begs the question of why the art director chose him."

Bliss raised her hands in a who-knows gesture. "Probably because every halfway talented kid actor in New York is away for the summer and the casting director figured what the hell, send Freckles. Basically, his mother made the kid do it. I understand that she kept whispering instructions from the side. 'Smile, honey. Hold up the product. They want to see the product. Don't forget to *enjoy* the product.' No wonder he looks disgusted."

She played the clip again, fast forwarding to the outtakes, using her mouse to raise the volume. The kid's whiny voice blared out. "Aw, Ma. Do I hafta take another bite? I hate this stupid pie."

Bliss nodded and switched it off. "No problem, kid. You didn't get the job."

"That's not worth showing to the HT board," Jaz said. He looked down at the different ad layouts on the table, putting a hand down on one she'd set way over to one side and scooting it over the glossy surface of the conference table in front of her. "I like this," he said, laughing.

Two identical young women in microscopic bikinis were feeding each other MyPies, and licking juicy filling from their lips with pretty pink tongues. Bliss could practically hear them giggling.

"You and the art director," she said. "Bill was drooling over those things." Bliss pointed to the huge, oddly symmetrical bosoms overflowing the models' teeny tops. "The implant twins would be great in a beer ad but not for HT snacks. Not if you want to get the moms."

"Not even lesbian moms?" Jaz gave her a sorrowful look.

"I wish them well but they're not in this demographic break-down," she said, waving that particular sheet of paper under his nose. "Which is not to say that there isn't a pot of gold at the end of that rainbow. Gay purchasing power is a big deal."

"Okay. You're the expert. But could I keep this layout for, uh, reference?"

"Just so long as it doesn't mysteriously show up as part of the final presentation. I can just see that bald accountant from the Leonardville office checking those two out. The old guy with the big wrinkly ears. Could be hazardous to his health."

"You mean Vern. You're probably right. He had a triple by-pass recently. I will have to keep these." Jaz rolled up the twins and went back to what he was doing.

A few hours later, they ordered in from Shun Lee and ate a deliciously drippy order of moo shu in fifteen minutes. Then they traded places. She was working with the multiple monitor set-up and he moved to the paneled outer office to go over her marketing research. Alf Sargent had scrawled notes all over the material that made Jaz rake a hand through his hair and sigh with exasperation.

"If Alf knew what he was doing, he'd be dangerous. Nothing like an outgoing CEO to make life difficult for the one coming in. Geez, he's a pain in the ass."

Bliss had to agree. And Alf really was a lech. He'd given her one too many fatherly pats on the back on her last visit to the Leonardville factory and even brushed up against her butt in a wide corridor where there was plenty of room for the two of them to pass each other.

She reviewed the last of the layouts and decided to do something ridiculous to make Jaz laugh. Bliss opened up InDesign and slapped together a collage of digital images from the Leonardville meetings.

A photo of Alf Sargent with a smirk on his face looked a whole lot funnier with two big Nutty Balls and a long banana added to the fly of his pants. Now for some pixel manipulation: she fiddled with the squiggly icing on the dancing cupcakes until they read Bite Me, and printed Alf and the cupcakes together. Then she found a little old lady in an image bank who resembled Alf's mother, teeny flowered hat and all. Bliss put a miniature Pomeranian on a leash and a Chippendale's dancer with major man-titty on another leash in the old lady's hands. She printed it out on a separate sheet of paper. Not bad.

Jaz thought it was pretty funny, stopping work for thirty seconds to crack up. He gave her a big smooch, then set the collages to one side and sent her away so he could finish his work.

Which was okay with Bliss. She shut down the computer and reclined her chair, treating herself to a brief, delicious nap. When she woke with a start, she listened for signs of life from the conference room.

Nothing. She got up and went to see.

There was Jaz, still there, not making a sound. He had kicked off his shoes and put his black-socked feet up on the long table. His tie was off, tossed aside in a coil of luxurious silk. Even with no shoes and no tie, he was doing a pretty good imitation of a hard-driving, well-groomed, studly CEO. She smiled, thinking of the contrast between executive Jaz and beach Jaz.

There was a bottle of expensive single malt whisky, older than she was, by a stack of printouts, and a full shot glass next to the bottle. He was sipping whisky from another shot glass, which was almost empty.

"Hey, sleeping beauty. I've been waiting for you."

That grin. That dimple. That look in his eyes that said it all. She wanted, really wanted, to jump in his lap. "Oh. But I don't like whisky."

"How about something else? Allow me to seduce you." Jaz swung his feet off the table and got up. He tossed the second shot of whisky down his throat.

"You sexy tycoon. I wish I wasn't so tired."

"Sit down. I'm sure there's something in this bar you'll like."

She kicked off her shoes too, and sat down on the end of the table. At least she could swing her feet and not be folded up at right angles in a chair. Bliss stretched out an arm and supported herself with one arm, watching Jaz bend over to look through the ranks of bottles in the conference room bar. What a butt. Talk about hard-driving.

"Okay, let me guess," he said, unaware of her interest in his ass. "You want a girl drink. Something sweet with a kick. How about a Dublin Dream?" He pulled out a bulbous green bottle of liqueur with a rather inebriated-looking cow on the label. "I understand this is pretty tasty, because Dora likes it—"

He stopped when he saw the expression on your face. "Oh, sorry. Your archrival. I almost forgot."

Bliss rubbed the back of her neck with one weary hand. "Could we not talk about Dora?" She hated the idea of Jaz and his assistant working late nights and easing their tension with a raid on a well-stocked corporate bar. She had vowed not to ask questions, sworn not to obsess, but that didn't mean she couldn't indulge in a touch of irrational jealousy now and then. It helped with weight control. Her archrival had no hips to speak of.

"You got it. Want some of this?" He waved the bottle of liqueur.

"Okay. Dublin Dream probably counts as dessert."

Jaz chunked some ice into a glass sized for a man's hand and poured out a healthy slug.

He brought it over and she stuck the tip of her tongue into the gooey sweetness, making him smile.

"Atta girl."

Bliss drank it down, swirling the ice cubes in the dregs. A happy, boozy feeling suffused her brain.

Jaz seemed to sense it. "Want more?"

"No, thanks. But that hit the spot." She set the glass aside, licking her lips.

Jaz took a chair right in front of her and put her feet in his lap. He picked one up and began to rub her pantyhose-clad toes, tugging sensually on each one and making slow circles with his thumb on the ball of her foot.

"Ooh. *Ooh*. You are not allowed to stop."

He finished that foot after a few minutes, and started in on the other one. The rush from the drink and the relaxing effect of a foot massage was a heady combination. Bliss rested her feet on either side of his cock and wriggled them.

"Love that toe action. Give it to me, girl."

Laughing, she pressed her feet lightly against his groin in a rhythm that produced a remarkably stiff hard-on in less than a minute. But he grabbed her ankles and made her stop.

"Lie down on the table."

"You mean—"

"That's right. You look good enough to eat and that's just what I'm going to do."

"What about you?"

He shrugged, as if he didn't care about that right now. "Later."

Jaz let go of her ankles and Bliss edged her butt into position, lying down on the table. He stood up and pushed her knees apart, but what he was after was still concealed by her dress. "Comfortable?"

She was, except for the ultramodern light fixtures overhead. "Could we do something about those?" She pointed.

"Right." He walked over to the switches, bringing the illumination in the room down to a glow. "How's that?"

"Perfect." Bliss stretched out on the cool surface of the table, feeling wanton.

"Pull up your dress. Real slow."

Having him stand there and watch her do it was exactly what she'd hoped for. Jaz held her gaze for a long moment as she reached down for the hem of her dress, sliding it over the smooth nylon of her pantyhose and up to her waist.

He looked down. "Wow. Somebody's already wet." He touched a finger to her concealed pussy. "Let's get the stockings off. And the panties."

Bliss kicked her legs up, putting her ankles together and raising her hips so he could reach the elastic waistband. In less than five seconds, he had bared her below the waist, tossing the ball of pantyhose and panties on the floor, and separating her legs again.

Bliss closed her eyes. Way to go. She felt him stroke the inside of her thighs, pressing them apart until her labia opened. He didn't waste any time, sitting down and burying his head between her legs, eating her avidly.

His tongue penetrated her first, good and deep, and Bliss arched her back. His hands clasped her thighs and held her hips still. He stopped to nip the sensitive skin on the inside of her thighs, following each nip with a warm, breathy kiss. Then Jaz moved back to her pussy.

He did a masterful job of clit-teasing, taking it expertly in his teeth so she didn't dare move. Then he let go and suckled it with little pulses until she began to moan.

He lifted his head, wiping his wet mouth on her thigh. "Play with your tits. Right through the dress."

Bliss rubbed her breasts in slow circles and pinched the nipples, erect and easy to find under the light material of her summer dress.

"Yeah," he growled. "Make yourself hot."

He watched for a little longer, then put his mouth over her clit again, sucking with such tenderness that she came in a rush of sensation, releasing her nipples to clutch his head and force him against her pussy.

He savored every second of her orgasm, licking tenderly between her labia when her clit got too sensitive to take any more stimulation.

She gave herself up to it, feeling almost like crying when he began to rub her lower belly with one heavy, warm hand, easing the last of her sexual tension into a glow that didn't quit. "Ahhhh . . . oh, Jaz . . ."

He stayed where he was, watching her drift back to reality, resting his head on her thigh, still stroking her. "Beautiful. You really are beautiful."

A little while later, she was putting on her pantyhose, unrolling them lazily up and over one leg and then the other. Bliss gave him a satisfied smile and sat down, smoothing her dress demurely. Jaz laughed softly. Then he clasped his hands behind his head and gave her a speculative look. "Want to go out?" he said casually. "I'm not ready to call it a night."

"Go out where?" She was thinking more along the lines of a late-night diner hamburger. Plus a monster pile of fries that could be dipped in ketchup.

"This place I know," he said offhandedly. "It's fun. Lots of, ah, unusual entertainment."

She shot him a quizzical look. "Meaning what? A flea circus?"

His cock was stiff, she noticed. That was to be expected, considering she'd come and he hadn't.

"No. An upscale sex show."

"Huh." She had never been to anything like that.

"Feeling adventurous?" Jaz had a wicked grin on his face to match the gleam in his eyes.

"Tell me more."

"It's a private club called Night Moves. A stockbroker pal took me there last fall. I had a great time."

"Of course. You're a guy."

"Guilty on that charge. But it's a cool place in its freaky way, and like I said, upscale. Not raunchy, not like a frat party. Couples go there too."

"Okay," she said, surprising herself. "But I have to go home and change first. I look like hell."

He sat up straight and rose out of his chair to kiss her. "I told you already you look beautiful."

"Yeah, with my dress up."

"Any which way. But whatever you want. Let me call for a limo. There and back. Nothing's too good for my lady."

All dolled up in a short scarlet dress with a flippy skirt, Bliss sashayed through the lobby of her building, checking her smooth French twist in the reflection of the door before stepping outside. Even though it was after midnight, it was still disgustingly hot and the gritty breeze made her blink.

So where was the King of Oral Sex anyway? She was pretty sleepy from the delicious session on the conference table but she figured she owed him one. Still and all, her makeup was going to melt off if she had to wait out here much longer. Bliss fiddled with one of her red-beaded earrings as she looked anxiously down the street.

A limo wove around double-parked cars and glided to a halt in front of her. Bliss sighed with relief. It was so hot out she was getting blisters just standing around in high heels.

Without waiting for the driver to do his obsequious thing, Jaz opened the back door and waved her in. The leather upholstery was ivory-white, a stunning contrast to the gleaming black of the limousine. All she could see of the driver were uniformed shoulders and the cap on his head. Evidently he had been given his instructions because the panel between front and back was already closed.

She settled herself on the seat, pressing up against Jaz. With the air conditioning on full blast, his body heat felt good. He leaned closer and captured her lips in a lascivious kiss, sliding his big hand up her dress and stroking her between her legs. He pulled up the flippy skirt and took a look. "No underwear? Bliss, you're too much. Just don't stand over a subway grate. I don't want everyone in New York staring at your sweet pussy. Especially since I just licked it."

"Believe me, I have no intention of going anywhere near a subway. I heart limos, all the way."

Night Moves was as upscale as Jaz had said. Maybe a better word was opulent. Black velvet banquettes were filled with members—mostly men from what she could see—knocking back drinks. They were well-dressed but the lateness of the hour meant that quite a few of them had a raffish look, ties loosened and faint stubble on more than one masculine chin. They looked at her appreciatively but not too boldly, aware of the contained power in Jaz's walk and the protective way he had her by the arm. He nodded to a few of the guys without introducing her, and they headed toward the private rooms he'd told her about, in the back of the club.

A strikingly sexy woman clad in a bias-cut satin gown was positioned behind a narrow reception stand, paging through a reservation book. Her high, full breasts weren't quite contained by her bodice, especially not when she leaned over the book. She looked up when Bliss and Jaz approached and came out from behind the stand to greet them.

"Here comes the hostess with the mostest. But you're sexier. A lot sexier," he whispered.

"That's because I'm the harlot in scarlet," Bliss shot back. She strutted past the ranks of admiring men, definitely in touch with her inner hussy tonight. If there were couples here besides her and Jaz, she hadn't seen any.

But she did once the hostess opened the door of the room Jaz had selected. There was a cabaret-style stage at one end of

132 / Noelle Mack

the space, and four or five couples, each sitting at an individual table with an encircling booth, discreetly lit for shadowed privacy.

The hostess in the satin gown showed them to the last table, well in back. Bliss was grateful for that—somehow she felt more self-conscious doing things like this around women than she did around men.

A hot-looking waiter in a silk shirt open down to his narrow waist took their drink orders and left. A moody blue light illuminated the empty stage and heavy, dark blue velvet curtains fell into rich folds on the glossy, black-painted boards.

"So what goes on here?" Bliss whispered curiously.

"Private club, consenting adults," he whispered back. "Those who want to can explore their fantasy on stage. No names. You can't really see their faces. But it gets wild."

"Did you ever do it? Get up on stage, I mean."

He kissed her cheek and she could feel his smile. "No. I was only here that one time, and that was awhile ago. I'm not a member. My friend got me on the list for tonight."

"So it's members only."

"That's right. Some like to show off, some like to watch."

Another glamorous woman, not the hostess, but as beautifully dressed, came on stage and spoke into the mike in a sultry voice. "As you all know, Night Moves is a private club. What happens here stays here."

Some of the onlookers murmured assent. Their waiter brought their drinks and left again. Bliss sipped hers, listening to the music that swelled through the room, a smokin' rhythm-and-blues groove that got under her skin.

"Tonight's show is all about ass. Big, beautiful asses that need what they're going to get. Spanking. Anal teasing. Full penetration. It feels so good. And tight male asses are going to get their share of the action too. Wait and see.

"Ever wonder what goes on in the executive suite after hours?" the emcee purred.

Jaz winked at Bliss. "Now you know."

"Meet Janeen," the woman at the mike was saying. "She's going to get exactly what she wants tonight. Her boss is hard and hot for her . . ." The sultry voice trailed off.

Bliss looked up, startled when the curtain rose. The set was amazing: a perfect illusion of an office building window seen from outside at night. A voluptuous, small-waisted woman sat on a swivel chair, wearing high heels and a short, tight lace skirt. She turned and spread her legs wide, slipping a hand between them, rubbing and sighing.

A man appeared behind her, tall and strongly built, his face in shadow. Something about his stance, even in silhouette, told Bliss that he was older than the woman he was with, but not by that much. He stood behind her and put his hands on Janeen's shoulders without saying a word. Tailored shirt. White cuffs. Expensive cufflinks. That oh-so-masterful look of an executive on his way up and having fun with the best-looking women in New York while he was at it.

Oh yeah. That was a fantasy Bliss had entertained herself with many, many times during her first couple of years after graduating from college, doing temp work all over New York. How often had she wished for a super-sexy alpha male to come out of his corner office and sweep her off her feet? And fuck her silly? About a thousand times. It hadn't ever happened until now. Until Jaz.

He could take care of her desire to get sexed up by a Mr. Big Shot in one swift session of excellent head. She thought about Mr. Beach Bum—admittedly with a very expensive beach house—and how great he looked in ragged shorts and bare chest. Life was good. Bliss got to have both, wrapped up in one fabulous man.

She wondered how far the fantasy about to unfold on stage would go, because she had a feeling this couple was for real. Why they wanted to have sex in front of others, she didn't know. But Bliss couldn't take her eyes off them.

Janeen ripped her tight blouse open, letting an awesome pair of bare breasts bounce free as she breathed her longing, talking dirty in a low voice. Her lover took her nipples in his fingers, rolling and pinching them until Janeen cried out. But she cupped her tits and offered them up to him. The couples in the darkened room watched in silence.

He caressed her, holding her big, soft breasts in his hands and squeezing so that her nipples stood out even more. Janeen rose slightly in her seat, hungry for his touch.

The man pushed her down and turned her around in the chair. She unzipped his pants, took his erect cock in her hand, and began to suck. Bliss could see that the back of the woman's tight skirt was made of stretch lace—and that her ass was bare underneath.

So Janeen wasn't wearing underwear either. Bliss could imagine what was coming next. The mistress of ceremonies spoke into the mike again but she was invisible now. The lights illuminated only the couple on stage. "I hope we're going to see more, don't you?" Her soft voice echoed in the darkness.

The man onstage pulled Janeen out of the chair and made her stand in front of him. A little unsteady on her high heels, she pulled up her lace skirt, completely baring her behind. She stood on tiptoe to whisper into his ear, tightening her buttocks in a way that made the men in the room suck in their breath.

The man on stage sat down in the chair and patted his thighs. Janeen lay down over his knees, bare ass up. Bliss felt her face flush and her pussy get wet. "Does this turn you on?" Jaz said softly.

"Yes," she answered after a while. She had never seen another woman get spanked.

Janeen's man wasted no time, bringing his strong hand down on her trembling buttocks again and again. Her lips parted and her soft, intense cries broke the quiet of the room as she begged for more, enjoying being disciplined in front of onlookers, even if she couldn't see them.

The man in the chair stopped and rested his hands on her behind. Janeen arched up, and tried to look around at him, but he got her under control again by holding her around the waist and delivering more pleasurable punishment to her bare flesh, spanking her harder. Janeen bucked on his thighs, then grabbed the legs of the chair, hung her head down, and waited. He gave it to her.

Bliss could feel Jaz's hand resting on her leg but he didn't make a move upward.

She looked back at the stage. Janeen was off her lover's lap and kneeling now, displaying her punished buttocks to the people silently watching as she sucked her lover's cock. He made her stop, stood up, and stepped back into the shadows, reappearing after a minute completely naked, his huge erection sheathed in a condom that was slick with lube.

He made Janeen bend forward, resting her hands on the chair, and gave her a hard pussy fucking first. Then he pulled out and spread her cheeks with strong hands, stretching the tight hole. He slid his sheathed cock into it, giving her the ultimate in deep anal pleasure, fucking her spanked ass with slow thrusts. All she could do was hold still and take him.

Bliss didn't quite believe she was seeing this. Yes, it was happening on a stage, but it was totally for real. The man thrust harder and deeper. Janeen began to moan, reaching a hand between her legs and touching her tender flesh. She and her lover came explosively at the same time, rocking and crying out.

An unseen someone dimmed the lights and the stage went black. Bliss could feel Jaz nuzzle her neck and nip her ear, whispering words of pure lust. But he still didn't touch her pussy.

Good. She wanted him to drive her crazy. He hadn't come yet and the thought of how he would, after eating her out and seeing these two go at it, made her unbelievably hot.

The blue light filled the empty stage again and a young man walked onstage. Cute, Bliss thought, very cute. Crew cut, great boyish grin, and built like a varsity athlete. She checked him out from head to toe without a twinge of guilt. Coming here had been Jaz's idea, after all. He was busy ordering another drink for her and for himself, and didn't seem to notice that she was looking at the new guy.

The office window set had been replaced by a cubicle of sorts, built in several levels. "This is Brian," the emcee said. "The new guy in our fantasy office. Young and yum and full of cum. His boss is a woman—"

"Lucky for him," Jaz said into Bliss's ear. "And here she comes now." Bliss heard stiletto heels strike the boards of the stage before she saw the woman who wore them. She was as masterful in her way as Janeen's lover had been, wearing retro black-framed glasses, her hair drawn back in a gelled ponytail.

The woman put her cubicle cutie through his paces in even less time, whipping off her man-tailored but very fitted suit to get her pussy worshipped by his tongue. She told him to put on a condom, he said no, and she spanked him hard for his defiance. He wanted it, craved it, accepting her stinging slaps with closed eyes and sweat running down his handsome young face. Whoever he was, he was totally into obedience training, needing to take it from a dominant woman. His partner let him max out on the pleasure of it, but finally he obeyed her, so erect he could barely roll it down past the head of his cock and over the thick shaft. Then she backed him up against the desk part of the set, straddling him and thrusting down on his sheathed erection.

She pushed her breasts into his face, scratching and clawing at his hair as he sucked her long nipples, and reached around to grab his shaft at the base, riding and pumping hard until she came first. With efficient moves, she got up and pulled the condom off her stud. He got the same treatment as Janeen, bending over to get a lubed dildo thrust up his willing ass, groaning in a low, ragged voice when his lady boss began to work it hard. Then she stepped aside and left it in his behind, watching him with her hands on her hips as he sprayed into the air in hot jets, excited by her assertive demands and eager to satisfy.

Jaz still didn't make a definitive move. He traced a fingertip around Bliss's knee and up between her thighs, but not all the way up.

"Let's go home," she said, wanting to leave while the lights were still low. She didn't suppose they ever got turned all the way up in a place like this but even so.

"Had enough?"

"Yeah."

"Hot and bothered?"

"What do you think?" On a scale of one to ten, the spanking had been a nine. The second fantasy was for those who were into it, so to speak, and ranked lower in her estimation. "Not that I'd ever get naked on stage. Not in a million years."

"I wouldn't want you to. I'd be jealous. Way too jealous." He tossed some big bills down on the table and they left.

The blue light coming through the windows of his apartment was eerily similar to the light on stage. Bliss twisted the slender rod hanging from the chrome mini-blinds to shut it out.

"Being watched doesn't turn me on. I don't know how people onstage do it."

"But I know that watching turned you on." Jaz's voice was deep, and a little muffled by the pillow his head was resting on.

"Yeah. It did," she said honestly. "It was raw, but it was real." She hesitated. "Just not . . . intimate."

"Yeah. Not something I want to do often. But what the hell. Summer in the city makes me a little crazy."

"I think it makes everybody a little crazy," Bliss said with a sigh. Watching a show like that at least made her feel that her most secret fantasies weren't such a secret. They were still hot and dirty, but other people had them too.

"You could be right. So what's your fantasy tonight?"

"Making love. No more and no less."

He sat up in the bed, the sheets tangled around his legs and his broad chest bare. "I thought you'd never ask for that."

Bliss walked over, shedding her red dress on the way. Behind the tinted windows of the limo, he'd managed to get her pantyhose off, but he'd still kept his hands away from her pussy, stroking her bare legs and ass until she relaxed. The limo driver never turned around, concentrating on getting through the chaotic late-night traffic around Times Square.

Bliss hadn't even noticed the brilliant lights and colossal video screens, blurred in the background as she surrendered to the tenderness of Jaz's kisses. She couldn't get enough, and he'd had to remind her to put on her shoes when the driver pulled up in front of the blue-glass tower that loomed over Columbus Circle.

Just looking at him right now, naked and ready to give her all the loving she wanted, and Bliss knew that she was a goner. The tears she'd almost cried when he'd had her on the conference table welled in her eyes again. Bliss swallowed hard and turned her face into the shadow, trying to get her emotions under control.

"Sorry," she said at last in a tiny voice. "I don't know what's going on with me. Maybe we—maybe things are just happening too fast."

He reached out and took her hand, drawing her down to him in the bed. "Come here, baby. I think we need to get next to each other. And I don't mean physically."

She rolled into his embrace, kissing his chest, feeling the faint pounding of his heart against her lips. Jaz stroked her hair and held her for a long, long time. They rested in each other's arms until she felt his cock grow hard.

Jaz sighed. "Can't help myself. Pay no attention. Don't touch it."

"I want to," she whispered. She moved back just enough to reach down and stroke the silky, stiff rod that nestled in the warm hair between his legs.

"Thought you wanted to slow down."

She smiled in the darkness. "I can't. Not when we're body to body like this."

Jaz rolled on one side so he was higher than she was. Bliss reached up and ran a hand over one mighty shoulder, tracing the line of his arm until she reached his hand. She rested her hand on his and he bent down to bestow a sensual kiss on her parted lips.

She clasped his cock again and he shuddered. Bliss remembered that she'd had all the fun tonight. He must be close to exploding. Jaz gently pried her fingers off his cock and rolled over to the bedstand, getting a condom. She watched him roll it on as fast as he could.

In another second, he had her pinned to the bed, holding her wrists above her head with one hand and fondling one breast with the other. The man never forgot that she had two, though. He was just as good to the other one in time. Bliss sighed with pleasure and let her legs fall open. Wide open.

Jaz stopped what he was doing to her tits and brought a hand to his cock, positioning himself to enter her. In one powerful move, he came down and thrust his cock deep inside her. He held her wrists in an iron grip, but his hand on her face was gentle. What he wanted was a kiss while he fucked her, and he got it.

Bliss kissed him with all the tenderness she felt in her heart. He stopped thrusting and stayed still inside her, letting her feel the size and length of his cock. She began to move her hips in a subtle figure eight, grabbing his ass to pull him inside her as far as he could possibly go.

Her body opened up to him . . . and so did her soul. They came together and the tears flowed at last, in hot trails down her flushed face. Jaz felt the wet sensation, brushing them away and kissing her closed eyes until she stopped crying.

6

After an afternoon barbecue in a neighboring community, Bliss and Jaz were headed back to Breezy Bay. They had decided on the scenic route that led through undeveloped National Seashore land. It wasn't the fastest way home but it sure as hell was the prettiest.

The wind rustled through tall reeds with feathery tops, deeply rooted in the marsh where the deer hid. Bliss had seen a doe and twin fawns on her morning run into town, walking across the sand path on slender legs and vanishing into the reeds again.

Jaz reached out a hand and let it rattle along the stems of the reeds, like a kid running a stick along a fence. The reeds bent slightly, then closed ranks as he passed.

"Impenetrable. Makes you wonder how Rocco ever found that wrecked clamboat," Jaz said.

"He's determined."

"And crazy. But your boss seems pretty happy with him."

"She is. She even says so." Bliss took Jaz's hand as they went around a bend in the path. A red-winged blackbird clung to the stem of a tall reed, its sudden cry echoing across the marsh before it flew away.

"How about you?" Jaz asked. "Are you happy?"

She nodded. "As a matter of fact, I am. I keep telling myself that this isn't going to last, though."

She wasn't sure how she had meant the words but he took them literally.

"Well, not forever. There are four more weeks of summer left. But September is when it's most beautiful out here. Cool nights, warm days. Not very many people on the beach."

"But we have to work."

"Yeah," he said. "But I can take three-day weekends. I don't think Vi will mind if you do."

"You never know with Violet Lentone. Right now I'm on her good side. The HT account is paying the office rent, put it that way."

"Good." He stopped at an open place in the reeds. Bliss saw a faint track between them she had never noticed before. "Hey, want to see the restaurant at the end of nowhere?"

She peered into the lush greenery. Basically all she could see were reeds, reeds, and more reeds. Here and there mallows grew, their immense, pale pink petals displaying dark maroon centers and a sexy little pistil. "Okay."

He went ahead of her, pushing back the encroaching reeds. They had to go single file. "This is the other side of Mrs. Drake's property."

"You mean that old lady who stays inside all the time when she's here?" In the last few weeks, Bliss had gotten to know pretty much everyone in Breezy Bay besides Mrs. Drake, although she had glimpsed her now and then. But the old lady kept to herself when she came out at all.

Jaz continued to lead the way, pushing the reeds aside and slapping a mosquito or two that landed on his arm. A high, stockade-type fence appeared at the end of the narrow path, almost hidden by the profusion of shrubs—bayberry and blueberry bushes—that framed it.

Bliss noted the weathered sign that had been fastened to its gate long ago, if the rust stains dripping down from the nails were any indication. KEEP OUT. THIS MEANS YOU. Another, larger sign bore only one word. BEWARE.

"Uh-oh," she said. "Well, I can take a hint." She turned around to go back.

Jaz grabbed her hand. "No, it's okay. We'll sneak through fast."

"What if she's there?"

"Mrs. Drake hardly ever is, you know that. She hates the beach." All the same, he seemed to be listening with a degree of caution. "I remember her sweeping the sand off her porch when I was a kid—she did it for hours."

"So how come she has a beach house if she hates the beach?"

"I don't know, but she's owned it since forever. She's hard of hearing now." He reached a hand over the high gate and pulled on a plastic-coated wire. The latch on the other side lifted and the gate creaked open.

Bliss looked through it at improbably lush, perfect grass. "A lawn? On Pine Island?"

"It can be done, if you remove every grain of sand with tweezers. And she probably did. Let's go."

They went through the gate, closing it behind them, and around the side of the Drake house. The curtains were drawn and no one seemed to be inside. Tom led the way over flat steppingstones and by a fence that enclosed property she couldn't see.

He stopped and pushed a wide board in, bending double to get under it and holding it up for Bliss when he was on the other side. "Right this way."

She bent down and followed him down another path that was even more overgrown. They came out into a clear area and there at the water's edge stood a shuttered building made of painted cinderblock. A dock had been built long ago from the bulkheaded shore that faced the bay to the front door, where fragments of a striped awning still clung to a metal frame and fluttered in the breeze.

Bliss walked behind him through sand that the wind had sculpted, seeing no signs of footprints other than theirs.

"Neat. Who owns this?"

"Right now, the Havertown bank does. They foreclosed on it. Someone tried to start a Mexican restaurant here, believe it or not, but they couldn't make a go of it."

"Did you come here?"

Jaz smiled. "Joe used to. I was working in San Diego then for another company. He said they served margaritas in mason jars, and that the waitresses were really pretty. Joe knew them all."

Bliss didn't doubt it. "So it folded. Too bad."

"By the end of the summer, they were slapping flies with the quesadillas. No customers. It's too hard to get to."

She walked around and surveyed the place. It was more peaceful than lonely, as far as she was concerned. "How long has it been closed?"

"Oh, at least five years."

She peered through a window. A collection of shells, bleached white by the strong sun, had been left on the inside sill. A small fly buzzed drowsily among the shells, the only sign of life inside the empty room.

Still, it was easy to envision bright tablecloths and bistro chairs and seafood dinners being served up. Or dancing. You could throw a party here that could go on all night. There were no neighbors and even the Drake house was some distance away.

He gestured to the dock. "Boats used to tie up here. But not many."

"Hm. So why would you want to open it up again?"

He took her by the hand and they strolled out on the weathered boards of the dock, sitting down together where they had a good view of the water. "For my friends. For the hell of it. My dad taught me that you have to do some things in life purely and exclusively for the hell of it."

She swung her feet and peered down into the water lapping quietly against the pilings and saw a tiny crab swimming sideways. It disappeared under the dock, not in any hurry to get where it was going.

Jaz turned to look at a windsurfer farther out who had caught a breeze and was making the most of it. His neon-colored sail swelled out as he raced by, leaving them alone again. The restaurant at the end of nowhere was a serene haven.

"So what do you think? Should I buy it?"

"Sounds like a wonderful idea," she said honestly. "I couldn't say why you should, but I understand why you want to."

He sighed with satisfaction. "It's completely impractical, of course. I'll never recoup my investment."

"You might. Pine Island property isn't going to go down in value."

"A full-force hurricane could wipe out every house on this island in about five minutes," he said. "And we do get them. That's another reason summers out here are so precious. Enjoy it while it lasts."

Bliss fell silent. His tone was casual, but his words troubled her. She didn't want to think about summer being over, or what would happen when her work on the HT account was done. She stood up, feeling a little lonely despite his nearness.

Jaz looked up at her. "Want to go inside?"

She shrugged and stuck her hands in the pockets of her shorts. "Okay."

They walked back to the front door, where Jaz felt up around a beam that supported the tattered awning and brought down a key. "Top-secret hiding place. Don't tell anyone."

She smiled. "I won't."

The key turned in the lock but the door stuck. He put his shoulder to it and gave it a good shove. It opened with a bang and they walked into a room that was uncomfortably warm and stuffy. But the air soon cleared—the bay breeze took care of that.

She kicked off her flip-flops and slid over the polished wood floor. Someone had swept it relatively recently. It was free of dust, and deliciously warm underfoot.

"Shall we dance?" he said, kicking off his flip-flops too and bowing to her with exaggerated gallantry.

"No music."

"We could fake it. I know a basic best-man wedding waltz and I can tango a little."

"I took a tango class once. Let's try it."

Jaz took her in his arms and bent her over backwards. "I have to give you a smoldering look." He lowered his eyelids and flared his nostrils. "How's that?"

Bliss grinned up at him. "Pretty good. You look like an Argentine gigolo."

He pulled her up. "Thank you, my little empanada. Know that I have for you the hots. I wish you to feel my largeness." Jaz pressed his crotch against her belly.

"I see what you mean," Bliss giggled. "But let us continue." They approximated the back-and-forth steps of a traditional tango, and she managed a few of the feminine little kicks without doing damage to his groin when he turned her.

Jaz hummed a melody in a minor key and made up lyrics that involved bingo players and bongo bangers, all of which sort of rhymed with tango now and then. He had her laughing almost too much to follow his lead.

They leaned against the wall, a little breathless.

"Had enough?"

"Yeah. But I wish I could really tango."

He nodded and took her hand as they walked to the front door. "That makes two of us." He slammed the door shut and put the key back in its hiding place.

By sundown, they were walking on the ocean side of Pine Island, down the beach. A steady, slight thumping they could feel through their feet made them both turn at the same time. Horses were headed their way, moving fast on the firm sand near the water's edge and kicking up sprays of sand and water as they came closer. Bliss saw that there were three. The first two were riderless, galloping, their manes and tails streaming behind them. A woman rode the third horse and shouted something Bliss and Jaz couldn't hear.

Tired, the first two horses slowed to a canter and then a walk. They stood back to let the horses amble by, as happy to be on the beach as Bliss and Jaz were, and as free.

"I didn't know there were stables out here."

Jaz nodded. "David Winters keeps his racehorses out here in the summer. He has a big place a few miles east. He likes to exercise them in the sand. Looks like these two got out somehow and did a little racing on their own."

"Sorry," the woman on the third horse called. She was still some distance away but catching up quickly. Her voice came to them on a gust of wind that was unexpectedly cold. Bliss shivered and Jaz put his arm around her.

"They were beautiful," she said with a sigh. "I wish summer would last forever.

Two weeks later . . .

Bliss was ready to take that back. She was stuck in New York and Jaz was stuck in Leonardville. The temperatures had risen into the high nineties and stayed there, with no relief predicted for the near future.

Thunderstorms that would have cooled things off had swept

well to the north and south of the city. Confronted by New York's glittering skyscrapers, radioactive with heat, the clouds said nah and headed to places that didn't want thunderstorms. Atlantic City, where power was knocked out to thousands of slot machines. Donald Trump blamed the mayor. The Catskills, which got hammered with six inches of rain in two hours. Her home town of Thurbeck had almost washed away. The mayor blamed the governor.

There just was nothing wonderful about New York in August. The humid air held the smells of street-cart hot dogs and overripe fruit, mixed with taxi exhaust and the smell of weary people.

Central Park, her favorite haunt in the summertime, was far too crowded. She wasn't about to take the subway down to Chinatown, which was even more crowded, for her favorite treat: ginger vanilla ice cream from the Chinatown Ice Cream Factory on Bayard Street. Bliss would have loved to consume an entire pint with spoon-licking slowness, fully aware that every molecule of it would embed itself in her fat cells until the day she died. Idly, she imagined her loved ones being nice enough to buy her a cool, pale blue, silk-lined coffin where she could rest in air-conditioned splendor with her eyes closed so she didn't have to look at the awful floral arrangements people sent to funerals.

Vi's shriek interrupted her soothing fantasy for a few seconds. Her boss had been running everyone ragged for days now. Bliss imagined Vi lying in a silk-lined coffin—it would have to be a designer coffin, of course. The thought made her smile.

Until Vi stormed in. "Why are you daydreaming? What's that smile for? Don't you know what just happened?"

"No."

"Take a guess."

"Bergdorf's is going out of business?"

"No! Kayla quit!"

Bliss wasn't surprised. Their passive-aggressive warfare had ratcheted up a notch during the heat spell, and she hoped Kayla would be happier elsewhere.

She half-listened to Vi's tirade on the topic of *ingratitude, interns guilty of* before her boss stomped out. Bliss decided to call up Allegheny Air and get on the next plane to Pittsburgh. She needed Jaz. Badly.

Of course, he had told her to use his house on Pine Island on the weekends or any day she wanted to. He'd even told her to stay at his apartment in the blue glass tower if her Chelsea sublet seemed too small and too confining.

By now she was keeping clothes at both places. But that didn't mean she felt like being in spaces that held no Jaz but were pure Jaz—serene and spare, with a whiff of clean, musky manliness hanging in the air to drive her insane with lust. Her own nest was preferable, now that it had a working air conditioner, pigeons and all.

Vi ran back into Bliss's office, a cell phone pressed to her ear. "Oh my God. The boat—the boat! Rocco's sinking! He's out on the bay—what if the ferry runs into him?"

"That's not going to happen."

"How do you know?" Vi hissed. "Shit! I can't hear him anymore—the connection is bad."

"Vi, he painted that crazy boat in so many colors and ran up so many flags on the lines, anyone can see it a mile off. Not to mention the stuffed seagull on top of the cabin."

Rocco's odd vessel was already famous, written up in the local papers. Jaz said someone had come out to interview its creator for a feature in *ArtNews*.

"Bliss, shut up. You simply are not a nautical person. What if it's foggy? What if the ferry captain is drinking his coffee and not looking out the window?"

"Rocco hugs the shore when he takes it out. He's not stupid even if he is sort of a lunatic."

"He may be a lunatic but he's *my* lunatic," Vi said. "I have to look out for him." She listened to the crackly call fading in and out with a tense expression. "Rocco? Rocco, where are you?" She gasped, then spoke to Bliss as the connection faded out. "He says he can wade in. But he sounds brokenhearted, Bliss— that boat was his baby." Her eyes grew wide as Rocco's deep voice bellowed something. Then the call ended.

Bliss hadn't been able to make out his exact words but she felt obliged to point out the obvious. "If Rocco can wade in, the boat probably ran aground. He's stuck on a sandbar, not sinking."

But Vi loved drama. She stared at the silent phone and closed it, giving Bliss a wild-eyed look. "We have to go out there and help him! You're not doing anything important right now, so we can grab a taxi and—"

Bliss held up a hand. "We are two hours away from Pine Island. Four hours, if you count going fifteen blocks in midtown traffic to Penn Station."

"We have to do something!" Vi wailed.

Bliss shook her head. "No, we don't. Rocco's next call will probably be from a bar, where he will get free drinks in exchange for telling the story. And everyone will wade out to help him pull his goddamned clamship off the sandbar. Count on it."

"Well . . ." The cell phone rang again and Vi flipped it open, pressing it to her ear. "Rocco? Rocco? Oh, dear God—how are you, darling? Where are you? What happened to the boat? Are you all right? The sandbar sucked off your left sneaker? Are you sure you're all right?"

"Give him a chance to answer," Bliss said, a weary edge in her voice.

"This is a crisis," Vi said throatily. "Someone has to ask the important questions."

Which weren't important at all. Something inside Bliss frayed, unraveled, reached the breaking point . . . and snapped.

"Fumf this snoff," she muttered. No matter what, she was a small-town girl at heart, who would never, ever have the nerve to curse out her boss.

"What?"

"I said fumf this snoff. I'm taking a few days off."

"You can't. I need you here."

Bliss swept the papers on her desk into a tote bag with an embroidered motto. *I Would Rather Be At The Beach Than Putting Up With This Crap.* Actually, it was plain white straw that didn't have a motto, but that one would have saved her the trouble of explaining where she was going and why. Bliss had had enough. Of Viola Lentone. Of Manhattan in the grip of a heat wave. Of everything.

Her boss would assume Bliss was headed for the beach, anyway. Leonardville, PA, did not have *vacation destination* written next to it in the atlas. It wasn't even in most atlases. But Jaz was there.

He was honestly happy to see her. Bliss was relieved. Some functioning part of her miserable mind told her that he might be shacked up with someone else. Someone slender and blond, who anticipated Jaz's every need and fulfilled it a few seconds later. Someone who had given Bliss the same look of cool appraisal when she walked into Jaz's office, tired from the flight and the usual ride to nowhere. The look that she hadn't liked the first time they had met. Dora.

Perfectly polite, Jaz's assistant showed Bliss to the corporate apartment that adjoined the executive office suite, and excused herself for not staying to chat. Bliss got the unspoken message: Dora had work to do.

She looked around, remembering when she had wondered

where Jaz stayed in Leonardville. So this was his pied-à-factory. The décor was masculine and vaguely reminiscent of a lawyer's office—there was a lot of maroon leather furniture with brass stud trim, and shelves filled with matching books.

But the bed in the next room was glorious. It was huge. The throbbing air conditioner made a down comforter on the bed a necessity, even in August. The comforter was huge too, shaken out and puffed up into lofty fullness. A slumber dome. Bliss set down her bag and flung herself at it. The down comforter collapsed around her.

She heard the door of the apartment open and snick shut. Jaz came into the bedroom and sat down on the edge of the bed, rubbing her back. Bliss didn't bother to turn over. What he was doing just felt too damn good.

"How are you doing? You sounded frantic on the phone."

"Better now," she mumbled. "Nice bed."

"Go ahead and nap. I have a lot of things to finish up. Dora's staying late. I can't get away, sorry—I wasn't expecting you."

"It's okay," she said, lifting her head. "This is a great place to suffer. I should have come out before."

"Why didn't you go out and stay at the beach house or my apartment?" His question held a note of mild reproof.

"You weren't there."

Jaz gave her a fond smile and ruffled her hair. "I'm flattered. Hey, I arranged a nice treat for you while you're waiting. A masseuse will be here in about an hour."

"Really? Thanks."

"You're wound too tight, Bliss. So when your massage is done . . ." He unzipped the back of her dress and slid a big, warm hand up her spine. "I want you to take off your robe or your towel or whatever she wraps you up in afterward." His hand moved in the opposite direction, down into her panties. "And get into a hot bath." A finger slid between her legs and into her pussy. "And play with this." She heard the very faint sound of him licking the taste of her off his fingertip. "And you'll be between the sheets and ready for me by the time I come back. Deal?"

"Deal."

She was padding around in a huge bathrobe with his monogram on the pocket when the masseuse knocked on the door. Bliss opened it.

"Hello. I'm Marina. You must be Bliss."

"Yes, I am. Come on in."

Marina was a tall woman, young, with short honey-blond hair, wearing stretch pants and a close-fitting T-shirt that showed off strong-looking arms. Which had to be one reason she could carry a folding massage table and a giant shoulder bag with relative ease.

The masseuse lugged the table into the room and set it up quickly. As if she'd been here before, Bliss thought. Jaz hadn't mentioned how he knew Marina or if he received massages from her.

"Scented candles okay?"

"Uh, sure."

"Some people are allergic to fragrances so I always ask. But I find they set the mood." Marina took them out of her bag and placed the candles here and there, touching a lighter to each wick in turn.

She took a bottle of massage oil from her bag and got it set up in a warmer that she plugged in. "Cold oil makes muscles tense up."

"Guess so. I appreciate the royal treatment."

Marina smiled slightly. "I do this for all my clients."

Including Jaz? Bliss didn't want to ask.

The masseuse went into the bathroom and came out with

towels that she spread over the surface of the unfolded table. "I'll put some over the parts of you I'm not working on. Ready?"

"Y-yes."

It wasn't as if Bliss had never had a massage before but she had never had one in a setting that was quite this intimate. She felt sexually aware of her own body in a way she hoped the other woman wouldn't notice. Jaz's brief caresses beforehand had gotten to her, big time.

Marina patted the table. "Hop on. Oh, one more thing. How about some music?" She went to her bag again and pulled out a handful of CDs, fanning them out for Bliss's approval. Without really thinking too much about it, Bliss chose one because the cover said *Slow Groove*. Slowing down was exactly what she needed to do.

When Marina turned her back to put the CD in the CD player by the bed, Bliss slipped off her bathrobe and stretched out on the table. She hid her face in her hands. She felt unbelievably naked.

She heard Marina turn around and the music started. Damn. She had chosen the rhythm-and-blues mix that had been playing at Night Moves. The sensual, throbbing beat was relaxing, though.

"Want to smoke a joint?" the masseuse asked casually.

Bliss kept her face in her folded arms. It had been a long time since she had done that. College, in fact. She decided against it, not wanting Jaz to see her with red eyes, acting goofy.

"Thanks, Marina. I don't think so. I don't have a problem with pot, I just don't feel like doing it."

Bliss lifted her head to see Marina put away the little silver case she had in her hand. "Okay."

"But I wouldn't mind a drink. Unless you think alcohol is poison."

Marina snorted. "I'm not that New Age. Whatever floats your boat. Bar's over here, right?"

"I wouldn't know," Bliss said wryly.

The masseuse squatted in front of a cabinet and opened the doors. Bliss could see that the cabinet concealed a small refrigerator next to a lot of liquor. "What's your pleasure?"

Bliss said the first thing that came to her mind. "Dublin Dream. On the rocks."

Marina fixed the drink exactly the way Jaz had, tossing ice cubes in a glass with abandon and pouring a healthy slug of the thick liqueur. She poured another one for herself, not as big. "Let's get creamy," she said lightly.

Bliss kept her upper body pressed against the table so her nipples didn't show. It was ridiculous to be so self-conscious around another woman, especially when all the rest of her was bare, but she was and there was nothing she could do about it. The masseuse hadn't gotten around to putting towels over her legs and butt yet.

She rested on her forearms and took a few sips of the drink Marina brought over. Then she swallowed it down all in one go.

Marina did the same and licked her lips. "Ahh. Sugar rush. Love it." She draped towels over Bliss's back and butt, and Bliss felt a little more relaxed. The drink worked quickly. When the masseuse poured warm oil into her hands and began to work it into Bliss's shoulders, she was almost limp.

Marina worked in slow, deeply soothing strokes. Bliss turned her head to one side, closing her eyes, but very aware of the masseuse standing so close to her and the subtle strength of her touch.

Neck, shoulders, spine, sides—Marina's hands moved with skilled assurance. Bliss had a marvelous feeling of being reconnected with parts of her body that had been missing each other.

Thank you, Jaz, she said silently. She didn't care if this woman had been rubbing him down. Bliss would bet he loved it if she had—and he needed this as much as she did.

As professional as Marina was, there was something extremely sensual about her caresses. Maybe it's the music, Bliss told herself. Maybe it's the drink.

When the other woman lifted the towel off her ass and oiled it up, Bliss realized how turned on she was getting. She buried her face in her arms again, enjoying the powerfully stimulating sensation of a really good booty rub.

"Like that?" Marina said softly. "You moaned when I touched you there. Doesn't hurt, does it?"

"No," Bliss whispered. "Not at all."

She heard a soft knock on the door. Oh, hell. That had better not be Dora, being capable and efficient about some little thing. She knew it wasn't Jaz. He'd said he had to work.

But it was Jaz. She heard him enter and ask Marina if he could speak to Bliss alone. The masseuse stepped into the hall and closed the door.

"Feels pretty good, doesn't it?" Jaz said.

Bliss only nodded. He stroked her hair, not touching her oiled skin. "Hey, Marina and I are old friends. Do you mind if I watch? I'm not trying to turn this into a two-girl show, but—"

"But you want to watch her rub me down. For some weird reason, that doesn't make me jealous."

He whispered into her ear. "She's not into men."

"You don't need to whisper. I don't think it's a secret." Bliss lifted her head, letting her hair tumble over her face and shoulders. "I'm going to go with the flow tonight. She's a great masseuse, no doubt about it. But the only person I want making love to me is you."

"All right. Fantastic. You're going to be so ready for me and I'm going to be crazy hot for you. Can I let her in again?"

Bliss giggled faintly. "She probably just fired up a joint. Give her a few minutes to enjoy it."

"Jesus. I hope Alf Sargent doesn't get a whiff of it. But he never comes to the apartment area. He thinks it's strictly for the hired help, like me."

"Oh, fuck him," Bliss said drowsily.

"Sweet of you to say so. Don't fall asleep."

"I'm not going to. I'm just more relaxed than I've ever been in my entire life. And I have to admit I'm turned on. She has the touch."

Jaz stroked her hair again, moving it away from her flushed face and getting her settled on the massage table again. Then he went to the door to let Marina in. As she'd expected, Bliss noticed the odor of pot smoke, not unpleasant.

"She says it's cool if I watch. But nothing else."

"Got it."

Bliss raised her head one last time and returned Marina's heavy-lidded, considering look. A flash of woman-to-woman understanding passed between them. *I don't like what you like, but I do like you.* "Have at," was all Bliss said.

She heard Jaz settle himself in one of the leather armchairs, which squeaked slightly under his weight. Marina resumed her slow strokes over Bliss's back, shoulders, and sides, getting her completely relaxed again before moving down to her buttocks.

She worked more deeply there, sliding her hands over flesh and releasing pent-up tension in a way that made Bliss tremble.

It felt so good. So incredibly good.

The masseuse's hands moved lower still, to the sensitive flesh at the top of Bliss's thighs, kneading and rubbing. She added in long strokes to the back of the knees, down into the calves, and all the way back to Bliss's ass, squeezing her cheeks together in a rhythm that was highly erotic.

It took a lot of restraint not to moan, and Bliss wasn't all that sure that she was entirely silent. The gentle pressure, up and down, matched her breathing and she couldn't hold back the satisfied murmurs that escaped her throat.

Marina pressed her hands down into Bliss's ass cheeks, an action that pushed her hips into the padded table. Up and down. Up and down.

Bliss heard Jaz draw in a breath. The sight of her laid out on a table and gleaming with oil in the candlelight as she submitted to the expert handling of a strong, attractive woman must be making him crazy. His balls had to be bursting with hot cum, his cock straining for release.

And there wasn't a damn thing he could do about it. What fun.

Marina had moved to the end of the table, where she picked up one of Bliss's feet, rubbing it with oil and playing sensually with her toes. She did the same thing to the other one. Bliss turned her head so she could check out what was going on with Jaz.

The man was leaning forward in the armchair, intent on watching Marina's every move. When the masseuse scrubbed the excess oil from Bliss's feet with a small towel, he leaned back, exhaling. Even though he was dressed, his cock seemed bigger than she'd ever seen it. How nice it would be to take it in her mouth while Marina rubbed her behind with the sweet-smelling oil and pressed her hips into the table. The indirect pressure on her pussy, snugly hidden between her thighs, felt amazingly intense.

But it would be more of a thrill to make him wait. Lazily, Bliss parted her thighs and let her calves hang down over the sides. The position tilted her ass up. This time it was Marina who drew in her breath. Bliss didn't care. She knew the masseuse was interested, very interested, in juicy pussy and having fun with willing female clients was undoubtedly something she enjoyed.

Marina could look all she wanted to. Bliss spread her legs a little wider. She was tempted to slide her hand under her hips in front and get her fingers into her labia. What if she told the other woman about how being stared at like that was exciting her?

Her teasing Marina so shamelessly was turning Jaz on to the max. He had to adjust the hot flesh crowding his fly. But he kept his cock in. Bliss was amused by his iron willpower.

She drew her thighs together again and Marina sighed. "Show's over, huh?" Bliss got the feeling that the masseuse was too mellowed out from the pot to want to control what happened.

Naked and vulnerable though she was, Bliss was the one in control. She kicked her feet idly, almost touching her heels to her butt. Jaz smiled at her. He put both broad arms on the arms of the chair and spread his legs far apart. She blew a kiss in the direction of his balls. They must be aching.

"Time for my front," Bliss said. "That was great, Marina."

She rolled over on the towels, stretching out, her arms at her sides. In this position, she saw Marina's face as the masseuse moved around her and bent over her. Again, Marina began at Bliss's shoulders, smoothing more warmed oil over her collarbone and the tops of her breasts.

Jaz leaned forward to get a better look. Marina poured a little more oil into her cupped hand and drizzled it over Bliss's nipples, so that it trickled down the rounded flesh. She caught it on either side of Bliss's rib cage and smoothed it over Bliss's breasts, making them bounce and jiggle.

"Very pretty," Marina said. "Sorry. But I guess he told you. I'm gay. And I love tits."

"It's okay," Bliss murmured. "What you're doing feels very good."

The masseuse caressed her breasts with light, spiraling strokes that ended at her nipples. That went straight to Bliss's pussy and the other woman had to know it. But they were silent, one giving pleasure and one receiving it, as the man who had paid for it watched the sensual display.

"Hold your tits for me," Marina said softly. "I want to do the musculature right under them."

Bliss closed her eyes and cupped her breasts so that the oiled, rosy-pink nipples stood out hard. The masseuse's strong hands did exactly what she said she was going to do, and then moved over Bliss's belly in deeper, curving strokes.

Bliss squeezed her breasts, matching the rhythm of Marina's belly rub, not stopping for a second. Why should she, when caressing herself—and being watched while she was caressing herself—was so incredibly pleasurable?

The masseuse's hands moved lower, creating new sensations by tracing the curving line at the bottom of Bliss's round belly. She parted her thighs almost involuntarily.

Marina laughed very quietly. "That's good, isn't it? You want to open up. Doesn't matter who does this to you, so long as they keep doing it." She continued her stroking. "Want Jaz to come and look at your pussy while I do this?"

Bliss nodded. She had almost forgotten that her hands were still on her breasts until Marina removed them and set them on her thighs. "You can spread your labia for him," Marina whispered. "Show him everything. This is for Jaz. I know that."

She motioned to Jaz, who rose from the armchair at last. Bliss opened her eyes, groggy from the incredible physical pleasure that suffused her entire body. He took hold of her ankles and gently spread her legs far apart, looking between them and then up at her face. His green eyes shone with delight at her wanton behavior. He helped her bend her knees and pushed them gently down sideways so her pussy opened wider, making a faint, deliciously juicy sound as the inner labia parted. He placed the soles of her feet together.

"Hot woman," Marina commented. "You're a lucky man, Jaz."

"I know," he said.

'You're all pink and pretty," the masseuse said to Bliss. "Your nipples and your pussy are swollen and tight. Wouldn't a tongue in your pussy feel wonderful right now?"

"Not yet," Bliss murmured.

"Oh, but penetration is what it's all about for you," Marina said softly. "But Jaz paid me to massage you, so I'm going to get back to work. You can put your fingers in your hot cunt. He'll like that and your hands won't be in my way."

Bliss grabbed her pussy and squeezed hard to keep from coming. Jaz took hold of her ankles. "Does it feel too good?" he said. "Don't come yet. Hold that hot feeling inside your pussy."

She let go and put her hands on her thighs. She could feel Jaz's breath on her labia. He was almost close enough to suck her clit but he didn't lower his mouth to her sensitive flesh.

Marina put her thumbs on Bliss's temples and began to rub. Her head was about the only part of her body that the masseuse hadn't touched. She moved to Bliss's cheeks with a light touch and rubbed her chin for good measure, relaxing and easing the tension from Bliss's sexual excitement.

The masseuse took a few moments to remove the oil from her hands with a little towel, then traced a fingertip over Bliss's lips. She opened her mouth involuntarily, electrified by the sensation. It was like a kiss—but not. Her lips parted and she moaned. Marina couldn't stand it.

"Oh, Bliss," she murmured. "I can see your tongue. Lick your lips. Show me how you use it."

Bliss did.

"Do I ever want to kiss you. But that privilege is reserved for Jaz. He's going to satisfy you tonight, believe me."

Bliss heard Jaz take off his shirt and toss it aside. He kept his pants on, although the masseuse wouldn't care one way or another about seeing his erect cock. She probably had something bigger that she could strap on, anyway.

"Time for you to go, Marina."

The masseuse moved away from the table and began to pack up. Bliss turned her head to see her squat, turned on by the athletic contours of what was nonetheless a very feminine ass.

"Leave the candles," Jaz added. "Great ambience. You can pick up the table tomorrow."

Marina got going with tactful speed but she paused to look at Bliss one more time. "The word for you is juicy." She slid a fast finger into her client's wide open pussy and took a taste, just as Jaz had done. "Very juicy. Have fun, you two."

7

The masseuse closed the door quietly behind her, and Jaz swept Bliss off the table and up into his arms. She didn't know if they were headed for the big bed or the bathroom and she could barely keep her eyes open. Jaz went through a door and switched on the light with his elbow.

"Ouch, that's bright," Bliss said.

"Sorry." He switched it off and set her on her feet. Bliss grabbed his shoulders to steady herself. "I'll go get the candles. Bath time for you, baby."

She put a folded towel on the edge of the bathtub and sat on it, pulling the faucet out with a yawn. Water gushed out into the sparkling white porcelain tub. She trailed her fingertips in the rapidly filling tub, adjusting the temperature a little higher.

It didn't seem possible to be totally relaxed and totally over-stimulated at the same time, but she was. Bliss pressed her knees together to control the throbbing in her pussy but the action only intensified the feeling.

Jaz came back in with two of the candles, placing them on the counter. Their soft light flickered in the dark bathroom and cast sexy shadows on his half-clad body. He extended a hand to Bliss, who rose, unselfconsciously naked, and stepped into the tub. She stood there and smiled at him, rubbing her arms. The contrast between the hot water and the cooler air of the room gave her goose bumps.

"Got any bubble bath?"

"No. I want to see you in the water. Come to think of it, maybe I'll scrub you down first and then let you soak." He pushed the faucet back in and shut off the water. He helped her out and over to a separate shower stall she hadn't noticed, getting the spray going and testing its temperature with one hand. "That's about right. Don't want to cool off that hot body. Want to pin up your hair?"

She'd forgotten about that and looked around absent-mindedly. Duh. Bachelor apartment. No bobby pins. Jaz shook his head and went to get her purse. Bliss pulled out a few long bobby pins and thrust them into the tangled knot she made with her hair. The effect was fetching and rather Victorian. Long tendrils fell down the back of her neck and a few curls framed her rosy face.

Jaz handed her into the shower, a fierce erection showing at the front of his pants. "Why are you still wearing those?" she inquired, letting the warm water sluice over her back but poking her head out to talk to him.

"To keep from jumping you," he said matter-of-factly.

"Well, it's time to take them off."

He handled the zipper gingerly, even though he was wearing briefs underneath, "Not that easy with a raging hard-on," he said. But he managed. Entirely naked, he turned his attention back to Bliss, who had her arms braced against the tile of the shower stall, enjoying the pounding of the shower jets.

"Mmm. This feels so good. I needed this. Thanks again for the massage."

He looked at her slick, wet flesh and his eyes glowed with

desire. "Turn your back to me. I want to soap you up and get the oil off your skin."

Bliss obliged, adjusting the spray to a gentler mode for her breasts and nipples. Jaz grabbed the soap and ran it over her back and ass, setting it aside to make foam with his big hands, stroking and rubbing. He held a natural-bristle brush under the water to soften the bristles, running the soap over them, and then brushing her back clean with deliberate gentleness.

She arched and swayed, relishing the erotic tingle that the soaped-up bristles gave her. Between Marina's touch and this sensual scrubbing, she was on fire with desire, but it was a whole-body desire so languorous and pleasurable as to not require immediate attention.

Jaz gave her buttocks an extra thorough scrub. "Nice color. Hot pink." He smiled wickedly. Bliss looked at him sleepily, lifting her arms and turning around so he could get the oil off her skin in front. The sight of her raised breasts and dripping nipples made him suck in his breath.

But he controlled himself. When she was completely clean, he shut off the water and let her step out. He didn't bother to towel her off, just helped her into the tub. "No rubber duck. Sorry."

"Not a problem." She lay back. "So you want to watch me in the water. Why?"

Jaz sat on the edge of the tub, his erection springing up between his muscular thighs. "I love wet women."

"Uh-huh. Go on."

"The way your tits float, the way your face gets all flushed, how relaxed it makes you—everything."

"Wasn't that the point of the massage?"

His cock twitched. "I will never, ever forget the sight of Marina's hands on you."

"You sure you don't want to get your hands on Marina?"

"You figured out that she's not interested in men."

Bliss nodded, reaching for a washcloth to drop into the water, and dragging the soaked terrycloth across her breasts. "So where do you know her from?"

"Dora."

She sat up suddenly, her ass squeaking on the clean porcelain.

"Whoa." He got a grip on her shoulder and steadied her. "All I have to do is say her name and you get that same damned look on your face. I think it's time I explained a few things."

"No explanation needed," she said. Her voice was tense. "I never gave you a list of my priors and you don't have to give me one."

"No?" He reached down into the water for the washcloth and rubbed it thoughtfully over her shoulders, watching how the water rolled down her skin. "But I never fooled around with Dora. She's gay, okay? She and Marina are lovers."

Oh. *Oh.* Bliss wanted to sink under the water, slither down the drain, and swim away. How embarrassing. She had taken Dora's look of cool appraisal as a jealous assistant's negative opinion of a rival for her boss's attention. It had never occurred to Bliss that she was simply being checked out. But she hadn't missed the meaning of Marina's incandescently hot gaze—and she had done a little too much to provoke that.

Oh, she hoped Marina wouldn't talk. But it was too late now. She looked up at Jaz, who was grinning down at her as if he was reading her mind.

"Dora's from around here. And she's not out of the closet. So I couldn't exactly explain it when we first met."

Bliss grabbed the sopping washcloth out of his hand and threw it at him. "You were getting off on all that complicated sexual subtext, weren't you?"

"Hey, I did try to reassure you. We were just getting to know each other. Still are. It's been a very interesting summer."

"A long, hot summer. Getting hotter. And you like it like that. You paid Marina to massage me."

He shrugged his shoulders and grinned. "I didn't know you were going to react like a cat in heat. But I wasn't looking for a threesome. She's not into them and neither am I. That was all about you."

"She loves women. She knew what she was doing."

"Look, Bliss, no harm, no foul. You enjoyed yourself. The world is not going to stop turning because consenting adults decided to indulge in mutual pleasure."

Bliss thought that over, a pensive expression on her face. "What if she tells Dora?"

"What's to tell? Nothing happened. Anyway, they've been together a long time. I understand it's an open relationship, to some degree. When they want to get crazy, they go to New York and hang out at City Chicks."

"Of course," she huffed. "The place to be, now that Meow Mix and the Clit Club are history. Not that I ever went into either one. So you and Dora never—"

"Never," he said firmly.

"And you and Dora and Marina never—"

"Never."

Bliss sloshed around, turning over and letting her ass cheeks cool off. "Did you want to?" Her question was soft, with a mischievous undertone.

Jaz patted her butt. "I want you. On all fours. On your back. Taking what a man can give."

"Oral first," she said in a breathy, bitchy voice.

"And what will you be thinking about?"

"Only you, honey. Only you."

She struggled out, a little waterlogged and a little woozy, still feeling foolish about not having figured out something so obvious. Just one more sign of how obsessed she was with Jaz, if she thought his gay assistant was his secret girlfriend.

Oh, well. Being stupid occasionally was probably good for her character. "Can I have another Dublin Dream?"

"Sure. Sweet stuff, just like you."

She remembered Marina's lighthearted comment—*let's get creamy*—and blushed. But she drank it down, wondering just how much crazier this night was going to get.

Jaz had her by the hips and Bliss was rocking back on all fours, taking him deep in her pussy, wild as she wanted to be. He came down and topped her fully, resting his body on her back but taking his weight on his hands—his cock was too long to slip out.

This way she could feel the swing of his balls with each stroke, something she craved. But he was getting tighter there, and closer to orgasm. His skin was slick with sweat, and his muscles slid over her yielding flesh. Jaz was getting wild himself, biting her on the neck and not letting go.

"Can I touch myself?" she whispered, gasping.

"No."

"I want to."

"Just—just let me ride you." His voice was ragged and he moaned, then thrust harder, one arm around her waist now, tight as a saddle cinch. She was sure he was going to come, but he pulled out, flipping her over onto her back and bringing his mouth down on one nipple, sucking so hard she cried out.

He stopped, resting his head on the pillow, nuzzling her tangled hair and keeping his big body above hers. "Sorry," he whispered into her ear. "Not in control. Making love to you— I can't get enough. You're so hot—and you're all I want. Makes me crazy if I think about it too much."

"Then don't think about it," she whispered. Bliss reached up to soothe him, running her fingers through his sweat-damp hair and looking into his troubled green eyes. For just a moment, she saw the vulnerability that every man hid so well—but not in the brief time before orgasm.

Hold me now. Love me hard. Love me the way I love you. Be mine, Bliss. He wasn't going to say it but she knew what she was seeing.

Overcome with feeling, Jaz closed his eyes but the emotional connection between them didn't break. He proved it physically, entering her again with a moan that shook his body and thrilled her to the core. He slammed into her, gasping and crying out, making her come once, then twice, and then a third time.

Then it was his turn for a shot at heaven. Bliss rocked him there and back again.

The sun brightened the room and she woke first, peering over his chest for a clock check. A seven, a colon, and two zeros came into focus. Too early. She buried her face under his arm and burrowed into his body. Jaz rolled to her and threw a leg, heavy with muscle, over hers.

"Time'sit?" he asked drowsily.

"Seven."

He groaned. "Gotta get up." He slid his leg, deliciously warm and furry, over hers. His soft genitals moved with it, just brushing her belly, and she fondled them affectionately, one hand cupping his balls and the other encircling his cock. "No can do. Gotta pee."

He gave her a closed-mouth, anti-breath-of-death kiss on the forehead, and rolled over to a sitting position, his back to her. Bliss reached up and ran a hand over the beautiful musculature of his back as he stretched. God, he was put together. There wasn't a part of Jaz that wasn't a treat to look at, from his broad, squared-off shoulders to his tapering waist and his solid buttocks on the bed.

She ended with those, giving his manly ass a trailing-off pat as he rose from the bed, heading for the bathroom to do what was necessary.

Bliss smiled and punched a pillow down to rest her head. "You piss like a horse," she said to the bathroom door.

"Yeah," he said proudly. "Me and Trigger got it goin' on."

She laughed. "That statement could be taken the wrong way."

There was a moment of silence. She could hear him scratch his hair and finish up. "Hmm. Guess so. I never used to be so kinky. It's all your fault."

"Right." She listened to the sounds of a man going about his morning ritual. Cabinet doors opened and closed, shaving gear was set on the sink, and the shower turned on full blast. Soap-scented steam drifted out until the water was shut off. The faint, brisk sound of a towel rubbed vigorously on skin told her he was drying off, and then she got a tangy whiff of shaving cream.

Bliss was just too content to move. "Do I have to get up?"

"No. Loll to your heart's content. I have a morning meeting with Alf Sargent."

She noted the sudden tension in his voice. "Not looking forward to it?"

"He's been bushting my chops for the last two weeksh." His words were a little slurred from making shaving faces. "Ouch! Fuck. I cut myself. Great." He opened the medicine cabinet for whatever remedy he used and dealt with it.

"What about?"

"Nutty Balls, what else. Stay tuned for the big battle of the pastries. He's a control freak. He's supposed to be retiring but the old SOB really doesn't want to let go."

"Why not?" Bliss asked sleepily.

"What else is he going to do? Play golf and pinch waitresses?"

"Some old SOBs would be happy with that."

"Not Alf. He keeps saying 'I'm a pieman. I'll always be a pieman.' And then he leers at Dora, so we all know what kind of pie he means. She shrugs it off, but I find it as annoying as hell." Jaz banged the medicine cabinet shut, but Bliss heard it swing open. He closed it gently, then brushed his teeth.

"He is kind of creepy that way."

Jaz came out of the bathroom, buck naked except for the small towel around his neck to catch the water from his wet hair. "Did he pull crap like that with you too? You never told me that, Bliss."

She raised her head from the pillow. "I could see it coming after the first time."

"Huh. You still should have told me."

Bliss rolled over on her back, letting the morning air cool the hot flesh under her breasts. "Yeah, guess so. We were both pretty busy, though."

He took the opposite corners of the towel in his hand and dried his neck. "Is that why you made me those collages?"

She smiled. "No, not really. I just wanted to make you laugh."

Jaz pounced on the bed, kissing her breasts and her neck. "You're sweet, you know that? Want to meet for lunch?"

"Hey, you know where to find me."

"So I do. There's coffee and box milk and juice in that cabinet, by the way. Hot Treats breakfast bars too." He pointed.

"Gah."

"Sorry, angel face. If I had my way, we'd be having brioche and café au lait in Paris, not hanging out in Leonardville."

"Some day."

"Some day soon. Wish I could stay and play."

He kissed her mouth and she kissed him back, hoping she didn't have the breath of death. "Me too, Mister Minty Fresh."

He pulled up the sheet. "Cover those tits or I'll never make my first meeting."

"Should I show up?"

"Eventually. Ask Dora for the schedule—you can reach her at extension 776."

"Okay." Now that she knew what was what, Bliss felt only a tiny twinge at the mention of Dora's name. A jealous reflex. Nothing she couldn't handle.

"Alf would admire your commitment to the campaign. We're going to talk about the energy bar concept. He loved the name you came up with. Jockablock. Can't miss."

"Of course not." She rattled off the copy she knew by heart because she'd written it. "On the go-go-go? Grab a Jockablock! Packed with organic oatmeal, ten essential vitamins, and super soy protein."

Jaz laughed. "Plus enough sugar to choke a horse."

Bliss sat up, keeping the sheet in place. "Right."

"Oh man. You look like a movie star. From way back, when wearing a sheet meant the lady just got laid."

Bliss fluffed her hair in a sex-kittenish way. "Does Alf have any idea how much fun you have in this apartment?"

Jaz shook his head. "I never had fun here. Not until you came along. Go back to sleep. You earned some R&R."

"Mmm. Okay, you talked me into it." New York in August, Vi's nervousness over Rocco, Kayla going AWOL—all of it seemed like a million years ago and a million miles away. Rural Pennsylvania wasn't the worst place in the world to unwind. She could think Amish for a few days, strive for simplicity. Just so long as she didn't have to jounce around in a horse and buggy.

She flopped down in the bed again to watch Jaz dress, realizing she wouldn't mind seeing him do that for the rest of her life.

Stop it, an inner voice nagged. *No matter what you think you see in his eyes, this is still a summer love. Maybe you'll get really lucky and it'll turn into a fall fling too. Maybe.* God, she hated her inner voice.

Jaz turned to her, jerking his pants up over his lean, briefs-clad hips and zipping up the fly. He winked at her and her heart went into freefall.

You are thirty. You are past the Age of Innocence ... well past. You are now entering the Age of Reality. Abandon hope.

He put on a subtly striped shirt and whipped an expensive-looking tie into a fast knot. "How do I look?"

"Mighty fine."

"Thanks, babe." He got on all fours on the bed, and claimed one more kiss.

The informal meeting was called to order, more or less, in the Leonardville conference room. What that meant: the guys in short-sleeved white shirts who were gnawing on bagels sat up a little straighter. The women in attendance didn't touch the bagels, Bliss noticed. One took tiny nips from a strawberry that had been meant for garnish.

Females and food were never an easy mix. Just getting women to eat in public was tough, as fast-food researchers had proved. They were much more likely to indulge in stealth eating, and fake eating—airpuffed snacks and sugarless treats. But the teeny-weeny MyPies might be a good fit for that behavior, Bliss mused, fiddling with a pencil as a few more management types entered.

She looked at the untouched platter of packaged HT snacks in the middle of the table. Then again, maybe not.

A female executive picked up a Jockablock and turned it over to read the nutrition label. Bliss observed her without looking directly at her—the company conference room was as good a place to do market research as anywhere else. Studying the bold, masculine lettering and steel-colored wrapper without much interest, the executive put it back on the platter exactly where it had been.

To eat or not to eat, that was the question. That was *always* the question where women were concerned. The executive's hand hovered over a package of cupcakes next. Bliss could almost hear the voice in the other woman's head saying no. She settled on a MyPie and unwrapped it partway, picking off bits of sugary crust and eating them furtively.

Bliss leaned back in her chair, looking up at the ceiling, waiting for the moment when the woman would actually bite into the pie. Out of the corner of her eye, she saw it happen—and it happened fast.

The woman sat very straight, licking a tiny crumb from her lips, as if she hadn't eaten anything at all. Bliss made a note on her yellow pad: *gone in two*. Jaz pulled out the chair beside hers and sat down, putting a toppling stack of folders on the table. He looked curiously at the note and then at her.

"You heading out?"

Bliss shook her head. "I'll explain later."

He pulled out two manila folders from the middle of the stack and leafed through the papers inside, preoccupied. "Meetings, meetings, meetings," he muttered. "I'm up to here with busywork, thanks to Alf."

Jaz looked around at the management team, still gnawing on their bagels. He leaned sideways toward Bliss and kept his voice so low only she could hear. "Fifteen years of working with white shirts and I'll be certifiably insane."

Vern, the head accountant, shot him a questioning look. Bliss had to wonder if those big wrinkly ears of his were better at picking up sound than most. But the older man only smiled in a friendly way at both of them, before he turned around, as if sensing the approach of Alf.

He was preceded by Dora, wearing a short and sexy suit with a metallic mesh cami underneath it. Bliss had to hand it to Jaz's assistant for blasting away the stereotypes about dowdy lesbians. Dora made the Office Barn $2.99 clipboard in her hand look like a chic accessory.

Alf pulled out a chair for Dora and flared his nostrils like a stallion when she gave him a frosty smile and sat down. Bliss was glad she was on the other side of the table but she felt a little sorry for Dora. Alf oughta know he had way too much nose hair to be flaring anything.

The meeting began . . . and dragged on . . . and on. It was two hours later when the white shirts stood up and readjusted their pocket protectors. The female executives stuck their paperwork back into bulky leather folders. Jaz wasn't the only one who had too much to do.

But Alf loved memos and reports and forecasts and Power Point presentations that essentially said nothing at all. He was big on corporate rigmarole and thought nothing of wasting everyone's time. Jaz had stared fixedly at a stray paperclip on the table during Alf's pep talk to the troops, almost yawning when Alf mentioned their mortal enemies in the battle for America's sweet tooth. Mrs. Beal's Bakery. Crumbleyum. Little Donna. Alf really had it in for Little Donna, for some reason. Good thing she was only a cartoon character or he would have set her perky pigtails on fire.

When the great and powerful Alf stood up, indicating that the meeting was at an end, Jaz stayed put. He turned to Bliss, chatting about the ad campaign while everyone else filed out. She got the idea. He wanted to talk to her alone.

He nodded at Dora, the last person to leave, who looked from him to Bliss, and smiled slightly. The blonde closed the conference room door behind her.

Jaz clasped his hands behind his head and leaned back so far that Bliss thought his chair might tip over. "Whew . . . glad that's over. Okay, shall we plan our escape?"

"I just got here. I came in yesterday, remember?"

"And you rocked me all night long, and wow, did I want to do you again this morning. You look great in a sheet." He grinned wolfishly. "But I gotta recuperate. I need sun. I need sand. I need to melt into my beach towel while you rub my back with coconut oil."

Bliss drummed her pencil on her stack of paperwork. "Ah, I

skipped out of the office. I can't head straight for the beach from here. Even though that's where Vi thinks I am." She made a wry face, remembering her boss in the middle of a meltdown. "I just couldn't take her craziness for one more second. But I still need to concentrate on this campaign."

He studied her for a long minute before he spoke again. "Got it. Battle of the needs."

"Well, I wouldn't go that far," Bliss hedged.

"Hmm." He leaned back in his chair, facing her, and crossed his legs, ankle over knee, in a way that emphasized his man stuff. She tried not to look. "How about we go back to New York, dump this blizzard of paper on Vi's desk so she can see that you've been slaving away, and *then* head out to the beach."

She thought that over. Air-conditioned limos, French restaurants with superb food and sexy waiters, freaky clubs, cool corporate apartment for hot nights—Jaz had done all right by her so far. "Ah—okay."

He let out a whoop and sat up straight, dragging her out of her chair and onto his lap for a not-at-all corporate kiss.

It was still sweltering in New York when they got back. Between the blasts of hot air from the subway grates and the gales of bus exhaust, Bliss could feel her work ethic shrivel up. There was no way she was staying in the city a second longer than she had to—Vi would just have to deal. Good thing that her boss liked Jaz so much. He really turned on the charm when he went into Lentone Fitch & Garibaldi with Bliss, and she didn't miss the interested peeks over the cubicle walls at both of them.

She and Jaz planned to head out tomorrow morning, and catch an alternative-theater production tonight, followed by a late dinner at some breathtakingly hip bistro. She hoped that the theater was air-conditioned. Jaz's college friend was playing the lead role of a mute guy living in a garbage can, that's why they were going. At least he couldn't forget his lines.

What to wear, what to wear. She pondered the question as she walked down Ninth Avenue, mentally reviewing the contents of her closet. Old Faithful, her black and strapless dress, would do, plus a light shawl in case she got shivery.

Several hours later, the shawl lay folded in her lap, her evening bag placed primly on top of it. Bliss fanned herself with the program. The air conditioning in the cramped theater was broken, of course. She applauded loudly when the actors took their bows, waiting until everyone had left to go backstage and find Jaz. A major piece of scenery was also broken, and his friend had begged him to fix it minutes before the curtain, a tattered relic of a Lower East Side burlesque house, went up.

Apparently the scenery was unfixable, which meant Jaz stood there for an hour and a half, holding it up. Bliss peeked around the curtain, which smelled like old panties, looking for him. He was on one side of the scenery piece, and his friend was on the other, as they leaned it carefully against the back stage wall.

"That'll do it," Eddie said. He turned to see Bliss standing there. "Is this your lady? Wow."

The admiration in his eyes made her feel even warmer. "Hi, you guys."

Eddie stopped gaping at her and turned to Jaz. "Thanks again, man."

"No problem." Jaz dusted off his hands. "Anything for art. But we gotta get going."

She took his arm, and they said a fast good-bye, then made their way to the street. This part of Manhattan, a mixed area of gleaming new buildings and restored warehouse lofts, was crowded with people. The heat hadn't broken and the air was even heavier, with a sultry charge to it that promised a thunderstorm.

Jaz kept Bliss on his arm, the width of his shoulders preventing anyone from shoving past. She was glad the bistro wasn't far away. Walking in high heels in a summer night was a great way to get a nasty blister.

The sidewalk tables were filled and a few diners were leaning on the railing that enclosed them. They paused to glance at the menu, posted under glass and framed in gilt, noting the gilt-edged prices. Jaz only shrugged but Bliss peeked through the window. Every table inside was empty. Their air conditioner was broken too.

"We're here," she said. "And this is as far as I'm going. Let's sit outside."

"You sure?" Jaz rubbed the back of his neck. His shirt collar was open and his tie had been stuffed into his pocket long ago. "I mean, you're pretty when you're sweaty, but we could get a cab and go somewhere else."

"There aren't any cabs. Order everything iced. We'll be fine."

He motioned to the hostess, who squeezed them in next to the railing. A waitress came over with menus, dropping them on the table with a few rushed words of greeting before she went away.

Jaz opened his. "Okay. We can start with a shrimp cocktail. But these aren't just any shrimp." He looked closer at the menu. "These are descended from Thai royal family shrimp, raised in golden cages on the shores of a secret sea."

"You're kidding."

"Read the menu. And if we are so inclined, we can dip our royal shrimp into tangy *ke-tsiap* sauce. Also known as ketchup, I believe."

"Marketing is everything." Bliss set her evening bag on the table, but Jaz picked it up and slung the delicate chain over his shoulder. "Um, that looks nice on you. I love a big guy with an evening bag."

"I don't want it to get swiped, that's all. It's too hot to vault over that railing and chase a purse snatcher."

"Nothing in there but lipstick and a $20 bill."

Jaz shrugged. "I don't care. Male guarding instinct. Can't help it." The waitress returned, brandishing pad and pencil. Jaz ordered two shrimp cocktails, two orders of chilled, poached wild salmon, and two salads, glancing at Bliss for her nodded confirmation. It was too hot to peruse menus, too hot to think. Her thighs were sticking together and her upswept hair was straggling loose. But she didn't look any worse than any other woman in the restaurant and she honestly didn't care. She was just happy to be with Jaz.

They polished off the cold dinner and ordered raspberry vodka frappes for dessert, lingering over the drinks long after he had taken care of the check. She heard thunder rumble and peered out around the edge of the awning at the black sky. They might be about to get socked by the wickedest thunderstorm ever or she might just be looking at dirty urban air. At night, it was hard to tell. Then a few huge raindrops smashed into the sidewalk and she knew.

Bliss scooted her wrought-iron chair away from the railing and ended up close to Jaz. "Looks like a big one," he said with little-boy glee. The rain pounded the sidewalk until it looked like it was raining up, not down. The spattering water cooled her hot legs and she wriggled her pantyhose-clad toes, enjoying it. The other customers squealed and chattered as they all edged back, sitting almost shoulder to shoulder and not caring. Toughing it out was part of summer in New York. Only the strong survived—and they usually managed to have a pretty good time doing it.

The rain turned to hail that peppered the awning overhead and pounded on the sidewalk. Infinitesimal bits of smashed ice stung her legs but Bliss still didn't mind. They were all in the same boat, sitting in safety as pedestrians ran for shelter, wading over the curbs hand in hand with helpful people they didn't know, cursing a blue streak and laughing.

A good big storm had a cleansing, invigorating power that most everyone enjoyed, despite the inconvenience of soaked clothes and squishy shoes. Jaz seemed to relish the sight of wet women in short summer dresses, Bliss noticed. She patted his cheek.

"You're gawking."

"Who, me?" But he turned his attention back to her, giving her a delicious, raspberry-vodka-flavored kiss that went on and on until the customers in back of them applauded. Then they shrieked as the awning above them split apart and hundreds of gallons of rainwater and hail poured over the tables. There was nowhere to run and nothing anyone could do. Jaz stood up, gasping, wiping water out of his eyes, and Bliss did the same, brushing hail out of her lap too.

"You look totally, absolutely ravishing." Drenched but debonair, he offered her his arm. Bliss waited a moment before she took it, pausing to brush more small hailstones from the tops of her breasts. "Now I know why hailstones are a girl's best friend."

She giggled and slid her evening bag off his shoulder, putting it back on hers. "Oh, shut up."

"Am I wrong?"

"Yes. That's not how the song goes, Jaz."

He flicked one last little sparkling hailstone off her skin. "Whatever. I don't know anyone who deserves diamonds more."

She looked up into his green eyes, not quite understanding what she saw there or where the emotion in them came from. Chalk it up to summer in New York. Everyone was crazy. He was no exception.

8

The storm system stayed parked over New York for the rest of the week, causing power outages and a lot of other headaches. Heading home from Lentone Fitch & Garibaldi, Bliss silently prayed that the elevators in her apartment building were working. She pushed the lobby door open with her shoulder, the plastic bags she held cutting into her fingers. She stood and watched the floor numbers light up in descending order, then entered when the elevator doors sighed open at last. With one free finger, she punched the button for her floor, praying that the air conditioner hadn't conked out while she was gone. Invocations to little gods were what got a girl through a heat spell.

The god of incessant rain was next on her list. Since the night at the bistro, it had barely stopped. Even inside her apartment she could sense the looming clouds, a uniform, oppressive gray. She looked through the glass door to the terrace, saying a silent hi to the solitary pigeon perched on the rail. You and me both, she thought. Fundamentally alone and living on crumbs. Indulging in a moment or two of flamboyant self-pity was deeply satisfying. Jaz had had to go back to Leonardville and their Pine Island plans had been set aside.

There wasn't much summer left. She'd stopped on her way home to look at the windows of the discount shoe store on the next block and still felt a little depressed. The season was about to change and shoes were already on sale, a jumble of pastel-colored flats and beaded sandals on a tabletop inside. The fall styles were displayed in the window, a mix of browns and blacks in everything from weird, spectator-style wedges to conservative job-interview pumps.

Her thoughts had drifted back to her newcomer days in New York and the temp gigs she'd suffered through before landing a job as Violet Lentone's gofer. The payoff: a yearly promotion, culminating in the Hot Treats account. Bliss's first big one.

Falling for the guy who ran the company—or who was about to run the company—probably hadn't been her smartest move. But the man was irresistible. Jaz's restless energy and take-charge air were what made him an effective executive . . . and a major stud. Was she wrong to want him as much as she did? Was she stupid to hope that it would last for a while? As in forever-a-while?

Feeling doleful, Bliss put away her groceries and went to sit on the foldout sofa with a box of cookies. She took a romance from the top of the pile on the table next to the sofa and read a few pages, then set it aside, ripping into the box of cookies and munching a few without tasting them. Nice if she could get through a few days without Jaz, or without thinking about Jaz. She used to have a life, she reminded herself. But life was better with Jaz. Bliss settled into the sofa and felt the remote nudge her bottom. The only effective alternative to reality was reality shows. It was time to get lost in one.

By Saturday morning, Bliss decided to head out to Pine Island, with or without Jaz. He'd promised to come but wasn't sure he could get away. Thank God for midnight confessions: she didn't have to worry about Dora anymore. He *was* working.

The ferry took the longer route around the flat islands in the middle of the bay, and Bliss had plenty of time to people-watch. There were young, nuzzling couples, and old, non-nuzzling couples. Many random children, more absorbed in pocket-sized video games than making mischief. An assortment of dogs whiffing the breeze and squinting into the glare. It wasn't raining and it wasn't sunny either. The sky was whitish-gray and the vast expanse of the bay was flat.

She looked down into the canvas bag at her side, and saw the book that she'd tucked into the bag next to fruit and cookies, about an indecisive young woman who hoped to find a meaningful life. The book jacket showed a fluttering hem and two bare feet. Bliss knew she wasn't likely to read it. The portfolio she'd brought along held layouts that needed final approval from Vi . . . meaning she had to work for some of the weekend.

The ferry captain blew the horn and the boat swung around, preparing to enter the dock. It bumped against the pilings and straightened out. She stood at the top-deck railing for a few moments, then spotted Jaz's brother and waved to him eagerly. Joe was standing next to a golf cart crammed to its vinyl rooftop with tools and lumber. He waved back.

"Want a ride?" he called.

"Sure." Bliss scampered down the metal stairs, catching up with Joe by the wagon rack about twenty feet away. "Can you take me to Vi's house? I have to go over revised layouts with her." She patted the portfolio slung over her shoulder.

"No problem." Joe stowed her bag and the portfolio on top of a toolbox and got behind the wheel. The small golf cart barely contained his huge frame but it was all that contractors were allowed to drive in the summer months. A bumpersticker on the dash that said *My Other Car Is A Monster Truck* made her smile.

"So what are you doing in town?" she asked.

"I was dropping off one of my guys—actually, this is his golf cart but he said I could use it. He's a reservist. Just got called up."

He waited a few moments for the last of the people who'd arrived with Bliss to disperse, dragging wagons piled high with duffel bags and weekend necessaries.

They made small talk for several blocks, until Joe came to a stop for a pack of little kids with wet hair and towels draped over their shivering shoulders. Two women brought up the rear of the back-from-the-beach parade, using mom magic to keep the kids together.

"Slow train," Joe commented.

"I see what you mean." She watched them go by, noting the long lines of small wet footprints that the children left behind. "Pine Island must be a great place for kids."

"You got that right. Especially when Jaz and I were growing up." He seemed lost in thought for a moment. "So where were you headed again?"

"Vi's house."

He nodded and made a left turn, coming to a stop in front of the angular structure. Bliss collected her things and waved him on. "Thanks, Joe. Stop by this weekend. I'll make meatloaf."

Joe grinned. "All right. I will. So when is Jaz coming out?"

"Last ferry. He's trying to escape Alf's clutches."

Joe made a face. "That old coot. He thinks he owns Jaz. But no one does."

"I know," Bliss said. She hoped Joe's remark wasn't some kind of warning. "See ya. Thanks again for the ride."

"No problem. Got everything?"

"Yup." She slung her bag and the portfolio over her shoulder and went up the ramp to Vi's house, hearing the faint whine of the golf cart backing up the way it had come.

Bliss tapped on the glass door, peering inside through the screen side of it with one hand cupped to block the sun. No one seemed to be home, but Vi was expecting her. And judging by the giant flip-flops someone had kicked off before entering the house—size fourteen—Rocco was around somewhere. Bliss knocked on the glass door again.

"Coming," Vi called.

Bliss waited until the older woman came out of a back room and crossed the living room to open the screen door. Barging into her boss's house just wasn't something she wanted to do. "Hi, Vi."

They exchanged air kisses. "I was just heading down to the bay," Vi said. "Rocco took the cabin off the clamship to lighten it. He doesn't want to get stuck on a sandbar again."

"It can't be fun."

"Oh, did I tell you that he named it? *Neptune's Folly.*"

Bliss grinned. "That fits."

Vi pointed to a plastic laundry basket filled with new life jackets. "I insisted on buying those. The marine supply store was having an end-of-summer sale."

"But it's not the end of summer."

Vi took a puffy orange vest out of the laundry basket and waved it around. "Just about everybody on Pine Island disappears in September, except for the locals and a few diehards. So the sales out here start in early August." She held the lifejacket up against her chest. "How do I look?"

"Good color on you. Neon orange matches your eyes."

Vi sniffed and flung the life jacket back in the basket. "Very funny. Just remember who signs your paychecks."

Bliss only smiled. Maybe a little of Jaz's attitude was wearing off on her. Couldn't hurt. She set her bag and the portfolio on a low table made of driftwood. "I brought out the layouts."

"Great," Vi said indifferently. "But we can go over those later. Rocco's waiting." She picked up the basket of lifejackets and looked expectantly at Bliss.

"Oh, you mean you want me to come along?"

"Yo ho ho and a bottle of rum. Yes, I do, Bliss."

In another minute, the two women were heading down the path to the bay. Bliss didn't mind. She hadn't actually been in Rocco's clamship yet and she was looking forward to it.

"Did you see the article on him in *ArtNews*?" Bliss asked.

"Of course," Vi said. "That damn boat is famous. A bunch of art college students came out to look at it. They smoked about a million cigarettes while they talked and talked about how symbolic it was. Rocco had to give them free ferry tickets and an etching apiece to get rid of them."

"Symbolic of what?"

"I forget. The struggle between man and oysters or something like that. But they didn't get into the Viking theory."

"I can't imagine that Rocco didn't explain it." Bliss had listened to several versions of that theory and a few others of his in the last weeks.

"Oh, I'm sure he did explain it and then he went off on some tangent. Once Rocco starts talking, he doesn't stop. And he's quite capable of getting from Vikings to oysters in the same sentence, believe me. It's one of his charms." Vi settled the basket of life jackets a little higher on her hip.

"You really care about him, don't you?" The question was out before Bliss could stop herself from asking. She prayed her boss wouldn't mind her nosiness.

Vi didn't seem to but she didn't answer right away. They rounded the last turn in the winding path. "Of course I do," she said at last. "Rocco Camp is the best thing that's happened in my life for a long while, crazy as he is."

Bliss gave her an I-understand-perfectly look. Not that she did, but she hoped Vi would start talking. Rocco and Vi seemed wildly incompatible to Bliss—she still couldn't get her mind around the idea of her perfectionist boss in love with a free-wheeling artist.

Vi rested the basket on top of a fence post and caught her breath.

"Want some help?" Bliss offered. "What else is in there?"

Her boss pushed aside the life jackets on top and showed her. "A thermos of iced coffee and some brownies I made. Ripe peaches. And a knife. He likes to cut up his fruit." Vi rolled her eyes. "Okay, I'm pampering him."

"Nothing wrong with that." But Bliss's tactful reply didn't match the surprised look on her face because Vi laughed at her.

"And I said Rocco was crazy. Guess I am too. Anyway, he's not that crazy—well, not totally. His paintings sell for several hundred thousand apiece. I mean, God knows where the money goes but he is making it."

"What you're saying is he's self-supporting."

"Right. And he loves what he does. That's very important, Bliss. Are you taking notes?"

"Mentally."

"A man who doesn't love his work is bound to drive you crazy," Vi went on. "Take that from a veteran of three marriages."

"I thought you were married four times."

"The first time was practice. I don't count it."

Bliss nodded. "Oh, okay."

"Anyway"—Vi picked up the basket and they continued down the path—"Rocco's a lot of fun. And he has to be one of the most interesting, imaginative men I've ever known. At my age I get to take risks. Our relationship isn't about deciding to have kids or picking out china or anything like that."

"What is it about?" Bliss asked cautiously.

"Loving each other," Vi said simply. "Looking out for each other. If you have that with a man, you have everything."

Bliss thought back on the amazing summer so far with Jaz. They did have that. How long it might last was another question. And not one that she wanted to ask him. "So-o," she said slowly, "how do you know when it's, um, the real thing?"

Vi looked at her narrowly. "You and Jaz are moving right along, aren't you?"

Bliss blushed. Had she been that obvious? Activating Vi's ever-busy brain on the subject of love might not have been such a good idea. While her question hadn't been specific, Vi had seen right through it and gottten personal.

"Well, I really like him. And I think he likes me. So, you know, I was just asking. In a general way."

"Uh-huh." Vi didn't sound like she believed that for a second. "The real thing . . . that's tricky. Sometimes it hits you like a freight train. Sometimes it sneaks up on you."

Bliss didn't answer, wondering if it was better or worse if both things happened. Because that was pretty much how she felt, like a freight train had snuck up on her. Whether Jaz felt the same way was another question.

"But real love is worth it. I know, you probably think I'm married to my brilliant career. And yes, I am . . . but you have to have someone in your life who you really care about or what the hell is all for? When Rocco and I met, we knew how lucky we were. That's one advantage of being—oh, that gacky word—mature."

They arrived at the end of the path and Bliss shaded her eyes to see the clamship, bobbing at anchor and not very far out. Even from this distance, she could read the new name. *Neptune's Folly* was stenciled in block letters on the stern. Of course, the shell chariot of the sea god had been drawn by dolphins and not propelled by an outboard motor, but it really was the perfect name for Rocco's creation.

He'd added duckboards beneath the motor, to make it easier to climb in and out. The stuffed seagull had been moved to the prow and made fast with several lashing of yellow nylon rope.

Rocco had rigged a substitute for the removed cabin out of lightweight PVC pipe and overlaid it with several colorful windsurfer sails, none of which matched, held together with duct tape.

The thing only added to the clamship's eccentric charm and it would provide a modicum of shelter. Bliss was glad they weren't going to be broiling in the sun. There wasn't a breath of a breeze and the painted sail with the golden lion was rolled up and tied.

Bliss and Vi stepped carefully on the mounds of eelgrass that washed up at the end of the walk. Some of it was dry and pleasantly prickly underfoot but it got slimy as they got nearer the water. Vi went ahead, putting the laundry basket on top of her head and boldly wading out.

"Yoo-hoo!" she called.

Rocco came out of the patchwork cabin. "Hello, beautiful!"

"Bliss is coming too. Hope you don't mind," Vi added.

"Not at all." Rocco waved to her.

Bliss followed her boss into the water. The tide was out and only the fringes on her cut-offs were getting wet. She paused halfway to look around, noticing that she could see the restaurant at the end of the world from here, half-hidden by the tall reeds.

She remembered the day Jaz had taken her there. It was probably a half mile from where she was standing and the place—what she could see of it—looked much the same, shuttered but peaceful.

Bliss heard splashing as Vi hauled herself up on the duckboards, assisted by Rocco, who must have already set the laundry basket on deck, because it was gone. Then he lifted his laughing lady up and over the back end of the boat in one effortless move.

The older couple kissed briefly and Vi moved around the

boat as Bliss waded closer. She got up on the duckboards next
and Rocco swung her on deck, just as easily as he had lifted Vi.

"Wow," Bliss said, looking around. "The cabin thing looks
great."

Vi came around it and Rocco reached out a hand to her,
drawing her to him and fitting her neatly under his arm. "You
think so? I scrounged all that stuff."

"I figured," Bliss said. "But it's really cool. *Neptune's Folly*
is one of a kind. A work of art."

Rocco inclined his head in an aristocratic nod that went well
with his height and his mane of silver hair. "Thank you, young
lady."

Vi went to untie the boat from its mooring. She seemed to be
enjoying the role of first mate, Bliss noticed with amusement.
Rocco got the motor going with a few good yanks on the
starter and a couple of curses, and they were off.

The calm water made for smooth cruising and they went for
several miles before they saw another boat. The people on it
waved and hallooed to Rocco, who waved back grandly.

Squinting in the sun, Bliss realized that they had reached the
middle of the bay where the low islands were, encircled by the
channel that the ferry company marked with buoys. The shift-
ing sands of the bay bottom meant the channels had to be
dredged, which was why, at low tide, the ferries didn't come
this way.

So Bliss was surprised to see a ferry in the near distance. It
was the oldest and smallest still in service—Jaz was sentimental
about the old boats and loved their all-wood construction and
sleek lines. He had pointed out this one to Bliss while they
were waiting at the ferry dock once, saying that it had once
been a rum runner during Prohibition days.

The top deck wasn't crowded with passengers the way it

would be toward the end of the day. And most everyone pre-ferred the spacious newer ferries. On an old boat like this, it was difficult to get kids and luggage and dogs on and off, and as the weekend approached, a lot of people traveled with all three.

Rocco brought *Neptune's Folly* about, killing the motor when his boat was still well outside the channel but keeping his hand on the wheel, every inch the captain.

"You're a glutton for attention," Vi said cheerfully. Several people on the old ferry's top deck came to the rail to wave to them and shout their approval of the crazy-looking boat.

It was shipshape in its weird way, Bliss thought, and it really did run. Jaz had said that Rocco knew his way around boats—he probably would've told Bliss to stay off it otherwise.

And speaking of Jaz . . . was that him on the ferry? A tall, well-built guy with black hair in a loose T-shirt that fluttered in the breeze came up to the rail. It sure as hell was Jaz. Bliss waved wildly at him, jumping up to get his attention.

"Jaz! Jaz!" she screamed.

"You're rocking the boat," Vi said, but she smiled indul-gently and waved too.

Jaz finally saw Bliss and threw her extravagant kisses, not caring who saw. She couldn't hear what he was saying over the roar of the approaching ferry's engines but it was probably something like *see you later*. Bliss couldn't read his lips either. The ferry went by, and half a minute later its wake hit their boat broadside, pitching it back and forth.

Vi swore and grabbed one of the PVC pipes of the makeshift cabin. Rocco stumbled and she reached out to him, holding his hand until he got his balance. It wasn't long before the water flattened out and Bliss let out the breath she hadn't realized she'd been holding.

"Life jackets," Vi said. "Everybody put one on."

"Let's just move out into open water," Rocco replied.

She gave him an imperious stare and scrabbled in the laundry basket for the biggest jacket, handing it to him. "Put it on. And don't be a dick about it."

Rocco winked at Bliss. "Aww. She's so sweet." He took the life jacket from Vi. "I know you care, Vi. And you're right about practically everything. That's why I love you."

From Vi's open mouth and startled look, Bliss could tell that she hadn't heard him say that before this moment. And before she could protest or argue, Rocco brought his mouth down on Vi's and shut her up with an ardent kiss.

Bliss turned away, waiting for them to finish. Her parents didn't act like this. On the other hand, her parents had been married for about a million years. Rocco and Vi seemed to be just finding out that love at any age was a many-splendored thing. She peeked over her shoulder. Vi was pulling her T-shirt down and smoothing her hair, and Rocco was yanking on the starter cord again. Whew.

The rest of the long weekend passed by in a blur of sun, sand, and . . . sex, of course. Lots and lots of sex. Jaz and Bliss made a pact to keep the real world at a distance and not listen to the radio or turn on the TV. Or say one word about Alf, marketing strategies, or strawberry anything. They agreed to make the most of being on Pine Island, especially since it was hot and miserable in New York.

Jaz took every opportunity to walk Bliss backwards into the bedroom of his beach house, and invented ingenious new ways to stimulate her with the outdoor shower. He even brought her to climax at a party, dancing slow and close in the dark and making her sway and press against his thigh.

She looked up just seconds before she came, seeing his face, shining with fine sweat from his own sexual heat. He'd been turned on by the way her tight shorts tucked into her pussy. He sat in a chair and made her bend over before they left for the party, so he could rub her between the legs with his fingers and get her hot for him in advance.

Jaz had slid his hands up inside the shorts when she turned her butt to him, pleased that she wasn't wearing underwear. He squeezed and stroked her cheeks, parting them and bending his head so he could get just the tip of his tongue in, allowing himself a taste of juicy pussy before the party.

The thick seam of her cutoffs felt nice against her clit, and he tugged the shorts higher, giving her a sensual wedgie and revealing more of her ass for his viewing pleasure.

Bliss rested her hands on her knees and stayed bent over, enjoying the experience of showing off in short shorts. Again Jaz slid his hands underneath the material, squeezing both halves of her ass and making her rock to his rhythm.

"Mmm," he murmured. "This is fun. A big, beautiful ass to play with, but I can't have it yet. All the guys are going to be looking at it when you start dancing, but I'm the one who gets to go home with you." He pressed several kisses on the material of her shorts. "Hmm. I don't think I'm going to let anyone else dance with you tonight, Miss Bliss. You're all mine. Agreed?"

"Uh-huh." Her tone was light but she liked his jealousy. Guys who were too casual just seemed like they didn't care one way or another.

Jaz's grip on her behind got fractionally tighter and he dug his fingernails in a very territorial, male-animal way. Bliss *loved* the way that felt.

"So it'll be just you and me, slow-dancing," he said softly, not letting go. "You can think about the way I eat your pussy . . . and get the shower pulsing on your clit . . . and most of all, how hot you got when you wanted my finger in your asshole."

Touching his fingertip to the spot with almost no pressure made Bliss tremble.

"Sliding in and out with plenty of lube. In and out. In and out. I used my thickest finger and rolled the rest into a fist to bump into your behind while you were on all fours . . . remember?"

"I remember," she whispered.

He squeezed her ass cheeks again. "I love to do you, Bliss. Orally. Then get my cock really deep in your pussy with you thrusting back and taking me all the way inside you. Anally. Any way you want to be serviced. I love being your man."

She was glad he couldn't see her face because hearing that made her so goddamn happy. Bliss still wasn't ready to tell him just how much she wanted him in her life when the summer was over. Right now she had him in her pants and that was about all she handle.

He sighed and slid his hands out, patting her fanny. "All right. Let's go."

She straightened and turned to face him. But Jaz didn't stand up, just pulled up her T-shirt and buried his face in her bare belly. His wildly affectionate kisses sent hot thrills through her body, and Bliss clasped his head, stroking his hair. He stuck his tongue in her belly button and twirled it, making her giggle.

"Like that, huh?"

"Yeah. Feels good."

"Then think about it every time I look at you when we're at the party. Think about everything I ever did that made your beautiful body feel good. And tell me what you want me to do when we get home."

"I'm not sure I can wait that long," Bliss murmured. And she hadn't been able to. His possessive attention had turned her on so much that by the time they were dancing barefoot on the deck, hardly moving in the crowd, she knew she was going to have an orgasm in the sensual press of anonymous bodies against theirs, lost in the dark and the throbbing, heavy beat that rolled out into the summer night . . .

* * *

They woke late, fooled by the ominous gray sky that made it seem like the sun hadn't come up. But it was eleven o'clock. Jaz rubbed his eyes and peered at the clock radio. "Mind if I turn on the weather report?"

"Nope."

He punched up his pillow, flopped back into it and dragged her into a side cuddle position.

"Hey," she protested. "I can't breathe."

Jaz relaxed his hold and gave her a kiss on top of her head. "Sorry."

"Howdy, folks. Looks like we have a storm blowing in from the northeast," the weathercaster said in a fake-friendly voice. "Time for tri-state listeners to hang up those beach towels and get ready for three days of rain and rough seas. Small craft advisories are in effect from Sandy Hook to Cape Cod and—"

Jaz switched it off. "That sucks. Wow, listen to the wind."

Bliss listened, then shook her head. "I don't think that's the wind. Sounds like a dog to me."

"Hmm." Jaz was quiet. "You know, you're right."

The sound died away. But somehow the echo of it stayed with Bliss. She got up, found her shorts and T-shirt, slipping them on. "I'll go see."

"See what?"

"Well, if it is a dog, it sounded like it was under the deck. Could be lost or something."

Jaz got up too and threw on jeans. "I'll come with. Gotta protect you. It's my manly duty." He scratched his chest, fluffing up the dark, fine hair. With a sexy shadow of morning stubble and his black hair sticking up every which way, he looked good enough to eat. She decided to grab a muffin on her way to check out the dog situation—after last night's super sex session, Bliss was absolutely starving—and jump him later.

She padded out of the bedroom with Jaz right behind her,

snagging a muffin in the kitchen on her way to the living room. She tried to slide the glass door open with her left hand because the muffin was in her right.

He snorted at her ineffectual attempt and put his hand over hers, pushing the door open smoothly. They stepped out onto the deck and Bliss was surprised at how cold the air was. The small community of Breezy Bay was quiet and the few houses she could see had their curtains drawn on closed windows and doors. Most likely a lot of people had already left on an early ferry, wanting to get back to New York before the bad weather hit.

Bliss could hear the heavy waves pounding the beach and she shivered. Sleeping next to the incredible warmth of Jaz's big body, she hadn't felt the temperature drop. He rubbed her arms while she took a bite of her muffin. A big crumb broke off and she brushed it through the boards of the deck, using the toes of one foot and looking down.

Two soulful brown eyes gazed up at her. "I was right," she said, startled. "There is a dog." The eyes disappeared as a streak of black fur moved swiftly, trying to get the big crumb.

"Where?"

She pointed down at her feet. "Under the deck. I just saw eyes. It's black. But I didn't get a good look at it."

Jaz moved away from her and went down the ramp. He stood just in front of the deck, several feet below where she was. "Yup. A stray. Poor thing is starving."

She balanced the muffin on the rail and followed Jaz. He and the black dog were looking at each other warily. The animal was painfully thin, with protruding ribs and a scrawny neck. It did have a collar but until it let them get close, there was no way to read the tags.

The dog didn't seem mean but it kept its distance, looking from Bliss to Jaz. Then it—okay, he, it was clearly a he—sat on his haunches.

"Good dog," Bliss said softly. The tip of its tail moved ever so slightly. "Good dog," she said again. The animal's eyes were bright and clear, and it seemed alert. She guessed that the blue metal tag was a county one, meaning it had been vaccinated against rabies. But how long ago?

Jaz reached out a hand and the dog's nostrils flared widely as it sniffed hard without coming closer. He took a step forward and the animal flinched. "Easy, pal," he murmured. "Someone's been jacking you up, I can see that. You're okay now—this is a safe place."

The dog stayed where it was, thinking it over.

"Bliss, go get the muffin."

"Is that healthy for him?"

Jaz shrugged. "I don't have any Iams, if that's what you mean. And he may not be able to eat kibble. Who knows what shape his teeth are in? Anyway, the muffin's soft."

She went back up the ramp to get it, walking quietly so as not to alarm the dog. When she came back, she set it on the sand under the deck. The dog looked intently at the muffin but didn't make a move.

Bliss put a hand on Jaz's arm. "Let's get farther away. Maybe he'll take it then."

"Good idea."

They moved back several feet and sat down. The black dog dropped to its belly, still watching them. Hungry, hopeful, he began to creep forward, as if he expected to get hit at any second. But he kept his soulful brown eyes on the prize. The dog gave them one last look just before he reached the muffin. Then he swallowed it in two breathless bites, licking its chops over and over to get every molecule into its mouth and from there, into its starving body.

The dog crept backward. Jaz and Bliss got up and moved to it, and this time it didn't flinch. She reached out a hand and patted the animal's head, giving it light, small strokes. The dog's eyes closed as its nervous tension eased.

"You've got the touch," Jaz said softly. "But I knew that."

Bliss took her time, letting the dog get used to her. She didn't want to do anything that might provoke an unexpected bite. But when it suddenly rolled over and presented its chest, looking up at her with doggish gratitude, she obliged.

She rubbed his breastbone, sharp under the skin and black fur, with one hand, and maneuvered the collar to where she could read the tags. "Okay. He had a rabies shot only two years ago. And his name is . . . hold still, silly." The dog wriggled and his muzzle bumped her hand. "Domino?" The animal sat up and looked at her. "Guess your name is Domino."

"He must be the domino with no spots. He looks solid black to me," Jaz said.

"Domino, Domino," Bliss crooned. The dog looked at her adoringly. "Uh-oh," she said. "I have a new best friend."

"Who does he belong to?"

She stroked the dog's neck and ears, trying to get a look at the tags again. "Don't think there is a name besides his. No phone number either." Bliss reached for the collar, then pulled her hand away when she felt hard, bumpy things in his fur. "Ugh, he has ticks. Lots of them. Okay, Domino, no more petting. We have to get rid of your passengers first."

Jaz stepped forward a little too quickly and the dog suddenly cringed, staring up at him, brown eyes wide with fear. "Oh, Jesus. Look at the white of his left eye. That's a hell of a blood clot. And there's a big cut on his forehead next to it that's almost healed—right there, can you see it under the fur? I'd guess he got hit with a two-by-four."

Bliss understood the quiet fury in his voice as she looked at the dog's left eye. She hadn't seen the cut when she'd petted his head. At least it had almost healed. He was a fundamentally healthy dog, despite his mistreatment.

"Some miserable fuck beat you up, pooch. Wish I knew who," Jaz said. "I'd beat the crap out of him."

"Yeah. Me too." Bliss kept her voice very soft. "But right now we gotta feed him something a little more nourishing than a muffin and get him to a vet for a thorough checkup. He's not lost. He ran away. Good for you, pal. You're a smart dog." She gave him an approving pat, selecting a tick-free area on the top of his skinny head. Domino looked ridiculously happy, though there was no telling what amount of abuse he had endured.

"Now what?" Jaz asked after a while.

"Whoa. Don't look at me. I can't keep a dog in a dinky sublet apartment." She made the mistake of looking into the animal's soulful eyes. "But if I could keep you, I would. Don't look at me that—oh, Domino. You're so thin and messed up, I feel like crying."

"I can't keep him either." Jaz sighed and raked a hand through his hair. "If you can't have a dog, you don't really have a life. Do you know what I mean?"

"Not exactly," Bliss said.

"Sooner or later, I have to turn around and go babysit Alf Sargent in Leonardville. I'm not my own master, is what I'm saying. So I can't be Domino's."

The dog gave Jaz a look of sincere regret, then turned to study Bliss.

"I think he understands."

Jaz shrugged. "Nah. It's the back-and-forth. I talk, he looks at me. You talk, he looks at you."

The dog settled down on his belly and put his head between his pitifully thin legs. From that point on, only his eyes moved.

"You know, when he fills out, he's going to be a big dog."

"What breed? Want to hazard a guess?"

She raised both hands in a who-knows gesture. "Your basic ASPCA black dog. Papa was a rolling stone and mama used to dance for the money they'd throw. Did I get that right?" she asked Domino.

The dog closed his eyes.

"I don't think he wants to talk about his parents," Jaz laughed. "I wonder if there's any roast beef left."

"Go look. He needs to eat. And what he really needs," Bliss said finally, "is a home. We're not going to take him to the pound. He's been through too much."

Jaz gave her a wry smile. "Now how did I know you were going to say that?"

"The same way I knew that you weren't going to take him there."

"You're right, Bliss. Maybe we can find someone who's out here full time."

They looked at each other and said the same name at the same time. "Rocco."

The dog banged his tail on the sand, picking up their mutual enthusiasm.

"Don't tell me you know him, Domino," Jaz said. "But you do count as a found object." The dog grinned.

Jaz turned to talk to Bliss. "Rocco hasn't had a dog for a while and he loves dogs. He used to take in strays and find homes for them, and he kept a few." He addressed his next words to Domino. "You're gonna love Rocco. And you can sleep on his sofa. He won't care. He found that somewhere too."

Jaz spent about an hour on the phone trying to find a vet in Havertown area who would see the dog on a Sunday, and finally reached one who agreed to meet them in his office. Proudly sporting a leash of nylon rope and an improvised raincoat crafted by Bliss from black plastic garbage bags and duct tape, Domino walked with them to the ferry in the steady rain, already looking stronger, thanks to the leftover roast beef and another muffin.

He wasn't the only one wearing black plastic. Weekenders who'd come out expecting nice weather had improvised raincoats of their own, and a few had just cut holes in the top for their heads and let it go at that.

The line for the next boat was long, and no one was in a very good mood. The ferry company was bringing over additional boats, which filled up with passengers and headed back to the Havertown dock one after the other, but the process was slow.

Domino noticed the other dogs waiting with their owners and even cats and other small pets in carriers, but he was well-behaved. Good sign, Bliss thought. She hoped and prayed that the vet wouldn't find anything much wrong with him. They couldn't ask Rocco to take on a dog with major problems.

The animal pressed against Bliss's wet leg, shivering a little. Bliss felt Jaz put an arm around her shoulders and give her an affectionate squeeze, and then the line moved forward.

What with one thing and another, they didn't get back to Pine Island until nearly midnight. Rocco offered to take the dog before Jaz was finished explaining the whole story, calling Rocco on his cell phone while they watched the vet's assistant patiently remove ticks from Domino, wearing rubber gloves and safety glasses in case the disgusting little monsters oozed blood when they were pulled out. She told them to watch for Lyme disease and other tick-borne ailments, giving them a brochure about the symptoms.

Domino didn't love getting the wound near his eye examined by the vet or receiving a full array of shots, but he didn't put up a fight. He seemed to know he was being taken care of. Poorer by five hundred dollars and richer by one healthy dog biscuit that Domino didn't want, they made the last ferry.

As Jaz had predicted, Rocco made friends with the dog right away, showing Domino to a shabby sofa, and letting him jump up. The dog sank into the cushions with an almost inaudible sigh.

"I can't thank you enough, man." Jaz said. There was a lot of emotion in his voice and real weariness, Bliss noticed. He planned to be on the six a.m. ferry, which would get him to the airport and into Leonardville by noon.

Bliss didn't envy him that. She didn't even have to go back to New York. Rocco had called Vi, and Vi, touched by Domino's hard-luck story and their rescue, gave Bliss the next two days off. Well, almost off. A modern slave had a laptop instead of a ball and chain. But ensconced at Pine Island, she could do the minor revisions Vi had in mind for the layouts just as well as she could do them in New York.

The rain had died down to a cold drizzle, but more rain was predicted for tomorrow. So Bliss would have to be inside anyway, and with Jaz in Leonardville, she would get a lot of work done. They walked back to Breezy Bay hand in hand, in silence.

"Are you missing Domino?" he asked after a while.

"How'd you know?" She wasn't really surprised that he did.

He stopped and gave her a light kiss on the forehead. "Dunno. Maybe because I was missing him too. He bonded with us."

"Yeah. For a little while," Bliss said. "Anyway, we can see him whenever we want."

"Yeah."

9

The storm stuck around for the predicted three days, then headed out to sea. It left sparkling, rainwashed skies behind it and a crisp coolness to the air. Heading back to New York on the ferry, Bliss felt refreshed and renewed. She didn't have a care in the world.

Yesterday she'd listened sympathetically to Jaz's recounting of his latest battle with Alf Sargent. In all seriousness, the outgoing CEO proposed a publicity stunt using human cannonballs to launch Nutty Balls on the unsuspecting public. A last-minute intervention by the head of the legal department—a quiet guy who was referred to behind his back as The Navy Blue Suit With No Sense of Humor Whatsoever—had effectively scotched that idea.

She knew that Jaz was getting more and more frustrated with his job. And that it was just a job to him, at this point. Alf Sargent showed no signs of stepping down. He pooh-poohed Jaz's ideas and tried to dominate every meeting.

All Jaz could do was fume. But he didn't believe in complaining. She bought a bag of small homemade doughnuts at the

Havertown ferry dock, fresh and warm and cinnamon-sugary, and gobbled one, wishing they could share the bag. Homemade doughnuts cured everything. She thought tenderly of him as she ate the other two.

Bliss daydreamed on the hour-long train ride, not really noticing the clapboard houses of Long Island morph into the brick apartment buildings of Queens. The train plunged into the tunnel that would take it to Penn Station, and she saw herself in the window reflection, looking tousled and summery.

Getting loved up by Jaz on a regular basis was doing her good. As-long-as-it-lasts. As-long-as-it-lasts. As-long-as-it-lasts. The mental reminder matched the sound of the moving train.

They slid into the station and Bliss stepped out onto the platform, working off the doughnut calories by taking the stairs instead of the escalator to the main level of Penn Station. She wasn't far from her apartment and decided to walk.

Most of the people on the streets still wore summer shorts and tops, but a few forward-thinking women strolled by in the newest browned-out fall fashions. Bliss noted what they had on: the Mad Monk look seemed to be big and so was Urban Wraith.

She felt almost dowdy in her sherbet-colored sundress and straw-soled espadrilles with the matching ribbon ties. Then an appreciative glance from a cute guy cheered her up—even though he had his tie thrown over his shoulder while he wolfed down a Hallo Berlin bratwurst from the quilted steel cart at the corner. So what if he didn't have an expense account. He was still cute and so was she.

She wandered back to her own neighborhood via a circuitous route that took her by as many flower stalls and dress shops as possible. A new sign on her block caught her eye. The Naughty Lady, huh? Looked like the place had just opened for business. Bliss crossed the street to check it out.

A pink corset fitted to a figure form in the window revolved under a spotlight. Around it lay an assortment of underthings, tossed with après-sex abandon on a rippled satin sheet. Someone inside the shop came close to the other side of the window and Bliss looked up at a bosomy lady who was very likely wearing the same corset as the one in the display. She had to be the owner.

Bliss studied the pretty things in the window, sort of aware that the shop owner was beckoning to someone on the street. Bliss looked over her left shoulder at a homeless guy pushing a shopping cart full of trash. Nope, couldn't be him. She looked over her right shoulder at a shaven-headed cult member passing out loony tracts and asking for small donations. Double nope.

She looked straight ahead again . . . right into the kohl-lined, smoldering eyes of the bosomy lady standing inside the shop, who crooked her finger again. Bliss opened her mouth and said a silent *me?*

The bosomy lady nodded, revealing perfect teeth in a luscious, lipsticky, pouty smile. Bliss wasn't sure if the woman wanted to make love to her or sell her something. She looked at the homeless guy again just to look somewhere else, but he had gone down the street with his cart, grumbling to himself.

Bad move. The proprietress came out the door and welcomed Bliss into her scented pink lair. She barely remembered crossing the threshold, overpowered by the mingled fragrances of rose essence and sandalwood.

The bosomy lady uncapped tiny vials of essential oil and waved them under Bliss's nose until she was dizzy. She held up tiny scraps of lace and chiffon that she said were panties, but Bliss couldn't be sure. No sane woman would pay $120 for an undergarment that barely covered her clitoris. She lured Bliss over to a rack of bras, flicking a manicured fingernail through the hangers. Bliss saw sheer bras in lurid colors, pointy bras with mean stitching, fake fur bras for cave chicks, leather bras for dominatrixes, metal bras for those special interplanetary occasions, and plain white cotton bras for imaginary virgins.

The bosomy lady went back behind the counter and withdrew a velvet-lined tray from the glass display case. Well, well. A snooty salesclerk at Tiffany's couldn't have done it with more hauteur—except this velvet-lined tray held sex toys.

The proprietress was obviously having fun, holding long vinyl dicks in her pretty, plump hands and explaining the merits of this one versus that one, handling and squeezing the lifelike, nicely heavy balls attached to the longest rod. Bliss wanted to walk out but she stayed rooted to the spot, hypnotized by the things and the woman's soft voice.

Should she buy a dildo? Bliss thought of Jaz's big, hot cock doing its cocky best to satisfy her and felt suddenly disloyal. She shook her head. The other woman shrugged and put the tray back . . . then straightened and set a different tray on the counter, with vibrators.

Hmm.

Her apartment looked just the same once she got into it. Maybe a little more dusty. Bliss set her bag and the portfolio and a hot-pink tote fastened with wee plastic handcuffs down on the foldout sofa. She had succumbed to the mystique of the Naughty Lady experience in the end, buying a vibrator, a corset, a small dildo, three gorgeous bras, and a men-in-uniform calendar from last year. Half-price. Not like the dates on it actually mattered. Women didn't buy calendars like that to write dentist appointments on.

She took the calendar out of the tote and looked at the thumbnail pictures on the back. A cop, a firefighter, a jet pilot, a hunky GI in ripped cargo pants, a delivery dude, and a tall doorman who wasn't wearing anything under the brass-buttoned coat he held open. She'd always wanted to live in a doorman building.

Bliss touched a fingertip to the photo of a bare-chested young waiter with a bow tie, black pants, and one hand around the neck of a cold champagne bottle, ready to pop the cork. She and Jaz had had fun with *that* fantasy.

Moving right along, she savored the tight shorts on the athlete, and the black lycra that cupped the ballet dancer's prominent bulge. He was really beautiful, with eyes like a faun, totally gay and totally hot. She imagined him expertly seducing the athlete, pulling down his jockstrap and letting the other man's erection spring out, going down on his knees to suck it hard and introduce his straight lover to the intense pleasure of man-for-man sex.

Clearly, watching the long vinyl dicks sway back and forth in the naughty proprietress's hands had been too much for her. Bliss only glanced at the remaining three photos—a sailor in white buttonfront bellbottoms, a guy in safari shorts, and a studly Santa to end the year—before she tucked the calendar back in the bag.

Bliss surveyed her apartment, deciding to do some serious dusting and spiffing up. She intended to invite Jaz over the second he got back from Leonardville for a playdate, but she couldn't imagine pirouetting for him in her cute new corset when the place looked like a dump. She untied her espadrilles, kicked them in a corner, and grabbed a rag and a spray bottle.

Spritz. Wipe. Spritz. She cleaned with a vengeance, eager to try on her new things but not letting herself have fun until the work was done. In an hour, it was. Full of housewifely virtue, she looked around and saw the dusty cheval mirror she had missed, attacking that last of all.

Wow. And whew. How sparkly could one mirror be? Not any sparklier than that. She shed her clothes on the way to the shower, pinning up her hair in the bathroom so it wouldn't get wet under the spray. She couldn't wait to get into that corset and try out a few seductive poses in front of the mirror.

Ten minutes later, she was hooking it up in front, grateful for the flexible boning and ingenious design. It was laced, but it didn't have to *be* laced. And ohmigoodnessgraciousheavenstoboobies. Did it ever lift. What amazing engineering. Major bridges spanning mighty rivers were not built as well as her new pink corset.

Bliss turned this way and that, admiring herself and practicing some sensual wiggling. Jaz was going to love this thing. She oughta call him up right now and let him know what he had coming. Flouncing down on the fold-out couch—and feeling a pang of regret that she'd cheaped out in The Naughty Lady and not bought the marabou-trimmed high-heeled shoes that went with the corset for a totally slutalicious ensemble—she reached for the phone and dialed the number of his inner office in the Leonardville factory.

He picked up after four rings. "Jaz Claybourn."

Bliss cooed a hello. He sounded amused by the sultry tone of her voice but his was almost . . . efficient.

"Hello, Bliss. Glad you called. Alf and I were just going over the revised Hot Treats layouts here in the conference room."

Aha. So he had picked up his private line but he wasn't in his private office. She heard Alf's affable hello to her.

"Don't put me on speakerphone, honey," she said softly. "Guess what I just bought. A corset."

"Oh. That sounds like an, uh, excellent idea."

Bliss got comfortable. Making him squirm was going to be a hoot. She knew he would stay on the phone as long as she did, Alf or no Alf.

"It's so pretty and pink. And it's nice and tight around my waist," she purred. "My ass and my tits are bare. You can do all the spanking and sucking you want."

"Really."

"I bought it at a new store called The Naughty Lady. And I

bought a vibrator too. It's small and flat so I can wear it under my panties. If I want to wear panties. Right now I'm not, though."

"Uh-huh."

"You know, it straps on right over my clit so I don't even have to hold it. I just step into the thongy thing that holds it and switch it on for hours of stimulating pleasure. It was only $29.95."

Jaz drew in his breath. "Good deal. Sounds just right for the marketing budget. Well, Alf and I were going over spreadsheets and—"

"Oo! I want to spread for you," Bliss whispered. "Can't you see me lying back on satin sheets with my legs far apart? I want you to tie my hands and ankles, and then turn the vibrator on. Pinch and suck my nipples while I'm tied and spread, and stroke my legs. Watch me have one orgasm after another."

He was silent for at least thirty seconds. Bliss imagined him loosening his tie. "Interesting concept," he said at last. "Very interesting. I think we should try that. Uh—hang on. Yes, Alf?"

She heard the old guy say something about wanting coffee, and where was Dora when you needed her. But Bliss didn't hear any sounds of him leaving the room. She could sense Jaz's irritation. He wasn't going to fetch coffee for Alf, but she knew all too well how demanding his boss could be. Alf would sit there until he got his goddamned coffee one way or another.

"I have to put you on hold for a sec, Bliss. Okay?"

"No problem." She waited patiently, listening to the forgettable music of the hold function and slipping a finger into her bare pussy. Nice and slick. Teasing Jaz was getting her hot.

A minute or so later, he clicked back to her. "Thanks, Dora," she heard him say to his assistant. The usual sounds of doors softly opening and closing, and the clatter of cups, reached her ears. "Still there, Bliss?"

"Yes, I am. Sitting on the sofa. Waiting for you."

"Okay. So, where were we?"

"You had me tied up and spread. You have your fingers in my pussy while the vibrator excites my clit."

"Good plan. Go on."

"I'm coming around your fingers," she breathed. "Bouncing my ass on the bed while you thrust in and out. My pussy is pulsing and I'm begging you to do it hard. I'm so wet . . ." She touched herself between her legs again. "I really am wet, you know."

"I don't doubt it, Bliss. As I said, it's a fantastic concept and I think you should go for it. Cream and sugar? Over there, Alf. Next to the little stirry things on the tray."

She heard Jaz take a sip of his coffee and choke a little.

"Is it hot?" she said softly.

"Oh yeah. Wish you were here so I could show you—um, show you my—our concepts."

Alf's booming, obnoxious laugh reverberated over Jaz's sigh. "We're geniuses," his boss said.

"Come on over as soon as you get back to New York," she whispered in Jaz's suffering ear. "Get naked and show me that big cock. Let me kneel and lick your balls before I take you in my mouth. I want you to lube your shaft and pump it in your hand until you—"

"Shoot," Jaz said suddenly. "Spilled my coffee. My hand's all wet."

"That's okay," she said. "I can just imagine that hot liquid dripping through your fingers. I want to lick up every drop of your cum. I know you're ready to explode right now. Good thing you can hide that erection under the table you're sitting at."

"Gotta make the best of it. Toss me some of those paper napkins, would you, Alf? Thanks."

She heard moppy noises and didn't say anything, just moaned into the phone, very softly.

"Sorry. Go on."

Bliss waited for a few seconds before replying. "See you soon, lover," she whispered.

"Right. Sure thing. Thanks for calling, Bliss." He hung up and she leaned back into the cushions, a funny little smile on her face.

He called when his plane touched down just before midnight and told her to be ready. He had a town car waiting and there wouldn't be much traffic at this hour. She'd slept in the meantime—in fact, she was still in bed when he called, entirely naked, loving the way his low-pitched voice seemed to slide over her skin even when he was talking on the phone.

But she got up and twisted her hair into a high, sexy chignon, put on the corset, and padded around the apartment barefoot. He was at her door, breathing hand, a minute after she buzzed him in from downstairs.

"Did you run up the stairs or are you just glad to see me?"

"Both," he said. He came inside and double-locked the door, then turned around to take in the full effect of Bliss in a corset designed for sex play, bare-breasted and bare-assed. "Turn around, angel," he said. "Nice and slow."

She did as he asked, rubbing her hands seductively over her hips and pausing to part her ass cheeks for a sneak peek at what he was going to get from her. In two swift strides, he came over and grabbed her, sitting on a chair and putting her over his knees. "So you get off on being a bad girl, hmmm?" His big, warm hands stroked her buttocks gently.

"Yeah." Bliss pushed her bare toes into the floor, straining up, craving his touch, wanting more. "Did I make you hot?"

"You know you did. You're good at being bad."

"Then I want what bad girls get. Give it to me, Jaz."

He kept on stroking her ass. "Where's the vibrator? I think you need to wear it. Let's make this spanking really intense."

She wriggled up and off, looking for the little toy, which she'd set out in advance. Along with the small dildo. Lubed and ready. What he would do with that was going to be up to him.

He looked at both of the sex toys, then at her, but he didn't say anything. Leg by leg, she stepped into the delicate elastic straps that positioned the curved side over her sensitive nub. Her breasts bounced when she leaned forward and he grabbed them, pressing the dull edge of his fingernails right where the areolas met the nipples. Bliss moaned. The feeling shot to her pussy, making it clench. He worked on her nipples a minute more, watching her face, hot desire in his eyes.

"Ready?"

She nodded as she straightened, then lay over his solid thighs, feeling Jaz open his legs wide to hold her comfortably— and to accommodate his huge erection. Having him fully clothed while he administered pleasure-punishment was even more exciting than when he did it naked. He seemed more in control, which meant she could really let go.

He played with the straps of the vibrator for a moment, adjusting the fit and making sure it was over the right spot. Then she guided his hand to the tiny switch, which she'd set to intermittent pulse in advance. He was right. She was good at being bad.

They switched it on together. The now-and-then pulse began, and so did the spanking. He brought his hand down again and again, making her ass glow. He used his other hand to hold her still, so the feeling was stronger. She couldn't get away, didn't want to get away. But he stopped, gasping. She twisted a little in his lap and saw him look to the side, catching sight of the small dildo she'd lubed up.

Bliss settled back down, her whole body thrilling with sexual sensations. Her hair swept over her face, hiding it, keeping her from seeing what he was doing. He began to stroke her hot, spanked ass and then he parted the cheeks with one hand. She felt the tip of the small dildo penetrate her anus and murmured her pleasure with a soft yes. It was as flexible as a finger and not much thicker. Jaz slowly pushed it into her, stopping when the round knob at the end, which kept it from slipping in totally, rested between her cheeks. "There you go. A toy in your beautiful butt and a clit tickler too. Doesn't get any hotter than that."

He let go of her ass and she tightened her cheeks to hold the dildo in. Jaz spanked her again, making sure to get the tops of her thighs as well as her buttocks. Each smack of his hand gave the ass toy a little push, and it wasn't long before she was rocking and moaning, surrendering to the extreme pleasure he was giving her. The vibrator did its thing, and Bliss gasped at every pulse, not knowing when they would come.

And then . . . Jaz stopped. She wanted to beg for more, was on the verge of ecstatic tears, ready to give it up, give him everything he wanted.

The man had amazing self-control. He parted her ass cheeks, took out the toy, reached between her legs and switched off the vibrator. He helped her stand up and watched her roll down the thin elastic straps and step out of it. He seemed to be assessing her sexed-to-the-max state, running his hands over her hips and thighs with undisguised admiration. He held her steady while he brought his face close to her pussy, touching the tip of his tongue to her overstimulated clit.

Then he buried his face in her soft curls, suckling her clit gently, pulling an endless, intense orgasm from her body that made her clutch his dark head and push her pussy against his tender mouth. She threw her head back and moaned long and low.

Jaz raised his head and wiped his mouth off on her belly. He began to unhook the corset and she helped him with trembling fingers. He picked her up and carried her to the bed, spreading her legs apart. She watched him shuck his clothes, watched him sheathe an erection that was bigger than any she'd ever seen on him. He got over her, positioned himself, and rammed into her.

He buried his face in her neck, moaning, trying to hold back. Jaz kept his body up by resting on his forearms. He clenched his fists, digging his nails into his palms, counteracting his uncontrollable response with a flash of pain.

But she didn't want that. Slowly, moving her hips up, down, around, and sideways, Bliss made him give it up, bringing him to orgasm with her body. He shuddered all over, gasped, and then it happened, rocking him until he cried out. Bliss stroked his back, drawing out the intense sensation, savoring his pulsing release.

Knocked out by pleasure, he rested on top of her for several seconds, breathing deeply and quietly. She put her hands on the front of his shoulders and pushed him up a bit so she could breathe too.

Jaz came back to reality. "Am I squashing you? Sorry." He showered her face and neck with tender kisses, and rolled off. "I'm pretty tired. But I had to see you. Never wanted a woman the way I want you, do you know that?"

They lay facing each other, and Bliss reached up to stroke his messed-up hair. "I'm getting the idea."

He gazed into her eyes, looking soulful. "So, uh, Bliss . . ."

She waited for the rest of the sentence but he seemed to be searching for words. "Yes?"

"What would you think about making this permanent?"

The question startled her. "Making what permanent?"

"You know. This. You and me."

"I'm not sure what you're saying."

"Me neither. Just thinking out loud." He turned his head and kissed her palm. "You got me all opened up."

"Is that good or bad?"

Jaz captured her hand in his big one and put it flat in the

middle of his chest. "Good. Very good. Especially for the heart. Feel that beat."

"Mmm," Bliss said. "Very impressive. But that could be just the aerobic effect of hot sex."

Jaz shook his head. "Not just. There's more to it than that. A lot more. But maybe this isn't the time to talk about it. I have to go back to Leonardville tomorrow. Alf insisted. I don't think he bought my excuse for leaving in such a hurry."

She patted his cheek. "What did you tell him?"

"Uh—that I was meeting a French manufacturer of fruit syrups and that Monsieur Sucre had to fly back *tout suite,* the syrups could be a possible new secret ingredient, blah blah. He gave me a weird look but at least he didn't argue."

"I should feel guilty."

"Don't. Not for a second."

Bliss nestled into his chest and he wrapped his arm around her, giving her long, luxurious caresses that swept from her shoulders to her hips. He stopped his hand on her ass and gave her a squeeze.

"Ooh," she said. "But you should sleep."

"I can sleep on the plane. You didn't have seconds yet."

She smiled into the hollow of his collarbone and pressed a kiss against his warm, musky skin. "Ready when you are."

10

Two weeks later . . .

Jaz was walking around the sand in front of the restaurant at the end of nowhere with a loan officer from a Long Island bank. He'd asked Bliss to come along, telling her to wear a tight top and shorts and dazzle the guy so he wouldn't see the holes in the roof.

She'd pointed out that she wasn't that dazzling, Jaz had disagreed, and they'd ended up in bed for a quickie. Which accounted for the lazy grin on his face when he looked her way.

Out of the blue, he'd asked for Bliss for her opinion on buying the place and she really hadn't known what to say. Turning it into a successful eatery seemed like a long shot, but she had no experience in that area, other than knowing that new restaurants had a notoriously high failure rate. Jaz's hard-headed business acumen didn't necessarily apply. He was sentimental about anything having to do with Pine Island, but then he had grown up here.

The loan officer, a young guy named Mike, had come out on

a motorboat, a new fiberglass model with no top and gaudy racing stripes. He cut the engine, came about, and bumped into the dock three times before he threw Jaz a line. He looked sheepishly at both of them when his end, which wasn't tied to his boat, fell in the water. Jaz pulled it up without comment and threw the dry end back at him, before looping the wet section around the dock cleat in figure eights, finishing with a half hitch.

Once Jaz had the boat tied up properly, Mike got out and got busy, alternately making notes on a clipboard pad and poking his pencil at the stucco surface of the cinderblock building. A chunk of stucco crumbled and fell into the sand, leaving a powdery trail in the air.

"Happens out here. The sea air takes its toll," Jaz said.

The bank guy frowned. "Yeah, but resurfacing a whole building is an expensive proposition. The owner couldn't afford the upkeep. That's why we had to foreclose on the property five years ago."

When you were in high school, Bliss wanted to say. Something about Mike's puffy face and much-too-white shirt told her he was as clueless about repair and renovation as he was about boats.

Jaz smiled blandly. "But the structure is sound. And I think I can keep those costs under control. My brother Joe is a builder."

Mike made a note of that and went inside the front door, peering at an old spiderweb to the side of it with what seemed to be apprehension. The spider was long gone and the gray wisps of its abandoned web would soon follow.

Bliss strolled out on the dock, shading her eyes with one hand, peering at the bay, wondering if *Neptune's Folly* was out there somewhere. There weren't any sailboats. The hot, muggy weather had returned in the last few days. The air felt heavy.

Looking in the direction of the reed-choked marsh, there

wasn't much to see except dragonflies zooming around. One whizzed by her in a flash of iridescent light and Bliss watched it return to the reeds.

She heard vague sounds from inside the restaurant: cabinet doors opened and shut, a stuck window being forced up, circuit breaker switches clicked on and off. Joe had asked a pal at the utility company to turn on the power to the building in advance, so it wouldn't seem so abandoned. Bliss listened to Mike's comments, figuring he was trying to seem knowledgeable. All he needed was to make sure the property wasn't inhabited by summer squatters or about to fall down.

Cinderblock endured. Even she knew that. Jaz wasn't going to lose money if he bought it; he just might not make any if he reopened the restaurant.

Her cell phone ring tone sounded faintly, reminding Bliss that she'd left it in her purse near the dock. She ran back, digging through the contents to find the phone, and pulled it out, looking at the little screen.

Vi. Oh, hell. So much for taking a day off on the sly. Vi must have come into the office, even though she'd said she wasn't going to. Bliss steeled herself to answer the phone, visualizing her boss drumming her fingernails on her desk.

"Hello," Bliss said brightly, trying for a not-guilty tone that would convince this judge. Tough to pull off when your bare toes were curling into warm sand. "Hello?" she said again when there was no reply.

"Bliss?" A crackle of static interrupted Vi's next words. "Are you there? This is Vi."

"Hi. Yes, I'm here. At Pine Island." Bliss decided not to lie. She braced herself for a nasty reply, but Vi surprised her.

"Me too. I'm out with Rocco—in *Neptune's Folly*—Bliss?"

"I'm still here."

"We're way out near the bay islands and . . ." Vi's voice trailed off, then came back. "Rocco can't get the motor started. It conked out and we started drifting."

Bliss looked through the window to see if Jaz was still inside. He and the bank guy must have gone up the steel ladder in back to check out the roof. She could hear their voices from somewhere overhead.

"Did you call the Havertown police? The marine division? They patrol the bay—"

"I don't know their number," Vi said nervously, "I had you on speed dial so I called you." She said something to Rocco that Bliss couldn't hear.

"Um, let me think for a minute. There must be something we can do. By the way, how did you know I was here?"

"I didn't!" The older woman's voice held a note of panic.

"Okay, okay, calm down." Bliss wasn't that worried, but she could tell that Vi was.

"Rocco, the motor is kaput. Quit fooling with it." Vi came back to Bliss. "Is Jaz with you? Can you two borrow a boat and get out here?"

Bliss kept the phone to her ear and scanned the horizon. No telling exactly where the *Neptune's Folly* was, but she figured Jaz could find the bay islands easily enough. How to get there . . . she looked at the fiberglass motorboat tied up at the dock. It was new and it would do.

"I think so, Vi—"

The connection crackled again. "Rocco says there's a squall line to the north. He doesn't like the looks of it. There must be something you can do. Bliss? Bliss?"

Someday her boss would figure out that things like the weather were beyond human control. To the rescue again, Bliss thought. Why on earth Vi thought that she would know what to do was beyond her. Rocco was right about the squall, though. Bliss could see a faint, very faint, line of dark clouds but it had to be miles off.

"Here comes Jaz. Listen, Vi, hang up so you don't waste the battery. I'll call you right back."

Jaz was coming out of the restaurant with the bank guy, not looking very happy. They must have found missing shingles on the roof, maybe water damage or holes. Oh yeah. Joe'd volunteered to deal with that in advance, but he must have gotten hung up on another job. She wondered if he would be able to meet them here like he'd promised.

Bliss took Jaz aside and explained Vi and Rocco's predicament in a low voice. Jaz cast a worried glance at the faraway line of clouds in the otherwise blue sky and turned to Mike.

"Look, we can discuss the roof later. But we have a problem. Friends of ours are out by the bay islands and their motor conked out," he said. "They're drifting near the ferry channel. Think you could swing by so we can help them out? We might have to bring them back here, I don't know. Their boat's pretty big, I don't think yours could tow it."

Mike thought that over. "Um, it's not my boat. It belongs to the bank."

The obvious question hung in the air. What was he doing with it?

Mike looked at them sheepishly. "It's a repo. I could get in big trouble if I gave people rides in it."

"I'm not talking about joyrides, man. Someone has to get out there." Jaz pointed to the gray line of clouds, which, Bliss saw, had grown thicker in less than a minute. But the storm was still far away from where they were. "See that?"

"Those little clouds?" Mike seemed unimpressed. "Miles away."

"Guess you've never been caught in a squall," Jaz said, irritation in his tone. "They're dangerous and they move fast, especially over open water."

"Not my problem, man. Sorry. Rules are rules."

And jerks are jerks, Bliss thought.

"You already broke the rules when you took the boat, right?" Jaz pointed out.

"Well, yeah. But I don't want to sink it."

Jaz blew out a long breath, his patience clearly wearing thin.

"Did you call the harbor cops or anybody like that?" Mike asked.

"No," Jaz said curtly.

"You can use my cell if you don't have one."

"You're a prince," Jaz said. "But Bliss has hers."

"Your friends should wait where they are. The ferry guys will see them if they're near the channel." Mike squinted at the sky. The blue was turning a hazy gray. "No lightning or anything."

"Not yet," Jaz said. "Wait a while."

That clinched it for Mike. "I don't want to be on the water if there's going to be lightning and stuff."

He headed for the restaurant's open door. Jaz gave Bliss a look she couldn't quite read and then turned to follow the other man in. Bliss heard him calling to Mike inside. "Okay. I understand where you're coming from. But there's one more thing—"

Bliss stared at Jaz's retreating back. How unlike him to give up so easily.

Jaz ran back out, slammed the door, grabbed the key, and locked it from the outside. "Asshole," he muttered.

Bliss, on the verge of calling Vi back, closed the phone and stared at Mike's furious face behind the window he was banging on. "Huh? But you can't—"

"I just did." He grabbed Bliss by the hand and they ran down to the dock to the boat. He scrambled in, getting busy with the key and looking at the gauges, leaving her on the dock where she tucked the cell phone into her purse and zipped it.

She didn't know as much as he did about boats and bad weather, but she could see how worried Jaz was and she wasn't going to argue.

Bliss kneeled by the cleat to untie the boat, struggling a little with the wet rope. She cast one last glance back at the restaurant where Mike's face appeared in another window, shouting something she couldn't make out.

"He'll stay nice and dry," Jaz said with contempt. He turned the key in the ignition and the engine roared to life. He put a hand on the gearshift, waiting for her. "Plenty of gas. Let's go." She scrambled in, pushing them away from the dock with the boat pole he handed her. "Good work."

He swung the motorboat out and away from the dock, and they left a broad wake behind them as they roared out into the bay. The squall line was closer and every trace of blue sky had vanished. Even though they were moving at top speed, the air was oppressively hot.

"Call 911," he shouted over the engine. "They'll connect you to the marine police. Tell them what you told me. They might get there ahead of us, they might not."

Bliss cast an anxious glance at Jaz's set features. His gaze was fixed ahead. The advancing winds of the squall brushed the water into whitecaps that slapped against the boat as they sped through.

"Kicking up fast," he muttered. "We're gonna get banged around. Hang on."

She clutched the edge of the windshield, ducking down behind it to avoid the wind. Bliss tried to call 911, and then tried Vi's number, but the oncoming storm disrupted the calls. She gave up. Jaz was doing his damnedest to get out to Vi and Rocco, and that was what counted. He kept a fierce grip on the steering wheel, and his arm muscles bulged with the effort it took to control the boat.

Five minutes went by. Ten. Fifteen. Bliss looked one last

time at the cell phone screen and then stuck it back in her purse, zipping it again, for what that was worth. She stayed down low, not wanting to look around but she knew visibility was rapidly decreasing.

"I see them!" Jaz yelled suddenly.

Bliss breathed a sigh of relief and peeked over the windshield, squinting against the wind and spray. There they were . . . but the *Neptune's Folly* was rocking hard in the waves.

The rain began, splattering on the windshield and drenching both of them in seconds. It was almost a good thing it was raining sideways instead of down—the inside of the boat wouldn't fill up with water. Bliss brushed away the water streaming down her face and waved wildly at Vi and Rocco, seeing a black head with floppy ears pop up next to Rocco's hand on the rail. Domino. Oh, geez. The dog was with them.

Jaz killed the engine, using the boat's momentum to come alongside the *Neptune's Folly*. The boats bumped and rocked together in the swells. Bliss got a line to Rocco, who fastened it quickly.

"I tried to call 911," Vi began.

Bliss shook her head, holding onto the rail of the other boat. "Explain later." There wasn't time to talk. There wasn't time to do anything but get the hell out of there. Bliss was glad to see that the older couple was wearing life jackets, and realized belatedly that she and Jaz weren't. She would look for them once they got Vi and Rocco into the boat. And Domino.

Rocco gave Vi a hand and she struggled into their boat, swallowing a sob. "Thanks, guys. You're amazing."

Domino had both paws on the rail, and looked up at Rocco for a second before he leapt, landing asprawl in the fiberglass hull but quickly righting himself.

Bliss reached out to Rocco, noticing that his strong hand was shaking when he took hers. He clambered in, pausing to slap Jaz on the back. "Knew you'd find us."

"Oh, yeah?" Vi pulled the shivering dog close to her. "I wasn't so sure. How'd you know that?"

"He's Will Claybourn's boy, isn't he?" The older man looked at Jaz. "Your dad would be proud of you. Always was."

"Never mind that. Sit down," Jaz yelled as Bliss undid the line. Vi and Rocco huddled together on a bench seat in back, looking miserable but not as miserable as Domino, dripping wet, between them. Bliss grabbed the boat pole and pushed them away from *Neptune's Folly* when Jaz revved the engine.

And then the squall hit for real.

Bending low to keep under the wind, she found life jackets in a long plastic box bolted to a bench, and got hers on somehow. She staggered forward and helped Jaz into his, one arm at a time, so he could keep a hand on the wheel while she fumbled with the Velcro straps.

"Thanks. Sit down," he muttered. His black hair was plastered to his head and he had to squint to see in the driving rain. She stumbled to a seat and clutched the edge with both hands, watching Jaz spin the steering wheel this way and that to cut into the choppy water as cleanly as he could. Rocco put a comforting arm around Vi.

The fiberglass motorboat banged up and down, and waves coming from the side splashed inside. Bliss felt queasy. She bit the inside of her cheek so she wouldn't throw up, and tasted blood. Oh, man. There was nothing she could do to help Jaz, nothing she could do to make their race to safety faster . . . she felt worse.

Then she realized the water in the boat was up over her ankles. Shit. She looked around wildly for something to bail with, and grabbed a cut-out bleach bottle stuck under the bench she was sitting on. She scooped water out just as fast as it was coming in. Shit oh shit oh shit.

Bliss looked over her shoulder at Rocco and Vi. He had

found another bailer and was using it, while Vi hung on to the dog, looking scared to death.

Several miles in back of them, a thin, jagged white line split the sky. She counted the seconds until she heard the thunder, and trembled when it boomed. Rocco's face was impassive, his silver mane flattened by the rain. But he kept at what he was doing, bailing with steady strokes.

Bliss turned around again to look at Jaz, seeing the tensed muscles in his back under his wind-whipped, drenched shirt. He hunkered down behind the windshield trying to see. A glimmer of light appeared in the near distance, and Bliss prayed that Mike had had enough sense to keep it on for a beacon. Jaz swung the nose of the boat that way and she stopped bailing.

Faint as it was, the light shone through the rain and spray, growing larger in the windshield. Jaz made for it. He turned only once to glance at them and Bliss noticed that he was gritting his teeth. With water running over them, his strong features seemed stronger.

Yeah. The Claybourn men definitely had what it took.

Bliss checked on the older couple. Vi was clinging to Rocco, her face buried in Rocco's chest, right between the two halves of the life jacket. He was patting her back in an absent-minded way and bailing at the same time.

Bliss set her bleach bottle aside, overjoyed when she realized that the light ahead had grown larger still, casting a halo through the murk. She made out the boxy shape of the restaurant at the end of nowhere, and in another minute, Jaz was coming about, throttling back and bumping into the dock pilings.

She grabbed the rope secured to a side cleat and made a wild toss at the cleat on the dock. The loop landed in the right place and she drew it in, pulling them alongside the dock and tying up as best she could.

The older couple rose, stiff and unsteady, and Bliss reached out a hand to Vi, giving her a boost onto the dock. Domino jumped for it, paws scrabbling on the splintery wood, almost falling back in the boat until Vi got hold of his collar and hauled him up. Rocco followed, pulling himself up on powerful arms, and getting Bliss out next.

"Go!" Jaz screamed. He took two big lunging steps, one to cross the boat and one to spring from it to the dock, where all five of them ran toward the restaurant.

Where someone was holding the door open.

They got inside, gasping for breath, and Mike slammed the door. He caught Jaz's eye. "Sorry," he said. "I didn't know what you were talking about."

Lightning cracked, bolt after bolt hitting the water where they had been only moments ago. The thunder was deafening and they stood there, dripping on the floor and looking at each other.

Then Bliss heard a familiar deep voice.

"Anyone want a drink?"

She whirled around. "Joe!"

He was standing behind the bar, had a bottle of whiskey in his hand and a row of ten shot glasses lined up. And a bartender's towel over one shoulder.

"Found all this in a cabinet. No salted peanuts. Sorry."

"That's okay," Vi said. "Make mine a double. Near death experiences are no fun at all. Any more towels where that one came from?"

Joe reached down and came up with a folded stack. "They're a little musty but they're dry."

Vi patted her face dry and wrapped her hair in the small towel. Then she took another and began to dry Rocco, reaching up to tousle his hair. Bliss took a towel too and tossed one to Jaz.

Joe ceremonially poured whisky, filling all ten shot glasses for whoever wanted one. Vi went over to the bar, tossed down a shot, and jumped when lightning struck again. "Yikes. Make it stop, someone." She looked curiously at Mike. "Hello. Who are you?"

"Our guiding light," Jaz said, grinning.

"Oh. Well, everyone needs one of those." Vi picked up another shot glass and held it aloft. "Here's to Mike. And a safe port in a storm."

Bliss and Jaz exchanged a glance. In an ass-backward way, they had him to thank for the motorboat. Not that they had to make a speech or anything. They just didn't have to explain it all.

The storm hammered Pine Island for the better part of an hour, during which they found chairs and talked, watching it rage outside the window. The men peeled off their soaked shirts rather than shiver in them, except for Mike, of course.

Bliss didn't mind admiring all that chesty glory and Vi didn't seem to mind either. On her third whiskey, she looked lovingly at Rocco and murmured to Bliss, "He's my home boy, you know. From Pittsburgh. But I'm all Italian and he's only half, on his mother's side. His father was a Camp."

"Oh," said Bliss, wishing she could have a Dublin Dream instead of whisky. But she was sipping from a shot glass anyway. "Are the Camps important? Should I know the name?"

"They were bus drivers," Vi said. "Actually, a cut above my people. I grew up on the wrong side of the tracks. Stop me if I get maudlin."

"That would be right about now," Bliss said, noticing the tears welling in her boss's eyes.

Vi wiped them away with the towel and used it to blow her nose. "Thanks."

They fell silent, listening to the guys talk about boats, and being on the water, and whether fish could think. It must be nice to be a guy, Bliss thought. Jaz was sitting with his foot propped on his knee, patting Domino, who moved to him from Rocco, who was leaning back in his chair, dozing a little.

The noise of the storm began to lessen and the sky became lighter over the bay. Bliss got up, setting her glass on the bar, and went over to the window. "Looks like it's clearing."

Jaz gave Domino one last pat and got up to join her. "You're right. I haven't seen any lightning for a while. Must be moving out to sea."

Rocco sat up suddenly, making harrumphy noises and blinking at Vi in an endearing way. "There you are. I was dreaming about you."

She looked at him wistfully. "Really? Was it a happy dream?"

"Very happy. Let's go home. I'll tell you all about it."

Jaz opened the door and took a deep breath of the clean air. "It's stopped raining. You're good to go."

The older couple thanked Mike and Joe, but Rocco only nodded to Jaz, a look of deep gratitude in his eyes. Jaz nodded back and then drew Bliss into an embrace, standing in back of her and resting his chin on the top of her head.

"Hmm. I think you have a keeper there," Rocco said, winking at Bliss.

"I know I do," Jaz replied.

11

The Leonardville boardroom was packed. Bliss had never realized just how many people could sit around the long table. Section managers and division heads were tapping pencils on legal pads and a few of them were squinting into laptops. At the very end of the table was Alf Sargent, chatting with a pretty woman sitting next to him.

Watch the hands, Bliss warned her telepathically. For some reason, Alf's obnoxious behavior had gotten worse in the last week. He yammered constantly at Jaz, in person and on the phone, breathing down his neck over trivial things. He leched more. Some of the female executives had complained to Jaz. Bliss figured that Alf just could not and would not let go gracefully.

To her surprise, Jaz seemed to take it all in stride. Since the day of the storm, he hadn't complained once about Alf or HT, as if the squall's fierce winds had blown away his feelings about working at a job he hated. He seemed resigned to it, in fact. Jaz didn't even want to talk about the restaurant at the end of the world, waving away Bliss's questions when Joe called to discuss the appraiser's report.

As for her—well, Bliss had to finish up this assignment before she could think about taking another. Her work on the HT account had been praised to the skies by one and all. Just because Jaz seemed to have lost interest in it didn't mean he had lost interest in her.

She walked into the boardroom behind Jaz, trying to look cool and composed. After several days of life-affirming sex to make up for almost drowning, it wasn't easy. She'd been so giddy she sometimes wondered if she'd been hit by a very small, erotically energizing bolt of lightning out on the water.

Dora handed out bound copies of the presentation to each person at the table, smiling politely and looking great. Bliss found her place and stacked her paperwork there without sitting down. She and Jaz would be giving the presentation together, complete with a digital album of the MyPies campaign so far. The tech guy cued up the first photos of the Pine Island children's parade, and the kids munching pies popped up on the screen.

"Go ahead and begin, Bliss," Jaz murmured. "Smile a lot. Use small words for Alf."

"Sure." She turned to look at the expectant faces and noticed that Alf's gaze was glued to her breasts. She imagined his head exploding into molecules of lust, then picked up a folder and held it front of her chest. She kept her explanation brief and to the point, and got a round of applause when she finished.

"Love it, love it," Alf said enthusiastically. "Just look at those cute tykes in that photo. We're going to make a killing on those teeny-weeny pies. Rodney here did a very interesting cost analysis. Ounce for ounce, we can charge double the price and shoppers won't even notice. God, I love being a pieman."

Jaz winced, but only Bliss was close enough to notice. He

covered the next thing on the agenda, a breakdown of anticipated revenue that she didn't pay much attention to.

Alf didn't either. He was leafing through his presentation folder when he drew out a sheet of paper printed in color and held it up to look at it. Then he perched a pair of half-glasses on the end of his nose and studied the sheet of paper very, very carefully.

Bliss turned pale. Through the back, she could just see the long banana and Nutty Balls on the photo of Alf. He was holding the caricature she'd done on her computer to make Jaz laugh the night they'd had to work so late. How in holy hell had it gotten into Alf Sargent's presentation materials?

Jaz seemed to notice her alarmed look but he didn't stop talking until Alf coughed in an affected way and held up the digitally created image for everyone in the room to see. "So. Who's the joker?"

An awful silence fell.

"I am. I take complete responsibility for that—that picture," Bliss said quickly.

He set the paper down on the table and folded his hands on top of it, looking at her over the top of his reading glasses. "Young lady, you flatter me. My banana isn't that big."

Was he going to shrug it off? That didn't seem possible. Unless he actually thought she had been trying to flatter him. That did seem possible. She felt a flash of indignation . . . mixed with raw fear. Lentone Fitch & Garibaldi could lose a multimillion dollar account in a hot second.

"Hold on. There seems to be more artwork here." He pulled out another page. Ohmigod. The collage of his sainted mother.

Bliss actually did regret doing that one. Making fun of anyone's mother, even though that wasn't actually a picture of Mrs. Sargent, was a one-way ticket to the seventh level of hell. She deserved to go there.

Alf poked a finger at the image of the gleeful little old lady leading a male stripper and a small dog. "So . . . I must conclude that you think my sainted mother liked . . . actually *liked* . . . having a good time." His voice was shaking with outrage.

Bliss didn't know what to say or do. This was a fight-or-flight situation that called for a split-second, instinctual response, so she just stood there. Jaz put a hand on her arm, as if he could read her mind. Fleeing the room was not an option and arguing with Alf that his mother really had liked to have a good time was out of the question.

He turned to face the people, a few of whom were looking surreptitiously through their presentation folders. Bliss had no doubt they were checking to see if they had the outrageous pictures too. It would make a great cubicle decoration, especially since Alf was an outgoing CEO.

Jaz cleared his throat. "Bliss Johnson didn't intend for anyone but me to see that. Mr. Sargent, I take full responsibility for this."

"Good. Glad to hear it. You're both fired," Alf snarled.

There was a collective intake of breath but no one spoke.

Stricken, Bliss looked at Jaz. Then she looked at Dora, who was visibly upset. Dora looked at Jaz, and Jaz looked at Bliss . . . and he winked. She had to be hallucinating. He had just lost one of the top jobs in the food industry. Not to mention a salary of $550,000. And a very cool apartment in the most expensive blue glass tower on the planet. And a town car and driver at his disposal around the clock. She swallowed hard.

He winked at her again. "Okay, Alf," he said easily. "You can take this job and—"

Dora emitted a squeak. "Jaz, don't."

Jaz shut up but only for a few seconds. He glared at Alf as if something had suddenly occurred to him. "Is Dora fired too?"

The glowering expression on Alf's face softened a little.

"Well, since I intend to stay in the saddle until we can find a replacement for you, Jaz, your lovely assistant can work for me."

"I quit," Dora said immediately.

The assembled employees couldn't remain silent indefinitely. A low buzz of conversation broke out and Bliss plainly heard her name and Jaz's mentioned several times. A strategic retreat seemed to be in order. Not meeting anyone's eye, she hastily gathered up her papers and backed out of the room, noticing that Alf was showing the digital collage to the pretty young woman he'd been talking to.

Pig. Lecher. Creepazoid. His banana couldn't possibly be that big. Her mind was in a whirl. The first thing she had to do was call her boss and give her the bad news before she heard it from anyone else. But it was Friday. Vi would be out at Pine Island. That gave Bliss the weekend to recoup—and think of a way to tell Vi what had happened.

Of course, she still didn't know how the pictures had ended up in Alf's folder. She dropped a few of her papers in the hall and kneeled to retrieve them as Jaz strolled out of the board room. Bliss leaned against the wall, trying to collect herself along with everything else. He rested his hand on the wall above her head and bent down for a swift kiss.

"Not here," she said, looking around wildly.

"Why not? I am officially no longer employed by Hot Treats. And neither are you. We could have sex in the hall if we wanted to."

Bliss clutched her papers as if they would protect her somehow. "I don't think that's funny."

He nuzzled her neck. "Don't worry."

"Easy for you to say. You probably have a zillion dollars in the bank, even if you did just get fired. I don't. And Vi is not going to be happy about this." She realized that she was shaking.

Jaz stroked her arms. The warm contact eased her nervousness a little but not completely. "C'mon, let's get out of here. You don't want to be standing in the hall when Alf leaves the boardroom."

Some other employees had already left the meeting and more were coming out. One or two nodded sympathetically but most seemed to avoid looking at Jaz and Bliss, as if making eye contact or saying an encouraging word might get them fired too.

Call it the pink slip reaction, Bliss thought numbly. Keep your head down and keep your job.

He guided her away from where they had been standing to a door that led outside. She followed him, not really thinking, until he stopped next to a car.

It was a banged-up, frog-green 1978 Buick with gangster whitewalls. There was no driver at the wheel. But Jaz was whistling in a jaunty way when he opened the passenger door for Bliss.

"Wait a minute. Where did this—vehicle, I think it's safe to call it a vehicle—where did it come from?" she asked.

"Borrowed it from a friend, just for today. Thought it looked like a good getaway car."

She got in, still in shock, placing the presentation folder stuffed with papers onto her lap. Bliss traced a finger over the label Dora had stuck in the lower right corner. *Bliss Johnson. Account Executive. Lentone Fitch & Garibaldi.* Her brilliant career had just ended. She was riding in a big, green, getaway car that was embarrassingly old. And her true love had lost his mind.

Look on the sunny side, she told herself. She tried hard, really hard, before she realized that there was no sunny side to this inexplicable situation.

Jaz got in behind the wheel and looked over at her. "Great

presentation, Bliss. The look on Alf's face when he saw those crazy collages was definitely the high point of my year at HT."

Bliss indulged in a little hyperventilating, then took deep, calming breaths. The kind of breaths that got a girl through tough things, like justifiable homicide.

"How did they get in there?" she whispered. Then her voice got louder. "I only printed out one copy of the Alf—and one copy of the little old lady. I gave them both to you." A queasy feeling assailed her. "You put them in his folder, didn't you? You really have lost your mind."

He started the engine and revved it. "No, I haven't. Buckle up."

She obeyed unthinkingly and stared at him, tears glimmering on the tips of her eyelashes. "Oh my God. I know you hate Alf, even if you have done a pretty good job of concealing that fact in the last few days. But even so—what possessed you to do something like that? I'm going to be standing in line at the unemployment office. Didn't that occur to you?" Her voice trembled with indignation.

"Vi won't fire you. She thinks I walk on water after that daring rescue. I couldn't have planned it better."

"Oh, right. You summoned up the wind and waves. You really are amazing."

"Thanks," he said smugly. "But we did rescue them. And I even paid to have the *Neptune's Folly* towed to the Havertown drydocks the next day."

"Nobody told me that."

"Huh. The Whitney Museum wants it, stuffed seagull and all."

"Nobody told me that either."

"Must be a conspiracy."

"I'm beginning to think so, Jaz."

"Settle down, okay? Back to what you were worrying about. Vi won't fire you," he said. "I fixed that in advance."

"Without asking me." She bopped him on the head with the folder. Pieces of paper flew every which way. It didn't seem to faze him.

"You're brilliant. And you can always get a better job, if you want to." Jaz put the car into reverse and backed out of the space, laying rubber out of the lot. Then he leaned forward to concentrate on the odd clunking noise the transmission was making. "What's that weird noise? Do you hear that?"

"Yes. It's the sound of a disco-era car trying to boogie down."

Jaz laughed, then patted the dashboard when the clunking noise died down.

Bliss scrolled back in her mind. "Wait a minute. You seem to be implying that I might as well quit, even though I'm fired. Was Vi—was she in on this crazy plan of yours?"

Jaz nodded. "Rocco asked her to marry him. She wants to sell the agency and retire."

"How nice of her to tell me. She's worse than you are."

He let the green plastic steering wheel slide through his curled fingers. "Love the way this car handles. I really feel like I'm in control."

"I don't. I happen to be completely baffled."

A truck honked behind them and Jaz gave a king-of-the-road wave out the window, signaling the driver to pass. "You know, it's best to have conversations like these in moving cars. That way we don't have to look at each other."

"Don't tell me. My eyes are going in concentric circles."

He patted her thigh. "Remember when we were heading out to Pine Island in the town car and we got stuck in traffic?"

"Yeah," she said. "Not perfectly, but I do remember it."

"I was talking about being able to do what was important in life."

"Uh-huh."

"Right now that means you. You are important. You are wonderful. It's been an amazing summer."

Bliss stared at his smiling profile without replying.

"Am I making sense yet, babe?"

"No." she mumbled. "Maybe we both got hit by lightning and didn't know it."

"Huh?"

"Jaz . . ."

He barely noticed her hesitation. "I made up my mind about you from day one. You just didn't want to notice. I admit I come on strong sometimes, but hey. You can handle it. You have what it takes, Bliss."

"Funny," she said at last. "I was thinking the same thing about you."

He let out a contented sigh. "So it's mutual. Good, because I don't feel like waiting another minute. Or wasting my energy on a job I hate. I want you in my life and I want you to be able to do what you want to do, whatever that is. By the way, I negotiated a fantastic severance package before I took the HT job, you know. They call them golden parachutes for a reason. And hey—what's mine is yours."

Bliss put a hand on each temple and let the warm pressure of her palms ease the pounding in her head. "Does that work in reverse?"

"Absolutely," he said with joy. "I'm ready to come live with you, if the pigeons don't mind. Until you're ready to blow a few million dollars on a really great apartment. Domino can come live with us in New York. He can have a diamond collar."

"I think he likes Pine Island."

"Whatever," Jaz said easily. "Then he can stay with Rocco. Or ride around with Joe. I'm helping with the down payment for the restaurant at the end of nowhere. He's going to try and make a go of it with a buddy of his. Decided that's not my thing, don't worry."

Bliss felt like her mind was full of marbles, magically going up and down little chutes in her head. This was a lot to take in. A *lot*.

"Anyway, let's get the hell out of Pennsylvania and go back to Pine Island. Want to get married on the beach or the back deck?"

"What? What did you just say?"

Jaz didn't answer until they drove onto the freeway. Once there he maintained a stately 55 miles per hour in the far right lane. "You heard me."

"Me marry you?"

He nodded.

"Me marry you," she repeated wonderingly. "It has a nice ring to it."

"Speaking of that . . ." He reached over her and opened the glove compartment to reveal a tiny black velvet box. "Diamond time."

Don't miss this sizzling excerpt from
MIDNIGHT CONFESSIONS by Bonnie Edwards,
coming soon from Aphrodisia . . .

Faye took a breath, smoothed her palm across her thigh to hike her dress, and crossed the threshold into the darkly lit hotel bar.

Alone.

On a mission she'd been planning for two weeks, and wanting for longer. Sex with a stranger. An I-don't-want-to-know-your-name kind of stranger.

Desperation was a harsh mistress and demanded sacrifice. And Faye was desperate. Propelled into the bar by a heat under her skin she could no longer deny, her craving seemed to explode outward, from her skin, her hair, the ends of her fingertips. She was on fire and it amazed her that no one in the hotel lobby had called 9-1-1.

She paused just inside the entrance to glance around for a likely candidate. At first she was disappointed. The sparse crowd was sprinkled around the edges of the room. Light came from table top candles and subdued ceiling bulbs made to look like the night sky. For a bar called the Stargazer, it made sense.

Faye noted couples having a quiet drink, men on cell phones

with laptops open, a woman with shopping bags sporting expensive logos at her feet while she sipped a martini. Her mouth was set grimly and she downed the drink fast, nodding for the next before the glass was set back on the table. An obviously bad day.

The only men of interest were a group of rowdy suits at a table left of the door. Four men in their early thirties, happy, celebrating. Her inner heat cranked up to unbearable at the sight of all those delicious-looking men to choose among. She kept her gaze forward, to hide her interest, but had to ease out a breath. She half expected to see fire blaze from her mouth she was so hot.

Need. She'd never felt such need.

Forcing her legs to take her past the men and toward the bar kept her focused.

A silence hit the table as she strolled by. She wanted to turn her head to look, but if she did, she knew she'd stop and one last shred of pride wouldn't let her. She would not stand there to be ogled openly.

Moisture pooled at the image in her mind of four men touching her with their eyes, skimming her arms, her breasts, her legs, taking inventory of all her secret places and wanting to be there, inside her hot hot skin. She took a hard breath, suddenly awash in heat.

If she wasn't careful, she'd end up with all of them at once! One could kiss her mouth, two could suckle her breasts and one could pleasure her lower. Melting in the heat of her own fantasy, she finally made it to a bar stool.

Her nipples peaked so hard the lace of her bra felt like burlap and scratched against the raised buds. She shivered with the yummy feel and imagined one of the men soothing the roughened nubs with an expert tongue. She imagined a wet mouth suckling at her and restrained herself from tilting her head back to offer more. She shivered.

One of those men at the table would surely read the signs of her arousal. One of them would want to tap into it, exploit it. One of them would want it bad.

And bad was what she needed.

This craving had built for months. At first it manifested as an unsettled feeling when her Great Aunt Mae Grantham had passed away. She'd put down her need for sex to wanting to reaffirm life.

That had seemed a natural response, but then the unsettled feeling grew into an itch she couldn't scratch. She'd had more sex, but she'd become even less satisfied than usual. All the while the craving tore and clawed at her, bringing sexual frustration to a pinnacle.

Everything she'd done, everything she'd tried had brought her to this moment, to these men. These strangers.

She kept her back to them so they could sort it out amongst themselves. In a few minutes, when they saw she was alone, one of them would stroll over, maybe lean against her forearm where it rested on the bar. He'd burn with the fire on her skin. He'd order a drink, see if she shifted away.

When she stayed put, he'd look at her and smile. She'd cross her arms under her breasts and without flinching, give him an eyeful. She'd chosen this bra for maximum uplift. The top of her areolas peeked over the edges of the cups, the rosy flesh obvious from above.

The dress she wore had practically chosen *her* instead of the other way around. She'd found it in her back room inventory, in a stack of men's fedoras, folded like a scarf. She never would have looked for a dress there. She'd checked the tag and found it had been worn by a B actress in a 1957 sex kitten flick. Not much cachet in the vintage clothing business, but a whole lot of "hot" in the seduce-a-stranger realm.

She smiled and felt her sexual aura shimmer again as she hiked up the tight silk hem to mid thigh and slid onto the bar stool.

She tilted her hips just so toward the men and placed her beaded clutch on the bar top. She smiled at the bartender and leaned toward him, her nipples grazing the round leather rolled edge of the bar top. Enjoying the pressure, she swished her nipples back and forth to ease herself.

Big mistake. At the faint abrasion, moisture pooled and slid down her channel to wet her g-string. She crossed and uncrossed her legs to appease her inner ache.

The bartender had been wiping up a spill a few feet over but let the cloth he used dangle as she settled herself. Her focus had turned inward when she'd felt the moisture between her legs. Now, she turned her gaze to him, sure he could see sparks from her eyes.

She tilted her head and he woke from wherever his thoughts had taken him and came over to her. Young, handsome and randy, he leaned across the bar, took a good look at her cleavage.

She shifted to make the flesh move. "Aren't you breaking some bartender's code by staring at my breasts?" But she squeezed them together again just to ensure his interest.

He grinned and looked into her eyes. "What can I give you tonight?"

"I don't know. What do you have that's juicy and wet? I'm a thirsty girl."

His eyes flared and he folded his arms on the bar. Strong forearms, with a sprinkling of hair showing out of the sleeves of his brilliant white shirt.

"You must work out. Your upper arms bulge with muscles. You look very strong."

One of the suits moved in beside her before the bartender could answer. "I'll have a whisky and soda, and for the lady?"

He followed the script and with a look that scorched peered down her scoop-necked bodice. She gave him a slow, welcoming smile and crossed her legs again. He caught the movement and traced a fingertip from the pink-painted nail of her index finger, across her knuckle and along the vein in her hand to her wrist.

When he stopped the delicate caress she thought she'd beg for more. She bit her lower lip, wetting it, plumping it, preparing it. He watched her mouth with deep focus. Their bodies turned toward each other, their heads dipping even closer.

A strong jaw, even teeth, and intelligent eyes made up her first impression. His control of the situation was apparent when he looked at the younger man and cocked an eyebrow. Quick as that the bartender bowed out of the equation.

Faye had found her man.

He smelled of success and money and she blinked up at him as if surprised he'd be so bold. His forearm burned along the length of hers on the bar, right on cue.

She swivelled her ass toward the other three men the man had left behind. An appreciative hiss came from one of them.

She imagined the man beside her skimming his hand down her back to cup a cheek and squeeze. She had to blink to dislodge the image.

His eyes were hazel and hot, his hair neatly trimmed, his hands the hands of a businessman. Clean, neat nails. She'd already learned his gentle strength when he'd traced her finger and hand.

Her lips were hard, though, just the way she liked them. She saw them bearing down on her own, demanding she yield her mouth to his. The strength of the fantasies she was having unnerved her. They were so powerful she wondered if she projected them onto her forehead for all the world to see.

She'd never been so imaginative. Never so hot, never so needy, never so alive.

"I haven't decided what I want yet," she said, finally remembering to reply to the stranger's question. "I can be very picky."

She cleared her fantasies away with great effort and took

stock of him. What she saw fit her requirements. Healthy looking, interested, no wedding band, and keen intelligence. Yes,
he'd do.

"I'm Faye Grantham," she said, tossing away her anonymous sex fantasy. Giving her real name came naturally and she
wasn't an easy liar.

"As in 'grant'im his wish?" One side of his hard mouth
quirked up.

"If you'd like."

"I'd like."

"Miss, can I get you something?" The bartender interjected,
all business now.

"Like I said, I'd like something wet, something juicy." She
arched her neck, trailed her fingertips down her throat. "Maybe
an icy drink, I like the way they cool me when I'm hot." Her
fingers drew down farther along the line of her cleavage.

There was a long moment of silence from the two men as
they watched her fingers trail between her breasts. Her nipples
stood out prouder, the areolas hard.

"Do you have something that will cool me off? Something
juicy and wet?" She emphasized the *t* sound, drawing it out
only to clip it off at the end.

The gulp the young bartender gave was audible. "A bellini.
You'll like it, I promise."

The man at her side, older, more experienced, narrowed his
gaze. Then he slid his hand to her back, just above the low material of her dress.

His fingertip drew slow hypnotic circles on her naked flesh.
Her spine straightened in response, lifting her breasts higher.
She looked into his eyes and saw the promise of a sure thing.

He was hers for as long as she wanted to play.

"I don't need that drink after all," she said. "I think I see
what I need right here."

She slid off the stool, making certain to brush the length of his body. Her pebbled breasts skimmed his chest, her knee bent as it caressed the side of his leg. Moisture gathered inside at the thought of sex with this man with the hot eyes and hard mouth. She licked her lower lip in anticipation.

"You have a room?" she asked him on a husky note, surprised at the deep timbre.

He nodded and turned his head to the bartender. She liked the sharp angles of his profile, took a complete inventory and burned again. "Champagne. Suite twenty fourteen," he ordered from the gaping young man on the other side of the bar.

She slid her eyes to the younger man. "Make it the best you've got."

She turned, took her clutch from the bar top, and headed toward the exit that would take them through the lobby and up to his suite. Her hips swayed seductively, her shoulders straightened, and she could feel the heat of his stare through the silk of her dress.

"My card," he offered. He took her elbow in a firm grip to guide her through the tables. She took the card, glanced at his name in spite of not wanting to know it. Mark McLeod.

It was a good name. She didn't recognize the company logo, but it didn't matter, they'd never be in touch again. She slid the card into the outside pocket of her clutch next to the very convenient letter from Watson, Watson and Sloane.

She looked up at his profile once more. Strong chin, bold nose, hard lips, and great shoulders. She warmed through and through at the idea of skimming his collarbone with her mouth, her teeth leaving small marks of possession along the path.

He did not look back at the table of companions he'd left behind. No, his focus was on Faye and on Faye alone.

She knew he'd keep it there. How refreshing.

They strode across the lobby together, his fingers firm on her arm. Her breath quickened with each step, her breasts bounced, each movement a secret abrasion on her sensitized nipples. Her knees quaked at the knowledge of what she was about to do. Sex with a stranger, in an airport hotel room.

Cool-headed logic flushed through her body, washing away the rapacious desire that had brought her here.

The inherent danger in her plan finally rattled her. Faye glanced at Mark out of the corner of her eye as they walked together. He looked like a decent man, a kind man. A normal man. A hot and ready man she'd deliberately enticed. She couldn't go back on her offer now.

Her body wouldn't let her, she realized as the warmth in her loins spread upward again. She tried to tamp it back, but it was useless. This was a battle she'd lost many times in the last three months. Her body wanted what it wanted in spite of her attempts to hold herself in check.

She wanted to scream her need out loud, but she didn't have to. Mark had picked up on her sexual craving, had responded and answered the call of woman to man. He knew what she wanted and he would give it to her.

Once alone in the suite with Mark, anything could happen. Any sexually deviant behavior he favored could occur and she'd be trapped in it with him. But wasn't that part of the whole thing? The fantasy of being unable to put a stop to things, of being swept up into something forbidden, exciting, and wild. Excitement mixed with a healthy dose of fear twitched and grew and made her pant.

Mark slid a finger over the elevator keypad and grinned into her eyes. "Okay?"

"I'm fine." Fear mixed with anticipation was a heady blend, arousing and spicy.

"You're more than fine, Faye. You're a dream come true." He let go of her arm and ran his hand down her back to cup her ass just the way she'd envisioned earlier. Thrill trails followed his movement. "You're perfect."

"Really?" She bit her lip. She shouldn't sound so ingenuous, so stupidly inexperienced. He'd be surprised enough by her be-havior once they were alone.

The elevator opened and they stepped inside the smoke-mirrored quiet. They turned as one to face the doors, bodies thrumming, heat rising, minds racing with images of what was to happen when the door closed, hiding them from public view. Mark frowned at a harried looking bellman with a luggage cart.

The bellman nodded and stepped back. The last chance to change her mind disappeared as the doors slid shut, closing Faye in with this stranger. This Mark McLeod.